NOTHING BUT DARKNESS

Darkness Series, Book One

MARIA ANN GREEN

NOTHING BUT DARKNESS
Copyright © 2018 Maria Ann Green

Cover design by Angela Fristoe
Covered Creatively Book Cover Design

Formatting by Jaye Cox
Formatting the Affordable Way

Other works by Maria Ann Green

In the Rearview, young adult poetry and prose

This book is dedicated to Travis,
the Bee to my Aidan.

Darkness (noun):

1. A lack of brightness; the quality of having no or little light: *he sat alone in the darkness of his corner*

2. A state of exhibiting or stemming from evil characteristics or forces; forboding: *she provoked a particular darkness within me the longer she spoke*

"Stars, hide your fires; Let not light see my black and deep desires."
—William Shakespeare, *Macbeth*

chapter One:

My eyes widen, watching the arrow fly toward its target. Leaves flutter, pushed aside. As it lands, into the sinew of her neck, my lungs fill with triumph.

Who knew death could be like this?

Pride radiates through my chest. I've accomplished what I came here to do.

The doe freezes, pain not registering yet. When it does she starts to dance, shaking her head and stomping her feet. A sad sound fills the air, ringing out my victory, as she stumbles through the trees. I'd have thought she'd die faster. The arrow must have missed her artery.

Rising from my hunting blind, I move toward the wounded animal. She tries to run, but her strength goes with her coordination. Falling head first into tangled roots, it's evident she won't last much longer.

I should put her out of her misery. Though, as the thought filters through me, I hesitate. My knife is ready, yet it remains still.

End it already.

I don't. I keep watching as she flails, screeching in agony. Red stains her otherwise pristine coat, standing out against the white. I don't think I've seen a more vibrant shade.

Fuck.

Snapping myself out of it, I raise my blade then stop as I watch the last moment of life fade from the doe's eyes. She dies while I kneel close enough to feel her last breath against my knees. The pink tongue lolls from her mouth. This hunting trip is a technical success, yet the experience feels inadequate now. I was supposed to be a man. I was supposed to end her before the arrow did.

I failed.

How could I fail?

Anger bubbles like acid from my stomach, coating the inside of my throat. I will not be a fuck-up. This weekend is for me. This is *my* time. I will not be weak. Without thinking any longer, as instincts take over, I act.

I plunge the metal into a soft spot under her chin. Only her head moves with my thrust. The second spout I've opened drains over my arm onto the cold ground. It flows warm at first, but chills quickly. The scent is overpowering. I've never been this close to such a significant amount of blood.

It's terrifying.

It's thrilling.

It's over too fast.

As the wound stops spilling, I stand, trying to clean myself off. She's going to be heavy on the way back to the cabin.

***

Work's been shitty lately, and the...rest, it's been lacking too. I needed a weekend away, a break, in the simple quiet country, a chance to let out my aggression, a chance to feel free.

So here I am, hunting up north at my uncle's cabin, soaking up the solitude. All alone; the silence is beautiful. No one asks me to hurry or to finish any work. No one speaks my name. No one speaks at all. There are no complaints, no shouts, no whining.

Everything's so wonderful, quiet.

The deer's been taken care of. After I did the easy work, I took her to a butcher to handle the rest. I don't even like venison, so I took his money, leaving the meat. Now I'm back at the cabin, flipping through channels next to a warm fire. There isn't much on, though I find a movie I haven't seen. Leaving it there, I sip my beer, and stoking the flames is all I have left to do tonight. No responsibilities other than staying relaxed, content.

Tomorrow I'll head back to town, back to the faster-paced city, forgetting how peaceful it is here. I'll be happy to be closer to everything I need and everyone I know. So for now, before I take this for granted, I put my feet up, relishing the silent darkness of tonight.

chapter Two;

Of course I forgot my goddamn coffee on the counter at home. That's the type of day it's turning out to be, after less than an hour since waking up. After such a great weekend away, I shouldn't expect anything else. My alarm went off so quietly I hadn't heard it until I'd slept in; I tripped over my computer's cord, sending it crashing to the floor (not salvageable), and the beginnings of snow are falling on my windshield. Plus now the coffee. The creamer will have gone bad by the time I make it home tonight.

Well shit. What else can go wrong? Hopefully nothing.

I sulk, starting the windshield wipers.

What a dumb fucking question to even think. I should be smarter than that, know better than to tempt fate. There's *always* something else that can go wrong. These are the moments when an accident crushes the fool dumb enough to ask the question. If I've learned nothing else in life so far, I've learned there's always something else.

And, as if on cue, I spot that bitch. That horrible, beautiful bitch, Eva Westfall. I let my eyes trail her from her parking spot until she's through the glass front doors. It's easier staring when I'm camouflaged by the thick snow falling from the crisp, gray sky. She makes the trip safely despite the flurries. *Damn.* I wish she'd fallen off those spindle heels and broken her ankle, or her neck.

There's always tomorrow.

With a sigh, I haul my 175 pounds out of my leather seat, into the cold Maine air. My 5-foot-11-inch frame isn't what most would consider intimidating, but I get by. Muscles help, so does charisma. As I enter the same doors Eva passed through moments ago, I walk slowly, hoping she's already been taken upstairs by the jarring, slow elevator. That piece of shit will break down some day, I'm sure, with someone stuck inside.

No such luck, though. She's held the door for me.

Her smile's revolting. What once sent a wave of excitement down my spine now inches me closer to vomiting down her cleavage, sizable as it is. She may have been the content of many kinky dreams, but now all I see when I look at her is the disgusting individual who stole my promotion.

Granted, she looks pretty good in her tight black dress today. But I still hate her. *Fuck* do I hate her.

"Hello, Aidan. How're you this morning?" As her red lips move I envision throwing her down a very, very long flight of stairs. I wonder how those lips would move then.

"I'm well. How 'bout you?" My smile's too sweet. I know it affects her as she leans almost imperceptibly closer to me. Not quite imperceptible, though. I notice more about body language than most. It's always been a talent. I'm also a fucking brilliant liar. Both come in handy. Eva's never once believed I'd rather gouge her eyes out than be in the same room with her.

A few months ago, my smile would've been genuine. Months ago, I would've been glad to have Eva beneath me in ecstasy with pleasure instead of pain. Those months have changed a lot, and now I want her fired. I want nothing more than for her to lose her job in some particularly embarrassing way.

I wouldn't mind for her to lose more than her job too, though there's no need to be greedy. Just the career will be fine.

My inner rant concealed, she continues to smile before sipping her fancy, store-bought latte. The bitch even has to rub it in my face that I left my coffee at home.

The elevator lurches to our floor, the seventh, so I wave my hand in what she thinks is a gentlemanly manner, to let her pass first. The truth is I just won't put my back to her any longer, not since she shoved a knife between my shoulder blades. She won't be allowed to twist the blade deeper.

Plus, despite her many drawbacks, she still has a plump ass packed into that black *business* dress. I'd prefer she exit first. "After you."

"Why thanks. See ya later." Again, her smile does little for me, but I return it, nodding as she walks toward her office. Her new, larger office. The one that's supposed to be mine.

Walking out, in the opposite direction of Eva, I take tally of all my rude thoughts this morning. Most toward Eva, and harsh. She gets under my skin. Plus I've been easier to piss off lately. I should work on that.

Coffee may help.

I round the corner then knock on the smooth space of wall between the doorframes of the adjoining office and mine. The other belongs to my closest friend.

"Hey, Jason, you up for coffee?" I ask, as I drop my briefcase on the floor just inside my office. I don't keep anything valuable in there, or in my briefcase, so I rarely shut the door. Never lock it. I get grief from plenty of others in the office, but I won't change. It's easier my way. Things I choose to do usually are.

Jason looks up only after my utterance of the word coffee.

"Fuck yeah."

"Nice. Isn't it a little early for that?" I'm such a fucking hypocrite—Jason is so easy to rile up. He always has been.

"Damn. Sh..." He catches himself on the latter half of his third offense, slapping his mouth with an open palm. It's so over the top, we both break out in laughter on our way back to the elevator.

"So how was your weekend, Aid?" Jason is one of the only people I allow to call me that. I'm not fond of nicknames, but Jason is too old a friend, and it's a pattern he's had too long now to try changing.

"Same old, same old. After our drinks Friday I didn't do a whole lot." I press the button, and we jerk downward. "How about yours?"

"Amelia and I took the kids to a movie, some stupid kids' cartoon, on Saturday afternoon. Then we got a babysitter for the evening, so we went out dancing. Let me tell you she's still got it, if you know what I mean." I always know what he means.

Jason's wife, Amelia, is as gorgeous as she was ten years ago when they met, though I can't say the same for him. He gained weight along with her for each of their three pregnancies. When she lost it, he didn't. His once-athletic physique is now what I'd call pudgy. That may even be generous. He's bordering on fat these days. In contrast, Amelia has legs that never end and a face like a model. Plus her rack is fucking mouthwatering.

Seriously.

"I'll take your word for it." *Lies.* I'd love to see her body moving to a rhythm. Friendship is stronger than lust. Almost all of the time. Though I've let my eyes linger longer than I should a time or two. But at least I've only looked.

"Any interest in going out with us soon?" I can almost taste the desperation in his question. He's a man hungry for his wife's attention. How sad.

He must not be getting enough, poor guy.

Well if I can't assist him into bed, what kind of friend am I? "Sure, buddy. Amelia have any single friends to bring along for a night?" Okay, maybe not completely unselfish, but at least I'll be helping him along with myself.

"Yeah. As a matter of fact she wanted to set you up with her friend from our neighborhood—Bessie, well actually she goes by Bee, Amelia is the only one who calls her Bessie." Or...maybe I'll just be helping Jason. I'd better score major points for this. Bessie isn't

7

the type of name that accompanies a knockout. He should've just told me her name was Bee.

"You'll owe me." Try as I do, I can't make that sound any better than a grumble as we exit the elevator toward the lobby coffee shop.

"Yeah I know..." He says it as an apology, though his smile doesn't convince me he's listening any longer. He's relieved he'll get a second weekend to watch Amelia's amazing ass shake on the dance floor. I can almost see the cogs turning behind his brown eyes as we walk up to the counter.

"Two strong roast coffees please. Both with room." After so many years we've just learned to take turns buying. It's easier. We've been best friends since college, and buying coffee together just as long. We needed a lot of coffee to get through some of those accounting classes.

His thoughts continue to churn behind his eyes as we collect our cups then head back to the rickety piece of shit up to our floor. While dancing, he'd get to saunter closer to her with each drink she consumed. He'd get to whisper things in her ear that'd make her blush if she were sober. He'd get to be riskier throughout the night, slipping his hand farther up her short hemline. So, maybe this night could be a possible opportunity for me. Besides, my date may not be that bad. I have no idea what she looks like yet.

Bessie...

"Big time. You'll owe me big." I lose the smirk I'd been wearing for a much more serious facade to break though Jason's steamy thoughts. "Plus you already do for checking in on your car two weeks ago. That storage door is a bitch to open every few days." Jason has a muscle car from the '60s that he shamefully hides in the winter. It's just sitting in storage until he, or recently I, takes it out, driving it occasionally to make sure everything's running. Before he went on vacation for over a week he begged me, *just one favor.* He needs to know I'm due.

"Man, you're right. Anything you say. I swear." Thank god. This'll come in handy. It never hurts to rack up favors.

"Okay. Then deal." And I let the corners of my lips turn back up a little as we round the corner, each heading into our respective offices.

chapter Three:

The day drags as I switch between typing on my computer and daydreaming about a few things. Slapping Eva across the face is one vision I can see playing out across my mind. But I don't only imagine aggression. Sometimes I see myself kissing her immediately afterward. I can almost feel our warm tongues intertwining, the heat of her body pressed up against me as her cheek reddens from the strength behind my hand.

Jesus. What the fuck? *Time to get my shit together.* I can't fondle or attack Eva. And definitely not both. She's my superior. My evil, sexy superior, who didn't deserve the job she got.

Traitor.

"Hey, you staying late?" Jason's voice breaks the trail of convoluted thoughts I'm strolling down.

"Nope. Hadn't looked at the time. Just need to save this, then I can walk out with you." We never arrive together, because, let's face it, getting out of bed in the morning sucks ass—I'd much rather sleep in. Though, we generally walk out together after one of us reminds the other to go home. Today's his turn.

"Any plans for the single man tonight?" Jason's always interested in living vicariously through me. Typically, I'm forced to disappoint him. Sometimes I invent lavish, dirty stories to satisfy him. But that's rare since I tend to forget what I've told him. A time or two I've gotten caught lying. He never seems to mind *too* much though. He's still entertained regardless.

"None so far. I may go down to Spot Z after dinner to see who's around." I'd sound lonely and boring to anyone listening.

I'm neither.

"Nothing wrong with that. There are plenty of hotties at Z every night. Not that I go there anymore since that asshole mugged me. It used to be fun. Did you know they never caught him either? Too cheap to pay for security cameras." He concludes with a sigh.

Spot Z is a popular bar just a ways down from my house. It seems to be on the corner of everything and everything-else in our town. Anyone who wants to drink seems to end up there at some point in the week. It's kind of a dive, a little dodgy, but that doesn't stop most. The lights are dim, the music's loud, they have typical bar games to play and a sizable dance floor, and the drinks are cheap. Even on a modest budget it's possible to get yourself plus a date drunk. Add to all of this well-endowed women and bartenders sporting tanned and toned muscles. Hence the popularity. There's something there for everyone.

The allure works on me too. I end up there two or three times a week. It helps I can walk there.

I can tell Jason misses trolling for ladies at Z by the wistful tone in his voice. As much as he loves his wife now, he used to love taking women home after a night at the bars. When we were in college, when he was thinner, he got plenty of ass. Now he has to be satisfied with the fact that the closest he'll get to another woman is playing wingman for me. Case in point why I'm not married.

"Maybe I'll get lucky," I add with a jab of my elbow to his chubby ribs.

"I hope so, if for no other reason than I'll get a retelling tomorrow." Knew it.

"You're a pig." I guess I'll have to try scoring just for him. How selfless and giving of a friend I can be.

"Hey, are you coming over for the game tomorrow night? Amelia said she's making food. I'll have beer." His hopefulness sounds on the brink of desperation.

"Count me in," I shout as I sink into my driver's seat, closing my door to the cold outside. I give him a thumbs up in return to his smile as we back out of our parking spots toward our respective homes.

***

"Fucking cocksucker!" I scream, honking my horn as a moron in a hybrid cuts too close in front of me. That's the shit that pisses me off. People need to learn to drive or get off the road. This isn't practice. It's real life. And this asshole needs to go back to driving school.

I need to teach this guy a lesson. It's a quick thought I don't analyze. So I speed up until I'm mere feet from his bumper. I lay my fist on the horn, leaving it there. I feel my blood pressure rise as my anger continues skyrocketing.

"Who the fuck does he think he is?" I barely notice I'm speaking to an empty passenger seat. "*WHO* the *FUCK* does this guy think *HE IS*?" One hand stays on the wheel, the other gesturing wildly.

With the sound still blaring, I move even closer as he tries to evade me. I'm inches from the back end of his car, and there's no fucking way he's going to get away from me. When he swerves right, I follow. Same when he attempts left.

As he moves back into the lane, speeding up, I follow suit, continuing my tirade. Eventually he raises his eyes to the rearview, meeting mine. When I realize I can see the color of his irises, dark brown, the part of my brain that's seeing red, the part that's lost control, fades away.

Holy shit.

"Holy shit."

I felt like I could've killed that guy. Is that even possible? Do I have such dark violence inside me? Even as I ask myself the question I already know the answer. I know if I hadn't snapped out of it, it was possible.

What the fuck?

This is how road rage gets on the news, why it's been studied. Such psychotic behavior from being cut off isn't a typical reaction. Some outliers can be dangerous.

***

"Home sweet home," I mutter as I cross over the threshold into my entryway. I've calmed down from my outburst, sure it's a one-time problem. I drop my work things underneath the end table by the door that holds my key tray. My briefcase never makes it past this point. Ever. I never work from home. There's no other way to keep a work–life balance. At work I work. At home I don't. Simple as that. I've never understood how others have trouble separating the two. It isn't difficult.

Just don't fucking work at home.

Looking around, I feel proud. Though the size is a luxury, I've also filled the space well. Every line is clean, sharp. The counters are granite, while the floors are dark hardwood. Grays, blacks, browns, reds, and whites might give a cold feel to everything, but it's a fresh, clean cold. The furniture, walls, and accents all bask in these simple colors, while the appliances shine in chrome. Despite the bachelor pad status, I have a painting in every room. No neon shit either. Only visually stimulating, and expensive, pieces.

My place may lack a woman's touch, but that's sort of the point. Most women don't complain when they come over anyhow. Plus they rarely stay long enough to admire my décor. And while they're here, their mind is occupied elsewhere. Most have no objection to the coolness of my decorating while in my bed, which happens to be king-sized and covered in a thick duvet to warm them up from said cold furnishings.

I can't help grinning at the possibility of some sizzling activity that could lie ahead for my night, so I head to the kitchen to fix dinner before heading to Spot Z.

chapter four.

Just as expected, at Z the lights are low, the music high. I can feel the *thump, thump, thump* in my chest as I walk toward the bar. It beats, vibrating against my ribs.

"Jack and coke please." My drink never changes. Once I found what I liked, I stuck with it. I don't think in all blacks and whites, there are definitely plenty of grays out there, but there's no point in branching out when you're already found your favorite. I doubt it'll change. What can I say, I'm loyal to Jack.

I've come to recognize most of the bartenders since I'm here often. A few recognize me enough to know my order as well.

"Sure thing." I forget this particular one's name, but he nods and has my drink ready faster than I can get the cash out of my wallet.

"Keep the change." I try to tip well—I've learned a little extra generosity goes farther than you can imagine, even if it's not genuine. *If you don't feel it, fake it. Just make sure to fake it well.* You never know when you may need a boost or a favor. For that exact reason I play nice as much as I can, on the outside at least. I've learned to play the game. Well.

"Thanks, Aidan." I should learn his name soon since he appears to remember mine. Though it's probably a rule instituted by the wait staff, to know the frequent flyers. I'm sure it works as well as my tactics. Be nice, get nice in return.

"Any fresh meat tonight?"

"A few ladies I haven't seen before, some young beauties on the dance floor. I think you'll do just fine." Exactly what I like to hear.

"Wonderful. Will you send Sheila over with another Jack in a few?"

"Of course. Have fun." He lifts his brows with an air of simple masculine camaraderie, acknowledging my attempt at conquest, and moves to help the other paying customers scattered along the lengthy bar.

I'm not much of a dancer. I'm not terrible, but I'm not far either. I generally avoid the dance floor until I've had a few drinks, and the skirt I'm chasing has as well. For this reason I make my way to a high-top about halfway between the loud, sweaty dance floor and the overcrowded bar. I enjoy sitting at these specific tables because they give me an excellent vantage point—in the middle of the traffic venturing between both destinations.

The more often I see a girl go by me, to or from the bar, the better chance I have of her coming home with me for a night.

I down several more stiff drinks, one after another. As I look around I spot a potential. Her hair is short, about to her chin, while her eyes are a tad glazed over. I let my gaze wander down to her skirt. It's as short as her hair.

Bingo.

Sheila comes over with simply phenomenal timing as Miss Nearly Skirtless walks by me on her way to the bar. Sheila sets my Jack on the table with a brilliant smile as I point to Skirtless. Both see my gesture, but I have to almost yell over the music.

"Another of whatever she has been having too, please. On my tab." Did my speech slur together? The words pass, and I'm not sure. At least they were loud enough.

Sheila's amazing at her job. I often wonder why she hasn't moved onto better things. She only nods, bouncing her ample cleavage, turning on her heel back to the bar.

"Well, well, well. What a gentleman. Thank you. I've been buying all my own drinks tonight. That's just not right." As she sits down in the other chair at my table I can smell the sugary liquor on her breath. Her big, blue eyes are clearly having a hard time staying focused. I'm interested in more than her eyes.

Her lips are incredibly full, pouty, and her blouse plunges to her navel before connecting with her impossibly short black skirt. Sheila drops off the second drink, winking.

This should be easier than I'd hoped.

"That's a damn shame. We'll change that right now."

Easy and fucking hot. She can't be more than 110 pounds soaking wet. *And I want her soaking wet.*

"What's-your name? Mr. Ten I bet." The slight slur in her pronunciation adds fuel to the fire that's starting to burn below the belt.

"Aidan, actually. Yours?" Her glazed eyes never stray from mine. *Hook.*

"I'm Melody, though I can't sing for beans. Isn't that just unfair?" As her hair falls into her sight line I take the split-second opportunity to distract her.

Leaning in to whisper in her ear, I simultaneously slide my hand up her smooth creamy leg to the hem of her skirt. "I bet I could make you hit the right notes." My smile's anything but gentlemanly. *Line.*

"I dare you." *Sinker.*

"Be careful what you wish for. I've never turned down a dare." I let my fingers slide past the hem, up her inner thigh. I can feel the alcohol seeping into my system. It's pushing me to be more brazen. But I couldn't care less about the consequences that'll follow these actions. All I can think about is the warmth my fingers are being drawn toward.

"Then I double dog dare you," she says, just as bold. And I'll never turn away from encouragement. Her legs part a fraction of an inch, giving me just enough space to meet my intended destination.

With the go-ahead I have zero inhibitions left. If I ever had any, I'm not entirely sure.

"Do you want me to fuck you right here in plain view of everyone? Or would you rather I fuck your brains out at my place instead?" Her gasp is loud as I lay out her options.

"How 'bout you show me what you can do with those fingers. Make me wanna go home with you."

"Can do." My two-word agreement is nearly all gravel in her ear. I slide my unoccupied hand into her hair, turning her mouth to mine.

There's no tenderness in the way my tongue enters her hot mouth. Pure lust courses between us. That's the way I enjoy it. She edges closer to my hand below the table, leaving her round ass on the edge of her stool.

Teasing is fun, so I refuse to give into her needs just yet. Instead I trail my fingernails along her inner thigh. I make little circular patterns up and down her leg each time, inching closer to where she's begging me to stroke, but I make her wait. My tongue is on a mission of its own as I drive her near insane with my movements along her leg.

"Please." Her begging is almost enough for me to bend her over the table right here, right now. On the other hand, I'd prefer not getting arrested.

"My place. Now." This isn't a request, question, or inquiry. It's a command, and Melody takes no issue with being told what to do. All she does is nod, hopping off the stool, following behind me.

chapter five:

Once we're to my front door I hand Melody my keys to let us in. Standing behind her, both of my hands trace the lines I was driving her insane with before. Her thighs are so smooth and warm. Her ass is firm, and it's at the perfect height to grind into me. This is my kind of heaven. *Dirty.*

Finally, I end her torture, finding the crease of her lips with both hands.

"*Fuck.* Crotchless panties? You dirty girl." My words are scarcely more than air. I see the goose bumps form on the back of her neck.

"I'm a naughty girl. Punish me." She hasn't even attempted to unlock the door as she's clearly enjoying my touch. She's soaking my fingers and her inner thighs.

"I'll teach you a lesson." Without warning I rip her skirt up over her cheeks, exposing it to the crisp air. In the same motion, without pausing, I swing my open palm back for momentum, slapping her porcelain skin with a loud crack.

"Shit." Her curse is a moan, followed by a loud exhale as she struggles to insert the key.

Fumbling, tripping over each other, we somehow make our way into the living room. Without hesitation I bend her over the back of the couch, tearing her panties in two pieces.

"Oops." My apology sounds more like a self-congratulatory boast, but she isn't complaining about it or the damaged clothing while I unzip.

"I can't wait any longer. Fuck me. Fuck me hard," she yells.

I debate making her beg, for about half a second, before responding instead with, "Abso-fucking-lutely," as I thrust inside her. Hard, quick. Her hips come back to meet mine with every assault as I continue pounding into her. Before long her legs begin to lose tension while her moans strengthen.

My hands circle around her neck, squeezing tightly as I build toward my own release. Behind my closed eyes I see black, then stars. My breath is rapid as Melody seems to be protesting something. Her struggle becomes more evident. With a little delay I understand her throat's constricted by my fingers.

She'd probably like to breathe.

It's all too much, and I finish. Sputtering as I release her, Melody's turned a few shades darker than the last time I looked down. Expecting her to unleash on my unexpected behavior, I pull out of her warmth, taking two sudden steps backward after coming inside her.

Her short locks are clinging to her sweaty pink face as she spins around as well.

"That...may be...the best lay I've ever had." Okay, definitely not what I expected.

"I didn't mean to choke you. Sorry I got a little overzealous."

"No, don't be. You can fuck me like that any time you want." She may have bruises tomorrow that she'll not be as excited about. Especially after sobering up.

At a loss for words, all I can think to do is smile, shrugging. With a swipe of her brow Melody leans down to pick up her torn lingerie.

"Thanks for a fabulous time, Sweet Cheeks." Her heels click on the hardwood floor as she makes her way to my front door. She only pauses for a second to put the remnants of her panties on the inside of my door handle and to blow me a kiss before slipping out of my house. In a matter of seconds she's left me standing next to my sofa with a dumbfounded look plastered on my face, my softening dick hanging out of my zipper.

"What the hell just happened?"

***

Knives scratch down my body, leaving lines of blood on otherwise pristine skin. I'm surprised I don't scream in protest. Instead bubbles of laughter burst from between my lips. In what world is this funny? I'm being tortured by a crazed stranger. That shouldn't be funny.

But for some reason it is. It's fucking hilarious.

"You think this hurts? I could do better than this."

What did I just say? I could hurt someone better than this? Whoa.

Deep in my belly I can feel the statement rings true. I utter one last sentence before steeling myself to grin and bear whatever pain is in store for me: "Give me everything you've got."

The psychotic does. I can feel each slash to my flesh; each one sends a tingle up my spine in a way that excites me.

***

With a jolt I wake from terrifying dreams. I can just tell I look horrible, because I feel about as bad. I need reassurance. I need grounding. *It was only a dream.* I reach a hand into the drawer of my nightstand. The cool metal of a sharp knife reminds me I'm safe. I'm protected.

After fully waking and calming, I forget what was so terrifying. It's buried back into my unconscious. My thoughts move to my cock and the enjoyment it had last night. I can't stop thinking about my adventure with Melody. If every night could be like the last, each with different women, I'd find my heaven.

Well, up in the pearly gates I bet there aren't hangovers. As my head pounds I neglect to shower, deciding against coffee too. Just the thought of the aroma makes my stomach churn.

I will not vomit at work today.

As usual the drive is quick, painless. Though sunglasses are hardly necessary, I don a pair to block the harsh, gray, clouded light filtering through my windshield. In my building the clunking of the elevator threatens to pierce my head as well as my nerves, but I exit on my floor in time to keep my temper in check. I certainly don't need any blowups today. Thankfully the ride was solitary, which is rarely the case.

Goddamn hangover. I should've stopped at three drinks.

I will not vomit at work today.

Fuck, I know better. Any more than three drinks on a weeknight is asking for a problem. *I asked and I received.* But thinking back to her once more, Jesus, this nausea is well worth it for everything I got last night.

Slumping into my desk chair, I wonder if I'll be lucky enough to bend Melody over any of the other surfaces in my house. Any time soon would be preferable.

With a start, I'm pulled from my momentary fantasy by none other than Miss Bitch knocking on my doorframe.

"Yes, ma'am, what can I do for you this morning?" There've been many times in my life I've been thankful no one can read my thoughts, and every time I've been around Eva since her theft of my promotion is on that list. I may stay civil, professional, in my actions and spoken words, but that bitch receives constant murderous commentary between every utterance. She'd shrink away if she could hear what I actually think about her.

She's just a pretty face attached to a soulless cunt.

"Do you think you'll be finished with the reports by lunch?" *Of course, you dumb whore. I finished them yesterday.* But since she doubts my abilities, and my memory, I think she can wait.

"Certainly. I'll have them to you by noon." Remember to smile.

"Thanks, Aid."

Do. Not. Call. Me. That.

"No problem Ev," I reply.

My smile's plastered to my face so tightly I fear my cheeks may crack with the pressure. I must look like a phony. Though she must be placated since she turns on the spot, shaking her cheeks down the hallway to her damn larger office.

Why a woman like that was chosen over me I refuse to understand. Apparently the wonderful world of finance is based more on fuckability than actual practical knowledge and experience. I could calculate circles around her.

She must have sucked the right dick to get the job that was promised to me months ago. I can just see her acting coy, shy even, to entice the right boss before sinking her filthy claws into him. I can't fathom her earning anything of value without showing off some of that pink undercarriage.

I wonder if I can fuck up her reputation with the superiors. How could I get her into deep shit without walking through the same? That's a thought I'll have to store to revisit later in more depth.

***

Gladly, the rest of my day goes by without incident. I don't plan my violent revenge upon Eva. I don't fall asleep at my desk pretending to finish reports that were already completed. There's nothing of significance to speak of, good or bad. For the first time in a long time, I'm somewhat perturbed with an uneventful day. I can't think of another time in my recent past when I believed I needed more adventure.

More sex yes, adventure not so much.

I generally find myself satisfied with my life. I enjoy having more than enough money (who wouldn't?). I find my work to be easy without crossing to the side of boredom. I'm not tied down to a woman I don't love. I don't have children crying or shitting in my clean home.

I've always been content.

Though right now I'm falling short of the contentment I've long since habituated myself to. It's almost as if there's something itching its way into my system, leaving me tingling and unfulfilled.

I need more.

I haven't a clue what it is I need more of, but I'm absolutely positive I'm missing something I hadn't needed before. I could be wrong. Maybe there isn't an emptiness burrowing inside of me, continuing to grow until I feed the desire with...with whatever I haven't found. Maybe instead, this dull, throbbing need to scratch at an unnamed, untapped excitement is simply an early midlife crisis.

It's possible.

Or maybe I just need more sex like last night in my life. Maybe I need a vacation. Maybe I need a new adventure.

Maybe I just need to get over myself and calm the fuck down.

I've little time to brood over my newly developed dissatisfaction, though, as Jason stomps into my office with too much enthusiasm. His large presence engulfs the entire doorway.

"You gonna go home to change before coming over?" *Shit.* I forgot about the game. Guess I won't be entertaining Melody tonight. Did I even get her number?

I head toward the door so we can make our way outside while hashing out plans. "Yeah, I don't want to wear this suit. I'll be over in an hour."

In the elevator Jason punches the button harder than necessary. I notice how fat his fingers have become with added weight. Time has not been as kind to Jason as it has to me. I wonder what our classmates will think at our next reunion. Will they be jealous of his happy family?

Am I the only one who has no desire to settle down with baggage?

"Sounds good." Jason's heavy cheeks flush with the cool air outside, and his smile is wider than his middle.

His constant upbeat outlook can be wearing.

chapter six:

Freshly showered and changed, with a case of beer in hand, I hesitate at Jason's door. There are so many other things I could be doing tonight. I know he's my friend, I like spending time with him, but honestly we don't need to watch football together every single week. We already see each other every day at work.

"Shit," I mumble. I'm a fucking terrible friend. Without any more hesitation, I knock.

"Well there you are, buddy. Food is sizzling. The drinks are cold. C'mon." Jason steps aside for me to enter. I only have time to take a couple breaths before his three little daughters come bounding toward us.

"Uncle Aidan!" My name's squealed in unison in a pitch higher than I should be able to hear. Truthfully Kayla, Sadie, and Delilah are beautiful little girls. But they don't encourage me to procreate when they shriek, bouncing around like this. These girls cause destruction wherever they go. Tornadoes. They're cute little tornadoes.

"Hey, girls." I stoop to hug each. "How're you tonight?" What could be new with seven-, five-, and three-year-olds, I have no idea. Maybe a new Barbie was invented since I was over last week.

"We're watching Fishy. Wanna watch with us?"

Hell no.

"Sounds like fun, honey, but Uncle Aidan told your daddy he'd watch TV with him tonight. Maybe next time."

Fat fucking chance, kiddo. You're cute, but not that cute.

"I want a fishy like Nemo. Daddy can we have a fishy?" Little Delilah chimes in before the other two can get too upset I'm not joining them. Thank you, Delilah.

"Er...ask your mom," Jason says. With that, all three are off as fast as they came.

"I bet you use that one all the time." When I walk into the living room, I drop my case of beer on the oak coffee table. My feet aren't far behind.

"You bet your ass I do. It's all up to Amelia. That way she can never blame me." His smirk shows a deviant satisfied with his bullshit.

"You shouldn't give away all your tricks or they'll stop working." Amelia's sultry voice fills the air, thick and sweet as honey, while she glides into the room with a sway to her hips.

Fuck me.

I've got to stop myself from dropping my jaw and drooling as she comes closer. Amelia's tits are prouder, perkier, than ever in a clingy purple dress. Her hips are as round as her tight ass. Aerobics have been good to Amelia.

"Oops, pretend you didn't hear that, babe." Jason breaks my momentary daze with his response.

"Hey, Mel. How've you been?" *Would you like to sit on my face,* is what I'd rather ask, but as she's my best friend's wife that'd probably be frowned upon.

"Great. Everything's good. How 'bout you?" Though I never see myself getting married or having children, Amelia's one woman who could've made me question my resolve. If I could fuck someone that gorgeous day in and day out, I might reconsider. But since she's taken I doubt I'll ever make a commitment.

"Same ol' shit. I'm always good."

I'd be better if I were between your legs, inside of you.

Stop that shit.

I mentally shake myself of the image, popping open a beer for distraction. I have to stop thinking such trashy thoughts about Amelia. I don't know what's gotten into me tonight. Something's in the air I think.

"I'll go get the food." She stops to kiss Jason's forehead before turning toward the kitchen and giving me another thought I shouldn't be having. Jason turns on the TV, allowing me time to get the lust out of my eyes.

"So how was your night last night?" Jason slops beer onto his chin as he tips his bottle back, then uses the back of his hand, not a napkin, to clear it away. It's a cringeworthy thing to watch. He isn't always the cleanest person. I usually don't like dirty people. I like dirty women. Dirty sexually. But dirty men are a whole different story. Dirty for men equals disgusting. And Jason used to be cleaner. Maybe each pound he packed on lead to the loss of a social skill.

"Well I brought someone home. She was so damn—"

"Here you go, guys. If you finish all this just let me know. I'll whip up some more." Amelia comes in before I say anything too vulgar.

"Thanks, baby. You're too good for me."

She sure is.

"I sure am." Her lashes flutter as she winks at her husband. She passes him a plate then sets the tray of wings, chips, dip, and pizza on the coffee table.

Jason's eyes are on the TV instead of the ravishing cleavage so near. He may be my best friend, but what a fucking idiot. I'd be ravenous.

I've heard even the most beautiful women can have a man get tired of fucking them, though I struggle with why. Well, unless you're factoring in their personalities, opinions, baggage, nagging...Okay I guess I understand.

"Game time," he barks around a mouthful of greasy cheese.

"And that's my cue to scoot." As Amelia leans over to hand me my plate her creamy skin is so close to my face. Closer than it should be. As the plunging neckline of her dress deepens with her bend, my eyes are glued. Unlike Jason I could never get tired of looking at this. Her delicate fingers brush my knee as she hands over my food, and there's something in her smile I've never seen before. "Have fun, boys," she purrs. Then in the next instant she's gone.

While I eat, watching the game, drinking too many beers, all I can think about is Amelia. What was in her odd smile? I memorize the tingle that shot from my knee to my dick with her—*surely* accidental—touch since it'll be the only time I'll ever experience it. It was something to remember, though.

By halftime my bladder can take no more alcohol. "Be back in a minute."

chapter seven;

Amelia, Melody, and Eva invade my thoughts as I walk upstairs and down the quiet hallways to the bathroom. Three women capable of inducing blood flow at a rapid rate.

"How are you two on food? The girls are in bed now, so I can make more if you need."

I yelp in surprise as Amelia's head pops out from around a doorframe. Her thick hair swings down toward the floor as she smiles at my flinch.

"Shit, you scared me." I laugh with her at my reaction.

What a baby.

"Naughty. You shouldn't be swearing. The girls aren't far away." Amelia's eyes light up, with what I think is mischief, then her smile's broader than before.

"Damn, I'm sorry." She steps out of her bedroom and my cock twitches at what I see. Her dress has been shed for a super short crimson silk kimono that should be tied a little tighter. She didn't expect to see me again tonight. Right?

"There you go again. What're we gonna do with you?"

Anything you want is what I think, but, "Uuhhh..." is the only appropriate thing I can come up with to actually say.

She takes my idiocy in stride, laughing. "I'll go down to make dessert."

"You don't have to. We're fine. Everything you prepared was delicious. As always." There, that's much more coherent.

"Don't be silly. I'm here to please."

"Okay. If you insist. I'd never turn down your cooking." I start to turn, reaching for the bathroom's knob, but stop when I see Amelia wink in response. I turn back to face her with my fingers still on the handle.

"See you downstairs." Did I imagine her voice dropping to a breathier tone?

Amelia smiles, bending over, slower than typical, to pick up one of her daughter's toys on the floor, and I'm shocked at what she reveals to me. I can see everything down her robe from her sweet, pink nipples to the creamy tops of her soft thighs.

Before I have any more time to think, I jerk the bathroom door open to run inside.

Mel's shaved. I can't un-think the thought. I can't un-see her body. She's toned. She's hot. And fucking shaved.

Fuck.

It feels as if my mind's blank and racing simultaneously. I hear Amelia head down the stairs, then I catch faint laughing from Jason. Maybe they're laughing at me. Is it possible I completely misinterpreted what happened, and now she's telling him all about my mistake?

But what the fuck did happen?

As I take too long to finish up in the bathroom, I decide I'm an idiot. Mel and Jason have been sickeningly in love for longer than I can remember. If she even realizes she showed me her goods it couldn't have been intentional, and she'll be embarrassed. On the other hand, she might have no idea what I saw. Best response is to pretend nothing happened.

I walk back downstairs with a slightly less embarrassed air, calmed. If I don't think about it, I'll move past it. Then we can *both* pretend nothing happened.

But, fuck me, what I saw was more phenomenal than what I'd imagined could be beneath those clothes. Especially after popping out kids. Three of them. Jason's too lucky. I don't know what he did in his past life to deserve that next to him at night, but I'd better start working on my karma.

"If my bathroom reeks, the next game is at your place. You took long enough. The game's about to come back on." Clueless Jason.

"I'll order pizza next weekend. My place is fine." That way I can actually watch the game instead of your wife's ass bouncing above those toned legs that go on forever.

"Deal."

I need to get out of this house before I take her by force, becoming a criminal and losing my best friend at the same time. I need to get home. Get away. I need to think rationally. I need to get out.

"I'll bring the beer," he adds. Ignorant Jason. Blissfully ignorant. Lucky, fucking-dumb-as-shit, blissfully ignorant Jason. At least he's happy. That's for the better.

"Great," I respond as I set my last beer on the coffee table and ease to my feet. My first instinct is to run out of the house as fast as I can, but I need to remain conspicuous. "Well this game is already lost. I think I'll head home. I've got a couple things I need to finish up before I head to bed." Jason's smile falls in an instant.

"Really? There's still a quarter left." His disappointment is pitiful.

"I know, buddy. But I have to go." I add a provocative wiggle of my eyebrows. Maybe Jason will assume I'm going home to fuck somebody else instead of fantasizing about his wife in her silk robe. His wife against the rough siding of his house. His wife in the shower...

Much safer assumption on his part.

"Ooooohhhh. Okay." Mission accomplished. "Nice," he adds.

Jason walks me to the door, and it takes every bit of focus I have not to turn around for a glimpse of Amelia's hopefully exposed skin. "See you in the AM. Don't drink too much when we lose. Eva will crack down on your ass for a hangover."

"She's such a bitch, isn't she?" At least I'm not the only one who thinks so.

"Huge one." I could say more, but even with Jason I don't want to chance anything biting me in the ass. I can think any evil thought I want about that woman. I just don't need to utter them out loud.

"Bye." I wave with the hand not pulling my jacket closed on the way to my car. I'm definitely rushing more than necessary, but I'm so thankful to reach my car. The cold air is refreshing, so I leave my windows cracked on my way home, trying my hardest not to think about Amelia's silky skin. I refuse to get hard.

I refuse, damn it.

I will myself to refrain. Maybe if I continue over and over with a mantra of, *I think I can, I think I can, I think I can,* I actually can.

Or maybe not.

I look down at my crotch as I pull into my driveway. Rolling my eyes, I yank out my incredibly erect dick and start to stroke. My eyes glance to the stars briefly before closing to imagine several erotic images I should not be thinking. Behind my eyelids, I envision Amelia's full lips wrapped tightly around the tip of my cock. I can see her knuckles turning lighter from the pressure of squeezing my lower shaft. What I wouldn't give for fantasy to become reality.

KNOCK, KNOCK, KNOCK.

chapter Eight;

I jolt out of my imagination to the present as masculine knuckles rap against my car window. Thank fucking god my jacket is covering my exposed crotch. What the fuck was I thinking jacking it in my car, parked in the open night air, instead of waiting until I got into the privacy of my home? I need to get my shit together. These women, they've hypnotized me with sex, used their sorcery to scramble my brain.

Fucking women. All they do is fuck shit up.

I finally look up to the man outside my SUV who interrupted my stroke session. And, while I zip up as discretely as possible under my thin fabric cover, I'm somewhat surprised to see I have no idea who he is. As I turn the key to roll down my window, I notice a small scar above his left eyebrow. His jaw is clenched and his nostrils are slightly flared as if he's uncomfortable or frustrated. He doesn't look happy.

"Can I help you?"

"Could I borrow your cell phone for a second? My car died a couple blocks back." He points southwest, toward Main Street. "I have no idea what's wrong with it. I was hoping you'd let me use your cell to call my roadside assistance." So he isn't a cop here to arrest me for indecent exposure. He isn't the angry husband of any women I've fucked. He isn't a nosey neighbor asking if I've fallen asleep at the wheel. He seems to be a normal guy in need of some help.

Thank fucking god for that.

"Sure." I get out of my car, making sure to lock it behind me before handing him my phone with a sigh of relief. His unfortunate circumstances explain his air of frustration well enough. I'm not here to be assassinated.

He smiles, displaying crooked, stained teeth as he grabs my cell.

"Thank you so much. I seriously appreciate it. My name's Mark, and you are?" He extends his hand to shake when he asks. As I connect my hand with his I can feel his calluses as if he works outside for a living. Mine feels too soft in comparison. An odd feeling ripples through my chest, but as quickly as it arrives it leaves, and I have no time to analyze it.

"Aaron. I'm Aaron. Nice to meet you, Mark." Why did I lie? Giving a fake name, requiring anonymity, aren't normal impulses of mine.

I don't even know this guy.

I start to feel the same odd sensation spread through me again. Only it moves slowly this time, lingering. I don't know exactly how to describe it, but the best that comes to mind is a cross between a tingle and a pinch. Both at the same time. On the inside and out. I feel it shiver across every cell traveling from fingertip to heel.

Maybe I ate something bad at Jason's and need to lie down.

Mark wraps his coat tighter around his wide middle, giving an appreciative smile as I warm my hands in my pockets. "Well it's wonderful to meet you, Aaron. I'm from out of town, so this looked like a horrible situation until you pulled into your driveway. I was beginning to worry I'd freeze to death."

"Glad to help." I neglect to meet Mark's eyes any longer, instead I stare down the dark street. I don't know how, but I can tell I shouldn't maintain eye contact anymore.

While he dials roadside and speaks, I think about his stained teeth near the mouthpiece of my phone. I imagine the little germs carried by rank breath finding their way into every crevice, just waiting for the opportunity to strike the next time I make a call. I can almost see myself heaving over a toilet, spilling my guts because of this dirty man's bacteria-infested orifice. My stomach begins to churn in an unsavory way as my eyes search the night for something else to think about.

Before I can wipe the disgusting thought from my mind, Mark turns back to me. I see his mouth moving, but I only hear silence. I know he's speaking to me, I can see it, I just can't seem to sharpen my senses enough to take in what's being said. He puts my phone into my hand, which I hadn't realized was open, and I fight the urge to shudder or gag at the gifts from this stranger now crawling over my skin.

Suddenly with a sharp metallic *POP* I can hear Mark's words once more. Not only am I able to hear, but also the strange sensation that was raging through me subsides with the return of sound; the anger I didn't exactly realize was mounting begins to fizzle out.

Not sure when I got mad, or what about, I'm just glad it's retreating. I don't need another road-rage-type incident with this guy.

"Thanks again, Aaron. Here's my card. If I can ever repay the favor please call me. Anytime."

Though I have my auditory functioning back I don't seem to have use of my mouth. First I went deaf, and now my motor skills are frozen. I'm falling apart. Instead of responding verbally I simply nod my head in agreement. I take his business card, again noticing how rough the surface of his skin is compared to mine.

"Well I'd better start walking back to my car so I don't miss the tow truck. Have a good night, and don't forget to call so I can return the favor." His smile seems genuine, but I notice a glint of something menacing in his eyes I hadn't noticed before.

"Will do. Get home safely." With that I turn to make my way

inside.

What a weird encounter. From the outside I can't imagine anything looked amiss, but there was definitely something off. At least something in *me* was off.

And let's not forget I was having a grand old time with myself when he walked up. That just started the whole thing with a real exciting bang.

As I step up to unlock my front door, a violent urge crashes through me like a heavy wave, and I can't fight it before acting. I whip the tainted cell phone from my hand toward the unforgiving concrete. My blood pressure spikes. I see red, literally, which I didn't know was actually possible. I'd always thought it was just a saying. My breathing picks up speed, making me feel dizzy. But then everything subsides as I look down at the pieces lying next to my feet. Instead of feeling scared or confused I, oddly, feel accomplished. Stepping over the threshold into my entryway, I don't regret my sudden action.

I'll need to buy a new phone though.

***

I see elongated faces with widening black spots growing like sores. Pointed gray teeth come at me, and before any get close enough to touch me I can tell each is sharp like a razor. Jagged fingernails scrape against my back, but I'm unable to turn around. I can feel the thick warm blood begin to trickle down my shirt.

I can't get away.

I can't run. My legs won't work. I try to scream, and nothing comes out but air. I can move my limbs and I can hear myself whimpering in protest to my attackers, so why can't I run?

Suddenly the horrible teeth meet my waiting flesh, and finally a piercing sound, with force behind it, escapes my lungs. I yell, thrashing, but I still can't move fast enough to separate myself from those inflicting the pain.

Then I hear sizzling.

This can't be good.

I know this to be an irrefutable fact seconds before I smell my skin melting against white hot metal. Now instead of screams all that escapes past my lips are hysterical sobs.

"Please stop. Please. No more. Please." I beg over and over, between cries, until I've become hoarse.

Why me? What have I done to deserve such torture? I let out one last plea while tears splash down my cheeks accompanied by hiccups.

When will this end?

***

In panic I awake from a nightmare I can't quite piece together. Another nightmare. Usually when I have a nightmare, especially one that forces me back to consciousness, I can't fall back asleep despite all efforts. I pace, or I lie staring at the ceiling for hours. As tonight's departure from dreamland was so abrupt, I anticipate needing a great deal of caffeine tomorrow. But not even coffee can replace lost hours of needed restoration. Yet this time, though I can't remember what I dreamt about, I feel myself fall back to sleep with minimal effort. No sheep or warmed milk required. I smile thinking maybe something has changed, and I'll rest deeper the rest of the night, or maybe it wasn't a nightmare.

***

"Hey, good morning. How was your evening?"

Fucking bitch, why does she feel the need to make small talk in the elevator? Does she not sense my boiling, acidic hatred for her? Is she that stupid?

Yep she probably is. Why are the hot ones always so bitchy or stupid? Or in Eva's case, both.

Her incessant chatter and unpleasant voice are grating on my nerves more than normal, but I remind myself Eva's my boss. She's my boss. She is my boss. She is my boss. "Great, thanks for asking. You look lovely today. Did you sleep well?"

"Oh you charmer!" As a near squeal of delight escapes Eva's throat, I know flattery will serve me well with her. Why I haven't attempted more of this earlier, I have no idea.

I need to remember flattery.

As the elevator doors creak open on our floor, I look into her eyes and wink with just the ghost of a smile on my lips.

"Good work on those reports, Aid."

It's fucking Aidan. Not Aid. Can't you ever get my name right? I'm not your friend. I'm your subordinate. Your subordinate who should actually be your boss. But, I'm not your boss because I didn't suck old and flabby dick to stab you in the back. Lucky me you're resourceful if you're not smart. You should be watching your back too seeing as Aid is also your enemy.

I nod and smile as she flips her hair, batting her eyelashes. Some women are so damn easy to manipulate. Turning toward my office I'm happier knowing today I'll be on her good side even if she'll never be on mine.

I wonder how I could stay on her good side without driving myself insane. Not sure that's actually possible. Can I compliment and charm her all of the time without making myself sick? Or is there some other way?

I let that question fester in the recesses of my mind while I sit down and get to work for the day.

Chapter Nine:

I've always been proud of my capability to compartmentalize. I can do my work while thinking of other things. Still I never screw up. Numbers have always come so easily to me, which is why I chose this path, even graduating early. There's always one true answer when it comes to numbers. There's no guessing, no opinions, no argument. Either your answer is right or it's wrong. You may have an extremely complicated equation, leading you to come up with an incorrect answer, but there's always a way to tell you're wrong. It's nothing like English, Psychology, or Philosophy where you can argue your way into believability with any point. Nothing's wrong, so the reverse can be true and nothing's right either.

No, I like numbers. They're easier.

With this being the case, I've always been able to have the math part of my brain working simultaneously while I use another compartment to work on something else. It's a pretty sweet-ass ability. Who doesn't love multitasking? So many people complain there's too much to do in too little time.

I don't have that problem.

Today as I go through various financial reports and spreadsheets, I think about my behavior last night. I need a new phone, but the oddest part is I feel no anger at myself for reacting so unexpectedly. I search deeper, expecting to find shame, embarrassment, or some form of discomfort regarding my reaction. But there's nothing to find, nothing except a dull acceptance of what happened. The rushing spike in my system that led to the destruction of my cell, though unpredicted, was exhilarating. I acted without thinking. I did what I wanted to do before I even knew I wanted to do it.

Maybe I should practice letting my instincts take over more. Though, I've no idea how to go about that.

On the other hand, something that does bother me was my reaction to the man's hands. Why did I care, in the least, about them? What *exactly* upset me? Even though I spend a great deal of reflection on these questions I don't come up with any answer. Maybe I just felt weak in comparison to someone who's tough, someone who works with his hands instead of in a comfortable office?

Maybe.

And what was that vibrating, that tingling, that numbing feeling? It spread through my system like a predator slinking through tall grass, toward juicy prey. What the fuck was that a reaction to? I've never felt anything like it before in my thirty something years. I don't know if it was his toughness, or his dirty teeth. Or it could've been something changing in my body. Did Amelia poison something I ate? Possibly.

Or maybe I have a tumor.

Of course, I wasn't' fucking poisoned. And I doubt I have a tumor.

But maybe it was all some sort of lingering reaction to my peep show from Amelia. Maybe the adrenaline, and whatever other hormones, were still floating in excess around my body to combine for an unpleasant, ill-timed effect. Almost getting caught stroking the snake could have spiked my blood pressure too. Maybe, when I was startled, everything together just added up to a nasty shock.

That's it. For sure. A shocked system is to blame for my unpredictable behavior and thoughts. Nothing more.

Don't get paranoid. Weird things happen for no reason. Though, someone once told me just because you're paranoid doesn't mean they aren't out to get you.

***

Around lunch time my kindness to Eva backfires. When I see her walking down the hall toward my office with a devilish smirk on her pouty, pink lips I have the urge to run. Or puke. Or both.

How I'd love to dig my teeth into those plump lips, drawing a metallic taste where the sharpest points meet.

"Knock, knock." Why do some people say "knock" while they're knocking? Redundant. Her smile is playful, and I'm annoyed.

She pauses to laugh, flashing her overly bleached teeth. "May I come in?"

I'd wholeheartedly love to say no. "Of course you may," I say, faking a smile and nearly choke on the sour-tasting words scraping my throat on the way out.

Strangely, Eva closes my door behind her as she walks in past the frame. Hmmm, that's odd. I doubt I'll like what comes next.

"Please, sit. What can I do for you this afternoon?"

She's already moving to sit before I start my gesture toward the plush leather chair across from my desk. Guess she didn't need the invitation. I hate myself for it, but I notice how her skintight skirt rides up above her knees as she sits. Eva flashes soft skin as if it better establishes her position of dominance in the office. And who the fuck knows, maybe it does. She doesn't cross her legs, simply holds them together at the knee with her feet tipped to one side of her frame. No matter how much I hate her, I'd love to look between those knees.

Shit.

Focus, Aidan.

She still hasn't started speaking, let alone stated her purpose for this drop-in. I'm getting impatient. Then her lips part and she leans just a fraction forward, dipping the hem of her collar a millimeter lower. I'd give even more to see under that shirt.

Good job focusing, Idiot.

"I was wondering if you'd like to join me for lunch today. I have a few ideas for our department I'd like to run by you."

Huh? What? Why me?

"I'd love to." I give my best seductive smile. It works. Eva's cheeks turn a shade warmer in appreciation. She's too easy.

"Good. Don't tell anyone else what we talk about today. I'm letting you into this first. I want your opinions before I solidify everything. I trust you, Aidan. I want you to know that."

Seriously? She honestly trusts me? That's both shocking and a terrible idea.

"I'm so glad to know that. You definitely can. Everything stays between us." *Yeah fucking right.* Fat chance. I'll stab you in the back the first chance I get, and I won't hesitate to twist the knife after it's deep between bones.

Eva smiles once more before standing, running her hands down her outfit. I can't tell if she's intentionally accentuating her curves or if this gesture has become a habit born from nervousness. Either way, when her fingers graze the sides of her ample breasts my mouth waters just a tad.

"Meet me downstairs in the lobby in an hour." She states. She doesn't ask. Although I'm glad to be on the inside, that way I can better watch her moves, her demanding instead of requesting rubs me the wrong way. My natural inclination is to do the exact opposite of what she orders me to do.

But I'll never let her know that. I keep in mind: keep your friends close, but keep your enemies closer.

Perfect.

That's just what I'll do.

***

I ponder what Eva has to tell me for the next hour, getting little work done. That doesn't matter, though, because I finished everything this morning. Ahead of schedule, per usual.

What could she have planned for our department? Is she going to stir the pot? The big bosses don't often like boat-rockers. Maybe she's unknowingly planning her own demise. God, that'd be wonderful. If she could kill her own career without my hands getting dirty I'd get the best of both worlds.

I stop to nod to Jason as I leave for my lobby rendezvous, giving him a mischievous grin.

"Where're you going?"

"Boss lady requested my presence at lunch." I stifle another smirk when Jason scoffs.

"Just you?" I wiggle my eyebrows to add to his, what I assume to be, incorrect assumption. I hope he's wrong.

I whisper, "Maybe she'll be walking funny by this afternoon. Keep an eye out." With Jason's shocked face behind me, I turn to head for the lobby.

Eva's ready when the jerky doors slowly open on the first floor to let me out of the death trap. Her tight nude wool coat is cinched at her waist, accentuating her hourglass figure, and my resolve to continue hating her is not helped as she bends at that waist to sip from the water fountain, pointing her round ass toward me.

Holy fuck.

With more effort than it should take, I shift my line of sight toward the glass front doors before she straightens. She doesn't need to know the effect she has on the flow and location of my blood. The more she has to vie for my attention the better.

Outside, the world is significantly different than the warm, clean lobby. The snow beyond the glass is gently falling on every surface it can reach. The sky is bleak, gray. Everything seems to have a dingy gloom stuck to it, clinging and taking over. Sounds are muted by the growing covering of flakes with mush coloring. Looking out there makes everything seem harder to accomplish than it does from indoors. I remember again why I put my back to the window in my office. Days like this make me want to crawl into bed.

"Damn snow." Eva slips her slender fingers through the crook of my arm after startling me. She giggles with what I think is supposed to be a flirtatious, youthful sound at my flinch. But the attempt just sounds pathetic, even desperate, to me, aging her.

At least she's always reminding me why I hate her. She never lets me go long enough to second-guess that.

"Yeah, it always starts too early, doesn't it?"

"And lasts too long," she adds with a nod.

"Well, shall we venture out into it?" Without waiting for a response, I lead her outside to the frigid air and slick sidewalk.

Eva leaves her arm in mine, using it to steady herself on the slippery surface beneath our feet. Her footwear, though it wonderfully accentuates her bottom half, isn't made for questionable terrain. I don't envy women's fashion. Yes it looks great, but most of the time it just can't be comfortable.

chapter Ten;

We head for the restaurant without discussing where we plan to go. There's only one place either of us considers. Delta's Grill is two blocks away, making it the most convenient location, especially since Eva's bare legs sprout goose bumps seconds after leaving the warmth behind. Plus Delta's also has somewhat secluded booths, which seem beneficial for today's discreet agenda.

"Thanks for consulting with me today. Your assistance won't be forgotten." Eva's features border on boastful, as if she's already moving up the ranks as we walk.

Not if I have anything to do about it, bitch.

"Absolutely. As the department progresses, so does everyone included in it. I may be helpful, but I'm certainly not selfless," I say. *Especially if you knew why I'm willing to "help" you.*

"Well put. Very well put." Eva laughs as I open the doors ahead.

We're shown to a booth toward the rear corner that's partially shielded by a wall of charcoal satin. I make sure to let Eva pick her seat first then sit across from her. I'm ready, sure this lunch will become interesting soon.

Our waitress makes an appearance quickly, ready for a generous tip. Her skin is almost orange with an obviously manufactured tan, and her hair frizzes outward in different angles, but her eyes are kind and her smile possesses genuine happiness.

"Hi, folks. My name's Kristi. I'll be helping you out today. What can I get for ya?"

I let Eva order first in feigned respect. "I'll have your chicken Caesar salad with a double vodka on the rocks." I look to Eva, ensuring I've heard correctly. Secrets and drinks. Interesting.

We're diving head first into the questionable pond.

"Sounds good, doll. And for you?" Kristi's laugh lines deepen as she turns to face me.

"I'll have the turkey avocado on rye, with a Jack and coke." Collecting the menus, I pass them back to Kristi's waiting hands.

"Can do, Love. I'll get those right in." She swishes back to the kitchen as quickly as she came.

"All right, Aid." I wish this cunt would stop calling me that. "I want you to be honest with your opinions, because as I said before, I trust you." *Well you're stupid to, but I already knew that.*

"Promise I will be. I'm ready." But before Eva can delve into her plans, Kristi returns with our drinks.

"Here's your vodka, and your Jack. Can I get anything else for you folks while you wait?" Her smile is attentive. She bounces while she speaks, too. I bet she gets a good amount of tips here, near so many high-end office buildings, and as friendly as she is.

"Yes, please, another for me." Again Eva catches me with her bold gesture to drink a second double. Does she plan on me carrying her back to the office?

Fat chance there, bitch.

"Of course." Again our waitress disappears.

I turn to Eva, ready for her proposal once more, watching as she downs the entire liquid contents of her first glass.

"Shit." I just can't keep it in.

Eva tips back, her long hair cascading toward her seat, and laughs a hearty sound I don't normally hear from women. So many hold back in attempts to sound dainty. But this laughter comes from deep within Eva's belly and sounds wonderfully real (possibly the only real thing I've ever heard from her) as it passes her nibble-worthy lips. It's the first time she's enticed a genuine smile from me in a long time.

Once she's finished she adds, "I just needed to loosen up. I hope you don't mind."

I raise my glass to her, duplicating her previous actions. Placing it back on the table, I turn my hand over, sweeping it across the table in a gesture for her to begin.

The less I say here the better. At least until I have a plan.

"I want to shake things up." Ha, I knew it. Goodbye, Eva. You *won't* be missed.

As I see many scenarios of Eva's leaving, her knee grazes mine, and I'm jostled back to the conversation in front of me. Though I pretend to not have noticed.

"Go on." I add a far-from-genuine smile to coax her along.

"I want to change a lot, actually. Here," she says. She leans over to extract a folder from her luxurious briefcase, again tempting me to peer down where her shirt's buttons are undone to the paler skin of her breasts. Despite my dislike for her, I can't refrain when the opportunity to look at her beautiful body arises. She may be awful, but I'd fuck her lookalike in a heartbeat. As long as those looks were attached to a different person entirely, with a different personality. "These are the ideas I've come up with." She pulls out an extensive list, beginning to detail all her daring thoughts.

Eva wants to cut half of our department to hire more seasoned, distinctly more expensive, field experts. She wants to purchase brand new software that hasn't been fully tested yet, which comes, again, at great cost. And after these changes, she wants to bid for competitive, wealthy clients. Her plan isn't out of the realm of possibilities, but if not executed precisely it'd crumble, losing the company an obscene amount. I hate to admit, it's smart. *I really,*

really hate that. It's also risky, very risky, and the heads will never go for it. The potential loss is just too great for them to get past.

During her rush of excited explanation, we receive our food from the haggard but sweet Kristi. Eva neglects to thank her. She eats slowly while the speed of her words increases.

I don't interject with more than a nod throughout, wanting to seem like a cohort, but not wanting to give her too much.

While delineating each bullet point, Eva drains her second glass, and her gestures move from subdued to boisterous as the alcohol begins to seep through her system. Yet she manages to keep her voice at an acceptable volume. She seems to be holding her liquor pretty well for a trim woman.

Somewhere she must have built a decent tolerance.

"So, Mr. Quiet, what do you think?" This time I don't mistake the touch of her leg as accidental underneath the table. It may have been if she'd removed it immediately, like last time, but instead Eva's knee lingers against my thigh, gently rocking up and down for just a few seconds.

She wants to impress me in several ways.

It takes everything I can muster to ignore her silent cries for attention. I'd, in other circumstances, do vulgar things to Eva, but right now I need to focus on her self-destruction instead.

"Fucking brilliant. You'll move up, and when you do I expect to be taken with you." I look into her slightly-out-of-focus eyes as I place my hand on top of hers. "This'll take you far. You're a damn genius." Okay I'm putting it on a little thick, but that won't matter with her buzz or her gluttony for compliments.

"I was hoping you'd say something like that." She squeezes my hand before winking and smiling broader than I've ever seen her before. For the second time today, I see something genuine from her.

"Can I suggest a few things?"

"Please do." She leans forward, ready to steal my ideas, passing them off as her own. That's exactly what I'm hoping for.

I lavish Eva with praise, feeding her horribly risky ideas to add to her list. I squirm with pleasure as she jots down equipment she didn't know existed, and individuals, geniuses, we could never afford. I also hint toward a wildly successful company that she should model her proposals after. It's not well known yet, but that same company is on its way to a destructive crash and burn. The bosses should know, though she clearly doesn't. I also sneak in a nickname for our VP that will piss him off, hoping she'll start to use it too.

Though I need better ideas to fuck her over, these are what I have for now.

"Danny will be putty in my hands." She's too easy.

Our check comes, further establishing Eva's stance on my side. And again I don't react when she utters her thanks and places her hand on my knee with an added squeeze.

"It's my treat, for being included and trusted."

"I think I see quite a few more lunches in our future."

"So do I, gorgeous. So do I." Eva bubbles over with laughter as we pass through the doors outside once more. Charming her can never be neglected again.

chapter Eleven;

Eva's face is contorted in what can only be described as excruciating pain. Her eyes bulge alarmingly as her silent screams crackle with hoarse desperation. She begs for it to end with both her words and her features.

I hear my own laughter before I feel it in my chest. My shoulders shake with each sound, and I can see my hands shaking as well. It's evident, maybe only to me, but they shake with excitement in comparison to Eva's fearful shaking.

She moves from pleading with her cries to simply moaning.

When I look past my hands to Eva's body, I see splotches of crimson. It seeps from holes all over Eva's naked skin.

I can't stop myself as I reach to fondle her large breast, pinching her delicate nipple.

She screams again. This time it's a piercing sound, and I slap her hard across the face, dragging my knife along as well.

It shuts her up as I'd planned.

"Now tell me you want me." The words are coming from my mouth, it's my voice speaking the demand, but it doesn't feel like it's coming from me. "Tell me NOW."

An odd floating sensation begins to roll through me as I hear Eva's words pouring from her bloodied lips. "I want you. I've always wanted you....So bad." She chokes on the last words, tears falling down her face, turning pink after mixing with the blood already splashing her cheeks.

"And now you die," I say.

I watch as the knife in my hand moves between her legs, lunging sharply upward. Seconds afterward her body goes limp, and I'm no longer pinning her to the cold concrete wall.

***

Again I wake up sweaty from a confusing, horrible nightmare. To my horror, I reach down to feel my cock throbbing and hard.

What the fuck, Aidan? But I don't have an answer.

Straining to bring myself back to reality, I see it's still dark outside. I look toward the clock. Fuck, it's only 3:30 AM.

Well, at least it's the weekend.

I attempt to remember everything that comprised my dream, but all I recall is the passion and urge to control, to conquer, Eva. I know I dreamt of killing her, and I know how dark the notion is that I wish I could. She's caused me nothing but trouble, and if I could murder her while getting away with it I probably would.

I'd be picked first for motive, though, with her theft of my promotion. So at least there's something, even if it's flimsy, holding me back.

I resolve to let my disgust go and think about it later instead.

Hoisting myself out of bed, I pad, naked, into the stone-covered bathroom. As steam fills the room, I look past what's in front of me. I envision Eva's naked body pressed between me and the wall as I step into the hot shower.

Beginning to rub myself, I close my eyes, but visions of splattered blood worm their way in, invading my fantasy. Eva's face hovers feet away from my closed eyes, her mouth contorted in pain once more as my moans of pleasure get loud enough to fill the entire bathroom just before I finish with one last yell, "Fuck," that's drawn out and breathy.

After my shower, I find it easy to slip back into a deep, restful sleep.

***

After an uneventful Saturday morning, excluding my dream, another trip to Spot Z is required. With Eva and Amelia's untouchable figures floating in and out of my head, I need to feel real skin beneath my fingers tonight. An actual body beneath me. I need to caress tits that aren't unavailable to me in one way or another. I need to get this frustration out with the help of my cock. With a real woman, not a mirage, or a dream, or just my thoughts.

If I get laid I should be able to think straighter, more rationally. Backed-up needs could be to blame for my troubles lately. Basically, I know I need to get my dick wet tonight. The possibility of running into Melody again brings a tingle to my stomach. She can make me forget these other convoluted complications with her silky curves and filthy words. She'll erase the pressing issues from my mind.

After making the decision to go, I dress quickly, in a hurry to make my evening exciting or at least eventful.

Dressed in hugging black pinstriped pants and a cream V-neck sweater to match the pinstripes, I check my reflection in the mirror. Satisfied that my clothes will get me some much-needed ass, I liberally slap on cologne, then call it good. Adding my sleek black winter jacket, I bound to the front door thinking about the dirty possibilities tonight may bring.

Grabbing my keys, I lock the front door, again deciding to walk the short distance to Z despite the chill in the dark night air. I want to be able to drink without worrying about making a dumb decision afterward. And with a slight bounce in my excited steps, I start walking.

On the short trip over I watch the houses as I walk by. Wondering what's happening inside each beyond the windows and curtains, I can't imagine living as these quiet little families do. I'd be sucked down into the thick, heavy monotony, and I'd decay inside from the boredom. I couldn't live with the responsibility of running every decision by another. No, I need to be in charge of my own bad decisions.

Again I realize I've made the right call with the life I lead.

The lights from Z grow bigger and brighter as I get closer. I can feel the vibrating punch of the too-loud speakers, too. There's no line outside, not even the bouncer, since the temperature's taken another dip. No one wants to stand in this shit.

As I near the dirty front door, my hand reaching for the handle, it swings open, almost hitting me in the process. A stumbling tangle of long blond curls and tight black spandex collides with me just outside the entrance. I react as quickly as I can, after a steadying step backward. I balance the woman who ran into me with a hand on both of her sides to prevent her from tumbling backward into the now-closed door.

"Holy shit. M'so sorry." Her slurred words send a shiver down my spine as she utters them breathily next to my ear. My hands slide down from her shoulders to her slender waist.

"No problem. Glad you're okay." I take another step back to look at my attacker's face and more importantly her figure. Her eyes are wide and light, with a slight glaze that can only come from lots of alcohol. Her lips are full and heavy, while her hair is long and begging to be pulled. Her tits are a hint smaller than average, but her ass is generous, perky, and all well-toned muscle. She's fuckable.

Yeah, she'll do.

"You come here with anyone, honey?"

"S'ur didn't."

"Planned to leave with anyone?"

"Only-you, Handsome." Her slur isn't improving with the cold, and she has to be freezing. Her dress is strapless, ending an inch or two below where her legs begin, but she isn't shivering yet.

"Good answer, beautiful." With an agreement reached, I make a quick decision to simplify the short walk back for both of us. I bend a little at the knee, running my fingers along the back of her tantalizingly smooth legs before grabbing them and hoisting her up into my arms to carry her home. Her drunken giggles fill the air as I walk as briskly as the added weight will allow.

This was a whole hell of a lot easier than I'd anticipated.

"What d'you want t'do t'me, baby?"

She starts to giggle again at the smirk I flash her before adding, "Probably more than you're ready for, but don't worry, I'll get you ready."

Oh, I'll get her ready all right.

chapter Twelve:

I look down at the alabaster skin shining below me, glittering with perspiration, as she screams high-pitched yelps of pleasure.

"Oh fuck. Fuck me, baby. Fuck me harder!" Her screams encourage me.

I grab her thin waist, flipping her over in one fluid motion. Running my fingers down her moist back, I let the waves of pleasure roll through me. This is what I needed.

This is what I deserve.

I pull out for a just a moment.

I earned this. Without question.

I reach beneath her to pinch her nipples as I reenter her from behind, and she starts to moan once again. One sound flows into the next, and she refuses to quiet while I continue to ride her hard, deep, giving her all I can.

As I'd anticipated, her hair is perfect for pulling while she begs for more.

***

Blondie (I never did catch her name) and I go at it twice more in the next few hours. After the adrenalin runs out, we both collapse from exhaustion onto the soft sheets. I start to sink into oblivion as soon as my head hits the pillow. But just before I let go, my prowess hits me: *I'm the rock star of fucking*. Then a deep sleep sets in that only comes after physical exertion and satiation.

***

This time I know I'm dreaming as I hear screams of terror entering my ears from what seems like a long distance away. It feels as if I have cotton in them as all sounds are muffled, distorted.

I look down at Blondie beneath me again as I straddle her, seeing her mouth wide open. Pure shock stretches across each of her petite features. She's horrified, paralyzed in terror.

I cover her mouth with my large hand, leaning close to her face.

"You asked what I wanted to do to you, baby. Well I didn't just want to fuck you. I had more in mind." I wink. "This is more"

I dip my pointer and middle fingers into her wet, warm mouth before switching hands to keep her from speaking. I've no desire to hear anything she has to say. Nothing can change my mind now.

Reaching behind me with the dripping fingers, I insert them into her waiting slit. Warmer than her mouth, it begs me to continue with my assault, and I'm happy to oblige for several moments.

After I'm satisfied with that task, I again lean forward toward her pretty face. Pulling my hand that was deep within her up to her face, I put my fingers back into her mouth despite her adamant protests. With the free hand I reach into my bedside table where I keep my protection. I wave the sharp knife before her frozen eyes.

I feel as if I've floated out of my body, now watching myself on top of her frame. I can see how securely I'm holding her down and how scared she looks. Then I watch detached as I plunge the blade deep into the side of her neck. She looks prettier now as the blood seeps from her body, onto my bed. She was too flushed before. Too alive. I watch as the life drains slowly from her eyes, her features slacking a fraction of an inch, sagging without the animation of life holding her together.

What a horrific dream.

I detangle my legs from Blondie's, lying back on my side of the bed. I'm glad it's over as the blackness of unconsciousness takes me over and out of dreamland again.

***

With a satisfied smile I blink away the lingering sleep from my eyes. It's still dark. The clock says it's just after 3 AM again.

I can feel in my lower extremities I've had a busy night. My cock is as satiated as my ego. I'm calmer, more relaxed, than I have been since Melody was here. I flash back to the sexual pictures of Blondie's body, and I harden once again. I needed everything I got. But I could definitely go for more

I reach over to wake Blondie up for another round and feel a cold wet spot.

"Fuck, did you piss the bed?" I know she was drunk, but I've never had anyone do this. How disgusting.

But it doesn't smell like piss. It smells of something entirely different, something I can't quite put my finger on.

I roll over, flipping on the lights, preparing to examine exactly what's gone wrong. Rolling back to survey the damage, I freeze.

The smell is iron, it's rusty and metallic, salty and red. I can't believe what I'm seeing.

I can't scream.

I can't breathe.

I can't move.

I can't think.

What the fuck did I do? Jagged breath escapes my dry lips, and I can't believe it's coming from me.

chapter Thirteen;

I stare at the pool of blood underneath a lifeless blonde woman next to me. In my bed.

Dead.

Dead woman.

Dead woman in my bed.

Dead woman, next to me, in my bed.

I thought I'd been dreaming. Could I seriously have been doing what I thought was playing out in the depths of my dreams? *No*. This can't actually be happening. I must still be dreaming.

That wasn't me. It's as if I hear my thoughts in a hiss.

I couldn't have done this.

But I can feel my blood pumping, my blood pressure rising, and my adrenaline kicking in. I'm absolutely awake, I'm not dreaming. This *is* happening right now.

My fight or flight response is kicking in. But I have no one to fight, and I can't run away either without expecting severe fucking consequences.

The first thing that breaks through the haze is determination.

I will not get caught. I will get away with this. Mistake or fate, there's no way I'm throwing my life away for Blondie.

No. I need to stop; I need to think. I need to figure out what the fuck to do.

What the fuck? What the fuck.

My breath is still ragged and my mind can't stop racing. I've killed someone.

I fucking killed someone.

***

I take a second to realize I'm not entirely remorseful. I don't feel ecstatic about what I've done, though, either. I'm torn. There's a red line traced down the center of my body in her blood; it runs from scalp to scrotum, and the two sides can't agree. Each pulls the other in a vicious tug of war. I don't feel all of anything, but instead I feel a little of everything.

That can't be good.

I'm not sure how I came to this point, this crossroad. I've become a killer, and didn't expect it to happen, never saw it coming. How can something like that just surprise anyone? After this is all cleaned up, I need to think. I'll need to process. But for now I need to get this bitch out of here and away from any trace of me. This analyzing shit can wait until I've taken care of this mess.

Right now, all I want to do is hide what I've done since there's no way to undo it.

I'm overwhelmed with no idea where to start. This isn't a problem I can discuss. There's no one to brainstorm with. Not even Blondie here can share in the delightful conversation. I look around my room, trying to call the answers to me. But nothing happens. I'm at a loss.

Fuck, fuck, fuck.

I finally jump out of bed, running to the shower. First I need to shower. I need to be clean in order to think straight. That'll help. I can't process through the coat of already-crusting blood; it's preventing plans from forming.

I blank my mind as the water begins to rush out of the head, heating the bathroom on this chilly night. I need a fresh start, a blank slate, in order to come up with the best plan. I need to let go of every feeling I'm struggling with, let go of every thought.

I wait until the entire bathroom is full of warm, steamy fog, and then I hop into the scalding water. The parts of my skin that are touched by the stream turn red. It hurts, but I relish the feeling, soaking in the pain. I close my eyes, push my palms into the contrastingly cool tile, leaning my forehead between my hands. The two different temperatures help to finish clearing my mind. Under the pounding water and surrounded by hot cloudy mist, coherent thoughts finally start to form, stringing together.

I let myself think back to the bedroom, back to what happened.

Envisioning it moment by moment, this time fully knowing it wasn't a dream, I try to look at what I did through the lens of reality instead of fantasy. This woman had done nothing wrong. She had satisfied me, several times, and I hadn't even known her name. I didn't seek revenge, as I would've with someone like Eva. She didn't provoke me. She was simply there when I was ready.

Wrong place, wrong time for her, but both right for me.

A switch was flipped inside, and I'm not sure if there's any way it can be reversed. But again, that's something to ponder after I take care of the dead body in the middle of my bed. *Holy fucking shit.* There is a dead body in my bedroom waiting for me to do something about it. Hide it.

A disgusting grin begins to creep its way across my face, and I'm both mortified and intrigued to have such a reaction. My cheeks rise, creating lines by the corners of my eyes.

Though, as quickly as the grin spread, it disappears. I smack my face hard, quick and biting, to wake myself. Fuck, I need to get a grip; there's still action to be taken. It works, but the mood swings better stop. Blondie was a living, breathing woman hours ago, and I ended that. I still need to pick up the pieces before they drip onto the expensive flooring.

The water swirls down the drain, each droplet representing a possibility for what to do next. I know I have options. I just need to pick one, and since emotion is getting me nowhere, I move to logic. I'm better with logic anyway.

No one saw her leave with me, and there was no way anyone could've known she was doing anything but going home alone. In fact, she said she had been at the bar alone. I didn't tell anyone I was going to Z tonight, and they have no cameras outside. *Thank you, Jason, for providing this tip.* He wasn't the first mugged outside Z. Probably won't be the last, either.

No one saw me.

I didn't even add the miles on my car since I walked. She didn't call anyone on her phone or mine since leaving the bar. I have no motive, and I have no connection to her other than her evening here, which no one else knows about.

If I can clean up sufficiently and create a plan to get rid of the body, I may be free and clear.

But how do I get rid of her? That's the big question of the day.

I turn off the water, since the heat is dwindling, and I need to get down to work. I dry off quickly, refraining from putting any clothing on. I'll need to shower again after my work here is done. This is going to be a messy job.

First I grab the knife, my weapon, bringing it to the bathroom sink. I've actually used a weapon. I've never used anything as a weapon before, well, nothing other than my fists when I punched my cousin in the stomach that time when we were in school. Now I've used an object as a legitimate weapon.

Shit, that's kind of cool.

Returning to the bedroom, I carefully strip the bedding out from under Blondie's body and throw them in the shower. She sure seemed lighter when she was still breathing. Logically, this seems odd since she should be lighter without all that blood she's since forgone. It's now marring my expensive sheets. Luckily, I have a protective plastic sheet covering my mattress. I have no idea how I would've disposed of a mattress if it too were soaked with Blondie's fluids.

Thank fuck for small miracles.

Grabbing the bleach, I douse both the sheets and knife to remove every trace of blood I can. I send additional pours of the acrid liquid down the drain to clean what has started down the pipes, careful not to get any on my swinging dick because that'd fucking sting, and I need to stay focused.

I doubt this clean-up job would pass any crime scene tests, but it's the best I can do for now.

Shit. I need to wrap up her body. I can't drag her outside like this. It wouldn't be too popular with the neighbors. And I don't have a shower curtain since the entire shower stall is constructed of glass other than the walls. I thought it looked sleeker, but right now a tacky curtain would help me a lot. Then again, I never anticipated being buck-ass naked standing in my bathroom trying to come up with something to wrap and dispose a dead body in.

Go figure.

I decide to use the plastic mattress cover to wrap Blondie's body in for the time being. That'll have to do, and I'll just have to buy another.

chapter fourteen;

Before I go any further, I sit down next to her on the plastic with a notebook in my lap, a pen poised above. I need to replace a few things after I get rid of her. I scribble several items that come to mind.

Sheets/bedding
Kitchen knives
Mattress cover
Leather gloves
Rope
Plastic bags
Bleach
Matches
Laundry detergent
Milk

I add the milk because I don't want to make myself seem too suspicious. What if someone found this list someday? I can't be too careful here. I need to consider things as much as I can from a detached perspective, from every angle, and I'm proud this list isn't too incriminating at first glance. Now it looks like any list I can take care of in one shopping trip.

Plus, well, I need milk.

I look over at Blondie, satisfied with what I've done so far, noticing for the first time her eyes are still open as well as her mouth, both in a shocked expression. Vulnerability and pleading read strong on her face. This was the last face she ever contorted, and I'll be the only person to see it.

I feel a tingle prickle on the top of my scalp, and a shiver courses down through my spine. I can feel my arousal kicking in quickly.

I killed this bitch.

I ended her life. I watched her last breath and felt the final pulses of heat emanate from her pussy.

Before I realize what I'm doing, my cock's in her open mouth. I can't reign myself in. I feel her tongue loll inside of her head, and I watch the finality of death in her eyes as I satisfy myself once more with Blondie.

When I finish a sinking feeling settles it.

I'm a fucking depraved, sick son of a bitch.

I really, probably, shouldn't have done that.

***

I know my DNA is all over her, and it was even before that last assaultive mistake. I need to dispose of her in a way that'll get rid of my mark. After the sheets and knife have dried, I wrap them in the plastic with Blondie, racking my brain for what to do with her. Where can I leave her? How can I get rid of all links back to me?

Water.

With the wonderful world of television, I've learned water washes away a lot of evidence. Not all, I'm sure, but a lot. And how convenient that Maine has an ocean close enough to dispose of her in.

But I don't want any blood in my car. That'd be bad.

And I can't rent a car to bring her to a disposal spot with the chance of spilt blood either, since my name will be linked with a rental as well. How can I get her from here to the ocean without leaving a trail that'll lead back to me?

Then I've got it.

Fuck me, it's brilliant.

I know how to do it without incriminating myself. But in the process I'll definitely be putting poor, innocent, unassuming Jason at risk.

Well that's too fucking bad for him, I guess.

Another pang hits me hard. I've become a selfish asshole. When I'm safe and have the time, I need to evaluate some things. I'm not entirely sure where I want to go from here on out.

I'd nearly forgotten I still have the spare key to both the storage locker and Jason's car. Even better, I'm not the only person with a set of spare keys. Amelia has a set, and I think his parents do too. He never asked for mine back. Plus I don't think he'd question for a second if I lied and said I had.

This is going to work. I know it will.

After devising my plan, I put on dark warm clothing and a tight winter hat. I don't want to freeze as I throw Blondie in the cold current that will wash her away forever. I add dark leather gloves to prevent fingerprints in the duct tape I use to seal her, her leakage, and the other incriminating items in the plastic sheet. It'd probably be good if my hairs stay out of the adhesive on the tape, too. I even add the rest of the tape roll in with her body to prevent two edges of tape being matched together with the roll still in my possession. No ties to me.

Tape just can't be my downfall. I can't be *that* guy.

Satisfied with my work, I grab the spare keys to walk to Jason's storage locker.

***

Jason's car is a thing of beauty, and I feel kind of bad looking at

Blondie inside of the trunk when I reach my destination spot. But I'm too distracted by Blondie's dulling eyes, ghostlike expression, and naked body to care as much as I could for the muscle car's interior. I need to get rid of her, and I need to do it fast.

Blondie is much heavier than I remember as I lift her out of the trunk. Dead weight is so much heavier than live, heavier than expected. I slip a few times trying to get her out, and swipe away the perspiration that leaks beneath my hat.

"Fuck." I definitely drop her on the ground. This is not as graceful as books and movies make it out to be.

I need to stick to skinny girls in the future.

Oh fuck me that was a slip. There won't necessarily be a future like this.

Thankfully the sky is still pitch black, and the streets are barren. I feel as if I'm alone in the world. This feels like a precious gift given to me despite what I've done. I have time to revel in the new reality I've created, not totally sure if it's sewage or a magic elixir I'm standing in. I feel as if I'm in it up to my chest, though. I can either stew in this forever, or I can debate the possibilities ahead of me and walk deeper into it or back away slowly.

There are two paths I can choose between, leading me to two different people I have the opportunity to become. I'm just not sure which road I'll take yet.

But quickly a hollow feeling creeps into my momentary self-absorption and moral dilemma. Uncertainty starts to burn at the edges of my mind, singeing deeper than I prefer. I can feel myself becoming more and more uncomfortable as I hold the lifeless body in my arms. She could either be my prize or the thing that unglues me. Even if I took the road of decided killer I can't be proud of what I've done tonight. It was not planned. It was not intentional. Hell, I didn't even know I was doing it until it was all over.

I toss her in the ocean with a sense of revulsion. She moves away, finally sinking, but my nausea doesn't subside. No matter what happens, she'll never count as my first victim. If I choose to have more she won't be included in my tally, and if I go back to a normal, moral life I'll do my best to erase tonight from my memory. Walking back to the car, I wonder if there's a pill for that.

chapter fifteen:

I've lost my watch, sleep chronically evades me, and I'm fully aware of how harried and unhygienic I look, yet I slough off the worry. I don't give much of a shit about what other people think right now. I do know this unkempt style won't fly for long, but for now no one's said anything.

Actually, I feel sharper than normal. I've been on my toes, ready for whatever's thrown my way. It helps too that I don't smell since I've showered, despite looking like I haven't. I've just slept on wet hair, not caring to fix it before leaving the house in the morning. I've had too much on my mind.

I've been struggling with the huge decision needing to be made. The one that's been following me around like a lost puppy, or a stalker. The decision I still need to make before it eats me alive. For days I've gone back and forth with what I could do, with what I shouldn't do, with what I want to do. It felt *so* good somewhere dark and deep within me to do what I did to Blondie. But at the same time, the little voice that is my version of a conscience reminds me how terrible it was, especially in the eyes of others and the consequences it leads to. It's not something most people do, or would approve of doing. Most people have more control over their emotions, their senses, their desires. I worry if I continue down the road less traveled I'll like it too much and lose all control. I'll get swept up in my excitement, then get caught.

I should be worrying about the guilt and moral issues, but those aren't the thoughts that have kept me up through the night. They're there, they just play a smaller role.

I'm treading both sides of the fence, which is making it hard to eat or sleep. I think about all the good and bad with each choice and end up getting nowhere. I can't let go of either stance, feeling as if I have two totally different personalities battling it out inside me. I wonder if they'll fight to the death, then to the victor goes the spoils of all future decision making.

Normally, I'd just make a list and pick the side that makes the most sense on paper, but this shit can't be put down as record. I'd be beheaded. I know which choice is the ethical one: to pretend like it never happened and move on never to do it again. Okay, it's the somewhat ethical choice, the lesser of two evils. Because the real moral choice would be to turn myself in right now. And fuck that. Plus, every time I start to prepare myself for this side of the coin I start to panic. My heart races and I become drenched in sweat thinking of what I'd lose with that path. My reaction is much less severe when I debate taking the dark road littered with more victims. Though thinking of getting caught is terrifying as well. Paralyzing in its terror, actually.

Thus my predicament.

It seems there's no perfect answer, which seriously pisses me off. I work with numbers, logic, facts. I don't do as well with gut feelings. My intuition is shit, and I've never been one to talk about how I feel. I tend to find the correct answer based on an equation, and I just can't do that here. Here I need to feel it out.

I fucking hate that I'm having such trouble with this.

***

"Hey, Idiot."

"Huh?" Jason is standing at my desk in my office. I missed him coming in here.

"You're out of it. I think you need a nap." Jason doesn't look concerned at all. Instead he looks like he's happy that, for once, I'm the one a little off my game.

"A nap on a day off," I say. Not to rest, but to continue this internal debate. I won't be able to focus until I've come to some sort of solid conclusion.

"Lucky you, the week is almost over. Then you can zone out all weekend."

"Yeah, yeah, yeah. Thanks a lot. What did you need, anyway?" *Hurry up so I can help you and go back to the deliberation inside my head.*

"Not much. I was just seeing how you're doing." Jason slowly looks me over with a twinkle of mischief behind his eyes, making me a little annoyed. Why does he get to be so carefree while I've been tormented for days since Blondie? Why doesn't everyone feel exactly as I do, and why doesn't the world revolve around me?

Okay not actually, but I'm still jealous he's in such a good mood.

"I'm great. Now get the hell out of here, so I can go back to doing nothing in peace." My tone is soft, so he can see I'm kidding.

"Okay, okay. You better beware, though, Mel's been hounding me to have you over soon. So watch out for an invite."

"Good to know."

"Hey, what time is it?" he asks.

I look down and when I see skin instead of metal I remember my watch grew legs and ran away.

"Hey, you haven't seen my watch anywhere, have you?" And the jerk laughs.

"The nice one Amelia and I gave you on your thirtieth birthday?"

"Yeah, I can't find it."

"She's gonna kill you." Jason smiles his annoyingly happy grin again and trots off to who-the-hell-knows-where, leaving me alone to go back to stewing in indecision.

***

The couch feels lumpy, uncomfortable, though I know it's only because I'm frustrated. It's a four-thousand-dollar couch; it can't be uncomfortable. Still I refuse to sit anymore. Instead I stand up, start to pace the living room. *Damn it*, now with all this movement my sweater feels scratchy and restrictive. So I whip it over my head, chucking it to the floor. There, now I can breathe better, sort of.

Nope...I'm cold.

Realizing I can't be happy with anything right now, I groan.

For almost a week since the eventful night I've deliberated, and now the weight of my unmade mind is starting to affect me. I need to figure it out. Tonight. *Now*. I need to stop being a little bitch and just fucking decide one way or the other what I plan to do about it.

Will I sweep it under the rug?

Or will I say fuck you to norms, fuck you to conventions, and feed my carnal, insatiable side?

Instead of making a decision, like a man, I stomp to the bedroom like a child having a tantrum. I rip a shirt at random off a hanger, shoving it over my head. In the process I pull on my ear and yell incoherently. This shitty mood has got to end. Grabbing my keys, I get the fuck out of the house, heading to Spot Z for a drink. Hopefully it'll calm me the hell down.

chapter sixteen;

Way too many drinks in and nearly falling off my stool, I've finally replaced my crappy temper with a much better one. I may be hitting on everything with a slit, but it beats the surly sulk I'd been doing. A few girls have caught my eye, but in the fumbling way I've asked them home no one's said yes.

Well fuck them, then.

I'll be leaving my car at Z tonight. There's no way in hell I could drive; I can barely walk. And I can't die on the way home, I still have a decision to make. It's time to go before I hurl on the floor. So out I stagger.

I know I should feel cold walking outside, but the alcohol has made it hard to tell. At least it's a short walk, so hopefully I don't get hypothermia or pneumonia or some dumb shit like that. As I look up at the sky, I feel my nausea bubble up. The stars are spinning. I don't think they're supposed to do that.

I should've stopped a few drinks before I did. I'm in for a rough night.

When I unlock my front door and stumble inside, I can feel the sick sweats start, my mouth beginning to water.

Fuck. I run to the bathroom, and luckily I make it to the toilet just in time. Even better, I got the lid up. I'm in no shape to clean.

***

Several hours go by, and I've lost count of how many times I've emptied the contents of my stomach into the toilet. One of the last thoughts going through my mind before I drift off on the cold hard tile is, *I'm never fucking drinking again.* Ever.

But how many times have I said that in my life? Probably too many to count.

When I wake up too early the next morning, there's drool crusted on my cheek, and my entire left side is red from sleeping on the floor. *Terrible fucking night.* The best thing for me right now is a hot shower then a couple more hours of sleep, in my bed this time.

I hop in without glancing in the mirror. I'm positive I don't want to see what I look like right now. It'll be bad enough after cleaning up. When I finish and dry off, surveying the damage, I'm taken aback by what I see reflected.

I look different somehow.

Nothing looks wrong exactly, but there's something different in the face I see now than the one I saw yesterday. Something's changed. I rack my brain for an answer, still coming up blank.

I get halfway to my bed when realization hits me.

I run back to the mirror and am greeted by a devilish grin on the face looking back at me. It doesn't even look like me. This face, the one that looks different than it ever has before, is the face of a killer. A ruthless killer. He's waving goodbye to the control that held the impulses at bay. The moral side lost out to the deep dark desires at some point during the hours spent drunk and sick.

I wasn't even aware I'd made any decision, but here I stand, completely sure in the new path I plan to walk. There's no looking back, and I'm more excited than I should be.

***

I'm flush with adrenaline and endorphins, and it takes a great deal of willpower not to begin giggling with sheer glee. My decision has been made, and with all of this surprising conviction it's pretty much sealed in stone. I'm ready to become what I must have been marching toward, unknowingly, for a long time. I'm ready to take the fork down the hidden path most people don't even know exists.

I'm ready to kill.

And I'm ready to enjoy it.

Minutes go by while I revel in the knowledge that I'll do it again.

The only thing that mars my elation is when I think back to Blondie. She was essentially an accident. She wasn't planned or intentional. She was a dream. Nothing more. There are so many people I've wanted to kill, but restrained myself because that's what's expected. How could I let an accident be my first?

And it's surprising we aren't all killers, that the world isn't made up of more people just like the new me. I know everyone has these thoughts. We are just taught to squash them. But no more squashing, no more restraint. And no more accidental killings, either.

I clench my teeth, balling my hands into fists as I make another quick decision. This one takes no deliberating since I've already jumped off the deep end. I'll make up for what I lacked last time, and I'll know what I'm doing with the next. I won't watch from above as if I'm outside of my body this time. I'll be inside of myself, fully conscious, watching and aware. I'll kill with a plan, with intention. And only then will I regain the satisfaction I should've let linger before.

When I do accomplish what I now intend to do, I'll allow myself to keep something. I'll save an item, but when I actually deserve it.

It'll be a donation from the recently, and dearly, deceased. I'll start a collection of donations. Donations from each pretty woman. Donations they'll give to me.

chapter seventeen;

For days I've been trying to brainstorm plans for my next adventure. The trouble is every time one begins to form I quickly find drawbacks. There's always a loophole, some way I'll surely be caught. Which is why everything I've come up with so far has been scratched. I never knew there would be so much to consider when planning to off someone.

Off someone...that has such a nice ring to it.

Kick their bucket for them.

Help them bite the dust.

Dim the light in their eyes.

Deliver their soul to the devil.

Send them to swim with the fishes.

Put them six feet under; food for the worms.

Take their life.

Murder them; kill them; destroy them; end them.

Okay, so I have no shortage of cliché sayings, but I'm still at a loss for my next plan or victim. Despite the number of days that have gone by since last Saturday, my excitement has yet to dwindle. Every time I picture The-One-Who-Doesn't-Count and her lifeless body, that it was my actions causing her exsanguination, I feel a sharp tingle in my scalp and my heartbeat picks up the pace. My endorphins are still in excess, and I just haven't hit my baseline from before that night. I know I'll come down eventually, but not yet.

I don't know what down will feel like, either. The thought sends fear rushing through me.

Jason even noticed an extra bounce in my step this week, though he attributed it to my mysterious lunch with Eva. I didn't give him any details after I returned, so my silence has led to dirtier and dirtier insinuations. He couldn't be further from the truth. But for obvious reasons I haven't corrected him. Instead I just smile, walking away. Every time. It's driving Jason crazier by the day.

He has no idea that instead of sex with the boss his best friend is happier than he's ever been because he assaulted and killed an unsuspecting victim. He'll never find out, either.

Ever.

***

It's Friday again. Somehow the week got away from me. I haven't gone above and beyond in my work like I normally do. I haven't gone to Spot Z, either, not once. I can't even remember where the hours have gone or anything specific I've done outside of the office. I stare at my computer with distinct lackluster. I need a plan. At the very least I need an idea I can run with.

Okay, maybe I just need a break so I can think straight. I can almost see my thought as it quietly fizzes out to die. And as if on cue I hear Jason next door heave his heavy frame up from his chair to stomp over to me. He makes a lot of noise these days. I wonder if he's gained even more weight. It's that damn marriage.

"Wanna get lunch? My treat." Despite the extra pounds he seems to be lugging around, Jason appears incredibly happy. The exuberance in his voice is apparent too as he hangs over the precipice of my office.

"Sure thing. Ready now?" I watch Eva walk past my office as I answer. I hope she backs the fuck off. But on her way to the kitchen she eyes me with suspicion written in her furrowed brows.

He nods. "Where do you want to go?" His eyes have a brightness to them that they only take on when he has good news or a secret to share.

"Let's do Delta's. They have a few new items. I wanna try their prime rib dip," I say. Plus I want to know what the hell he has to tell me. Please god, don't let it be anything about me. He doesn't keep track of his mileage on the muscle car, does he? I don't think so. Fuck, I hope not.

"Yeah, let's go now," he says.

Eva pops out of the kitchen as the doors to the elevator begin to close, and she moves as fast as her heels will allow. Is she trying to catch it?

"Can I join?" She sounds desperate.

Seriously?

"Sorry." I mutter as the doors close without her inside.

Please don't let her try to follow us.

We ride down in the death trap, without commenting about Eva, then head through the lobby with chitchat that feels forced. I can't remember the last time our conversation didn't flow freely. What the fuck's going on?

Stamping the snow off our feet inside Delta's, the warmth does wonders for my nerves. Oddly enough Kristi is our waitress again, though we aren't seated in as secluded of a table. We don't look as if we need privacy today, I guess.

"Hey guys, I'll be helping you today. My name's Kristi. What can I get for ya?"

"Two beers, please." Jason answers before I get the chance. It's a beer kind of afternoon. No arguments from me.

"Coming right up." Her hips sway as she scurries to the bar. Something about Kristi strikes me, giving me the spark of an idea, but then it's gone just as fast.

"So…I have something to tell you." *I knew it.* My ability to read people will come in handy with my new hobby. The pause grows. He's waiting for me to respond before he spills.

"You're killing me. What is it?" I lift my eyebrows in anticipation, giving him the reaction he's expecting.

"Amelia's pregnant again. It was a total accident, but we're having another baby!" Each of his words is punctuated with an exclamation. To Jason this is good news.

To me it would be torture.

I don't react as quickly as I should, and the smile isn't instant. His starts to fall. Before I can stop myself I ask, "But what if you have another girl?" Jason laughs, thinking I was joking, trying to trick him even with my hesitation. Then, finally, I realize what's expected of me and I put on the correct mask to fake it. "Wow, that's so great."

Well, great that it isn't about me, anyway.

"Yeah, we're excited. Just found out yesterday. Though I don't know how long she suspected, she just peed on the thing, and then confirmed it at the doctor this morning. God, I hope this one's a boy." He elbows me, and Jason's face is so full of joy some of it rubs off. I can't help to be happy that he's happy. Jason deserves to get what he wants. He's a good man.

"I bet this one is." There's too much estrogen in that house.

"Well, Mel and I were wondering…and you don't have to if you don't want to, but we were wondering…if you'd be Godfather again?" Considering both Amelia and Jason are only children there must be a shortage of acceptable candidates. Why else would they choose a bad influence like me? Twice?

"Of course. I'll be there."

Great. It takes all my brain power not to roll my eyes.

Through the rest of lunch we chat about the upcoming possibilities. Jason's excitement never ebbs. Not once. We both suck down two beers before we realize we should stop, knowing we've got to go back to work.

I can feel a little bit of a buzz, and I find myself considering Amelia's actions from the other week in relation to this revelation. Were her newly raging hormones driving her to bend the rules with me? Or was she just trying to do something dangerous, understanding how wrong it was? I can't decide which I'd prefer.

While Jason babbles on, and my focus fails a little, I swear I see Eva through the windows of the restaurant. For a brief moment I think I see her peering in, shivering without a coat, looking for someone. But then after nudging for Jason to look there's no one there.

And I don't see or imagine her again.

"Thanks so much; you two have a wonderful rest of your day." Kristi winks as she takes the paid bill and tends to her other tables. The ghost of an idea still lingers on the tip of my tongue, but again it slips away as Jason interrupts my thoughts while we stand to leave.

chapter Eighteen;

"So how about coming over tonight to celebrate? You said you'd meet Mel's friend. Mel's cooking dinner, and we can play drinking games after. I'd say let's go out dancing afterward, but I didn't line up a babysitter." Jason rambles on from one thought to the next, barely pausing for a breath while we make our way back to the office. His attempt at distraction is more obvious than he intended. And the fact that he won't let me answer between questions is another dead giveaway.

"Sure. But what friend was that again?" For the life of me I can't remember who I was supposed to meet.

"Umm...remember our neighbor?" I can see the slight cringe in Jason's features despite his effort to hide it. He refuses to look my way while we walk, preventing any possibility of eye contact.

Wait. Oh shit...

"Bessie," he adds. Yep, I remember now. How could I have forgotten? Jason's eyes stay forward as we enter our building and make our way upstairs. He changes his answer after thinking about it though. "Bee."

He never should have told me Amelia calls her Bessie. Twice now.

After a significant pause, I say, "I guess I said yes before. But may

I remind you I'm doing this for you, not Mel, and definitely not Bessie. I'll be there to celebrate your little parasite growing inside of your wife, but don't think I'll meet her again after this." I look at him and wait for him to turn. "You. Owe. Me. Don't even think for a second I'll let you forget it."

Jason smiles and the gesture's catching. He is one happy son-of-a-bitch right now. "Remember no one except Amelia calls her Bessie. It's Bee. Tonight will be so fun. Thanks." He drops his heavy hand on my shoulder to add, "Awesome. This will be so great. Yeah, yeah, I know. I know I owe you."

"Good, you better know." If he forgets I won't hesitate to remind him.

"I do."

"What time should I be over?"

"How about 7?" Just enough time to shower, get ready, and brainstorm how to plan my next kill before heading over to celebrate the great news of his next little brat.

"Yeah, that should work for me."

***

When I get back to my office it feels off. I sense it before I even turn on the light. Someone was in here. Maybe I should start locking it. Then I find it. There's a sticky note smack in the center of my computer. It's scribbled in angry red marker.

Aidan, you could be a better team player. Work on that.

Fuck you, Eva.

***

The shower's hot spray begs me to linger underneath the restorative pressure. I can almost hear the "please" sighing from the pipes. It's calling to relax every muscle, every nerve, every stressor. My thoughts seem to flow freely while the water cascades over me.

But I resist temptation, getting out before I'm too lost inside the corridors of my mind.

I need another unknown. That's what worked so well before. I had no connection to her, no links, no ties. That's why there haven't been any unexpected knocks at my door, and why I've never felt the need to look over my shoulder in suspense. I got away with it.

So to be able to again I need to be smart.

My picks must stem from coincidence instead of motive. I need little or no association to each. I don't mind waiting for my next rush, I just want to set my sights somewhere so I can start watching.

I'd like to stalk my prey a little this time before pouncing.

Pacing around my room, the walls feel like they're moving inward. It seems the creative juices have ceased to flow, and I still need to get ready before driving over to face the ogre. Man, I hope she isn't as hopeless as I've been picturing. And if she is, I genuinely hope Amelia does something unexpected to liven up my evening. Or there better be lots of beer.

I look to the clock in my bedroom, groaning. I need to be there in half an hour. Guess I can't rub one out like I'd planned. Poor time management on my part.

Searching through my closet, I do a double take at the label on a button-up shirt. Grabbing it off the hanger to throw on over my dark jeans, I lift an eyebrow. At first glance I swore it said Kristi. But I don't have any shirts by Kristi, not to mention I don't even think it's a real brand.

Taking a second look, I realize I wasn't even close. The only matching letter is the K. Duh.

But, "I wonder...," and then the thought that was dancing around in my mind without landing anywhere in particular finally stops to plant itself for growth. Kristi, the waitress, she'll be my next adventure.

Yes.

I smile, knowing I can let the fantasies begin.

Perfect.

And with that I put on the red shirt that's still dangling from my hand. Since it was a clear sign it's now my lucky shirt.

I doubt it's a coincidence it's red, either.

***

I breathe one last steadying breath before punching the doorbell at Jason's. This night will be awkward. I already regret agreeing to come. But there's no time to change my mind and run as the door swings open.

"Why hello, handsome." Amelia's grin stretches from ear to ear as she ushers me inside.

"Hi yourself, Mama."

Her face glows in response as she gingerly touches her stomach. "Isn't it wonderful? Such a happy accident." I definitely read too much into her exhibitionist exposure the other night. "I'm so glad you'll be Godfather for another round. We're just making sure you'll never get away from us." Her eyes linger on mine for a bit too long before she spins me to take my coat. After I've handed it over I'm startled by a smirk then a wink.

Or maybe there *is* something devious going on inside Mel's head? I don't know. She's too hot and cold to make sense of. I don't get women. Either way, I should be more opposed to the idea of her flirting with me, but that's hard to remember as her fingers run down my arm while we walk to the dining room.

"Hurry up, dinner is almost ready. Plus I just can't wait for you to meet Bessie."

"I've been waiting all day." I cringe toward the wall, my features out of her line of sight.

This should be a hoot. Turning back, I return her wink with one of my own, hoping to disarm her as she's done to me. But if my attempt works she doesn't show it. *Calm and cool as ever. Bravo, Mel.* She only smiles coyly, I see out of the corner of my eye, as her nails breeze across my lower back just before we reach our destination. She's so subtle I still don't know if I'm imagining or exaggerating these gestures.

My eyes scan the room for the new face of Bessie, or Bee. Whatever the fuck her name is. But all I see is Jason as I walk into the dining room. The ceiling is high, and it's clear Mel has been redecorating. Must be that nesting thing knocked-up women get. Everything looks crisp and new, in a warm color palette of honeys and chocolates.

Mel disappears into the kitchen, off to find Bee.

"Hey, we've been waiting on ya, kid."

"Jesus, I'm only five minutes late." Jason's brows knit together in concern. The sarcasm flies above his head, and he only gets I'm joking after I laugh.

"I hope you're hungry. I'm grilling steaks. The good ones." I guess as a father of 3.5 children he has to think about how much he's spending on food. I, on the other hand, have one mouth to feed, so I always eat what I like, meaning I always have "the good ones."

"Starving." I nod.

"So am I." A new, warm, slightly breathy voice comes from behind me in the hallway. I don't want to turn around. I really, *really* don't want to. How long can I wait before I'm the asshole? Jason's about to speak, looking so nervous. Not a good sign.

"Aidan, this is Bee Iverson. Bee, my best friend, Aidan Sheppard."
Okay it's now or never, Champ.

I turn around as she waddles toward us. No wonder she's hungry. She must always be hungry. Okay, *don't be such a mean fuck,* that's unfair. She isn't waddle-worthy. But she's no Amelia.

Maybe she only looks wider because she's standing next to Amelia?

"It's nice to meet you, Bee."

Chapter Nineteen;

It's easy to tell she was once prettier. Her face does have beautiful features; she has a nice rack on display, her eyes are big, round, and bright; her smile is straight and white, her hair is thick, swaying down past her shoulder blades. She just looks like those features have been slowly filling out for a few years. I bet she was skinny in high school. She dresses like a girl who was once skinnier.

She ate that prettier self.

Granted, she's better than I'd feared. She could be worse for sure. But to be fair she could also be better.

"Hi, Aidan. I've heard so much about you. I'm glad we're finally meeting."

I'm sure you are.

"Absolutely." It's all I can muster for the moment.

We chat about the basics, covering all the typical surface questions, and I warm up the more we talk. Bee may be bigger, but she's funny too. Her wit is surprising, and the more she makes me laugh the better she looks.

Plus she's legitimately intelligent. Her knowledge of politics, current affairs, and even history catch me off guard. She calls me on my bullshit answers a couple times, though not in an annoying way. In a surprisingly charming way.

***

Eventually, as the steaks sizzle above the charcoal, Jason and I wander into the back yard to talk on our own while the girls make their way to the kitchen. Somehow dinner parties like this always seem to separate by gender for a while.

After a lull in our conversation Jason's face pinches in anxiety. I know what's coming. "So…what do you think? Do you hate me?"

"Actually, no. I mean I probably won't be calling her, but she's not bad." I chuckle. "She's funny. Good company for tonight at least."

"Yeah, well, you fuck models, man. Your standards are way too high."

"Fair enough." I do have a nice spank bank of material. Though, it's not like I've never had a drunk evening, taking the best of the bad options home at bar close. But those aren't the things you counter with when given a compliment. Seems to be one of those smile-and-nod moments.

"Seriously, I don't know how you do it."

"Just lucky, I guess." He scoffs, shaking his head as if he's disappointed in his shallow friend, though it's obvious he's jealous. Sometimes I can feel his envy radiating off him, and I know if he could switch places with me temporarily he would. He didn't have a lot of luck before Amelia. Then he hooked her and that's all he ever needed. Rookie move. But trading places would only be temporary; he's such a romantic, clueless sucker.

"Yeah, epic luck apparently."

"We all have something." I think for a second before adding, "Tonight could've been a lot worse. You still owe me. Just not as much as I thought you would, I guess."

"How about I bring the beer Sunday and buy lunch Monday?"

"That'll do."

We make our way back inside to the ladies when the meat is ready. Dinner consists of way too much talk about babies and families. *Boring.* Even Jason participates more than I expect. I've nothing to contribute, so I find myself nodding a lot while zoning out. My mind begins to wander toward gruesome thoughts of Kristi the waitress. What can I do with her? What can I get away with? And how should I cover it up?

I want to do something different this time. Since I'll be fully present, and she's my new number one, I want to have an exciting experience. Monotony has never been something I've strived for, so I want something altogether new. Plus I don't want to buy more sheets again.

"What do you think, Aidan?"

Shit. Why does my opinion matter? I don't give a flying fuck about kids. I take a gamble. I have no desire to be lectured for not listening by either of the ladies.

"Absolutely."

"See, Jason, I told you he was ready to settle down." She points to him, shaking her finger before turning back to me. "You could only enjoy the bachelor life for so long, right?"

Wrong.

But it's too late to argue now, so I just go for short and sweet, hoping to move on quickly. "Right." Nothing else to add to that load of shit.

"Well, I'll be your best man, of course." Jason's in on it, too? What a bunch of traitors.

"Okay, let's not get ahead of ourselves." I've been ambushed.

Bee leans forward, blocking Amelia from my line of sight. For a brief moment I wonder if she's going to say something stupid about getting me to settle down, too. But I'm shocked to hear her ask, "Do you guys play fantasy football?"

Wow, another bonus point for Bee. I wink at her and she smiles before leaning back to let everyone into the new conversation.

This chubby bitch may be pretty cool. Who knew?

***

Several board games and beers later, it's definitely time to head home. I need the cool sleek lines of my house to focus my mind toward a new goal. I need to plan. I need to be alone.

There was no awkward exchange of phone numbers with Bee or promises to call when we both know I won't. And thankfully Mel keeps her dirty mouth shut this time while Bee packs up, leaving before me. But I know Mel will badger me the next time I'm here. She'll ask questions about how much I like Bee's personality, then chastise me for begrudging her weight, but hopefully it won't be in front of anyone else. I linger while Bee leaves, not wanting to have a forced conversation outside alone. I got away without false promises in the safety of numbers inside, but I can't guarantee I'll be as lucky twice, especially if cornered.

"We'll see you Sunday?"

"No, honey, I'm going to his place this weekend. Guys football day, remember?" Jason's voice kicks up a notch in anticipation of being told no. He's so whipped. And whiney.

"Oh, I forgot. Well, hopefully we'll see you soon, then." Jason tries not to sigh, but I can see the tension relax from his face as he got permission from his pregnant wife to leave the house for a mere few hours.

Sad.

"And you're bringing the beer. I plan to get shit faced, so don't skimp."

"Nice." Mel always gets judgy when she's knocked up. I forgot that.

"What a sad single life I lead." Remembering, I turn the antagonistic sarcasm up to push her buttons, keeping her in check. I don't berate her life choices, well at least not to her face, so she should keep her nose out of mine too.

"Play nice, you two." Jason, always the moderator. I wonder if his head would pop off if there were too much tension in a room. "Night, man. See you Sunday." He gives me a tipsy half hug and marches off toward the bathroom, leaving me standing in the entryway with Mel.

Alone.

I think back to the last time we were alone. Just a few feet away upstairs. I struggle to breathe calmly and give in to a small gulp before waving my hand in feigned nonchalance, looking like a spaz.

"See you when I see you."

Mel leans in for a hug, and I catch the ghost of a smirk pulling at the corners of her mouth. The hug lasts just a little too long. In that moment all I think to do is smell her hair. It smells spicy, like cinnamon. As I pull back her hand grazes my ass gently.

Whoa.

That couldn't have been an accident. Could it?

"Come back soon. We really, *really* miss you when you stay away too long." She plants a kiss on the corner of my mouth, and with nothing to say in response I nod, turning to leave.

What the fuck is going on?

chapter TWenty;

As I lie in bed I can smell the rank undertones of cheap beer tinged with potent garlic lingering on my stale breath. I should get up to brush my teeth. But I won't. The bed is too warm, and my limbs refuse to move. The relaxed state of inertia is too powerful. Hygiene can wait until tomorrow. A lot can wait.

Despite valiant efforts to fall asleep, I've been lying here for hours. My new sheets are soft. The house is warm. I should be able to drift off to dreamland. But I can't, and the longer sleep eludes me the angrier I get, making sleep even more elusive in a vicious circle. So I continue to look around the room, hoping for some inspiration. Nothing strikes me, though.

The streetlights outside make shadows dance around my room. Odd patterns creep along the walls in a slow, eerie waltz. I imagine them marching to their death and shudder. The dim glowing of orange gives off a sinister feeling. Anything could be lurking within those shadows. Anyone could be biding time to strike against me.

Settle the fuck down.

I need to watch the paranoid stuff or I'll end up getting caught and hung in the street for everyone to see. They'll groan in disgust as my body starts to leak what was once contained inside, those closest gasping or screaming as they notice my eyes open and hollow, void of emotion and forming red lines of petechial hemorrhaging.

Snap out of it.

I need to get planning for this Kristi thing tomorrow or my mind may start to have a mind of its own, taking over when I don't want it to. That could get pretty inconvenient at work. I don't need to be that creepy guy people avoid.

I finally give in, realizing I'm not going to get to sleep without pharmaceutical assistance. So I take a sleeping pill and count the seconds until I fall asleep.

2,978 of them.

***

I watch as rusted monsters march around my room. They're chanting something, but I can't seem to make it out. Their tongues sound too big for their mouths.

One of them has two heads; one for watching where he's walking, and the other for watching me. Another has dozens of hands, each wielding a different weapon.

As they circle the room, I'm paralyzed. I want to yell for help, but when I open my mouth only air rushes out. My limbs even move in slow motion as if I'm being weighted down.

One of the monsters, the size of my thumb, jumps onto the foot of my bed, starting to scream the chant the others are still mumbling. He scrambles across my body to shout in my face. And finally I can understand what he's saying, no longer sounding foreign. It's crystal clear.

"We will kill you if you don't kill soon. You must kill or we will. You must kill. You must kill. Kill now. Kill now."

Then it cuts my throat.

***

Fucking nightmares.

I take a shot of Jack, popping another sleeping pill. Hopefully the combination will slow my unconscious down so I can go dreamless for once.

***

Saturday morning arrives, and I finally get out of bed, heading into the shower. Again the water seems to bring out my best ideas, but I cut it off, jumping out quickly so I can write each down before forgetting. I move to the porcelain throne, writing furiously.

If anyone were to walk in on me sketching out ideas for violent murder while shitting on the toilet, I don't think I could come up with a believable excuse. I guess I could just go with the catchall: *it's for a novel I'm writing.* Totally believable, right?

I bark out a burst of laughter. I'll have to remember that one.

Looking down to my scribbling, I know my plan is somewhat elaborate. Okay, pretty elaborate. I wish I had someone I could brainstorm with. Someone who was like me that could look over my ideas and tell me where the drawback or mistakes are. It would be easier if I could collaborate with another killer.

I wonder if there's a website directory I could sign up for. Definitely not. So I could be the creator of the idea: Coldbloodedkillersnetwork.com, "A place to socialize and network with other psychos just like you." I could make some money off that idea. Right before getting thrown into prison, or right off a cliff.

I shake my head, leaving the bathroom in search of clothing.

Without someone to look over my plan, it'll just have to do. I'm going to wait a few days though, taking time to rethink everything through several times. At least. Have to work out any bugs I can catch on my own before jumping in. Plus, it never hurts to sleep on an idea before deciding or taking action. Especially when freedom and safety are at risk.

After fleshing out my special plans for Kristi the waitress, my Saturday goes by without anything else noteworthy occurring. The sky outside remains gray. The wind chill drops a few degrees. My phone never rings. Basically, I sit on my ass watching TV, relaxing. I have the vague feeling I'm missing something, but it isn't an urgent feeling, so I dismiss it.

Afternoon fades into evening, and evening saunters into night.

This is why I love being single. I can sit at home all day, like today, in peace and quiet without ridicule or nagging. I can walk around in my underwear, or naked if I choose (though I rarely do, because, well because it's drafty). I can eat anything I want, watch anything I want, and do anything I want without ever asking for permission, forgiveness, or consultation. When I want entertainment I leave the house. If I need human interaction I walk to the bar.

Maybe everything I've done up to this point has been leading to my new hobby. This lifestyle, my personality, everything. I think I enjoy what I've done because of who I am on a deeper level. There may be something missing from me that others have, and *that's* why I feel no need to pair up with someone. I don't want to be stuck with someone I'll eventually hate. And being alone just makes it much simpler to continue with my new adventures, my playdates. I'll never have to explain odd behavior or lengthy disappearances to anyone.

I can feel my eyelids slowing down with sluggish defiance, knowing I'll be able to sleep on my own tonight.

I wonder if there'll be a point when I'll need to make and execute (*perfect word choice*) playdates for exceptional ladies in order to sleep soundly.

Only time will tell.

chapter Twenty-One:

Ten minutes past kickoff I can hear Jason shuffle up my steps, followed by his muffled knocking at my door.

"About time. I've been waiting on ya, kid." I keep my face stern and my tone even-keeled.

"Yeah, yeah, yeah. Hilarious." He gets the reference. "The girls were whiney, and Mel didn't want me to leave. Though, she never said I couldn't." His posture is slumped, but his face radiates relief.

"Ah, the joys of family life." I neglect to move, effectively blocking Jason's entrance.

"Get the hell out of my way so I can warm up inside."

"What's the magic word?" Jason shakes his head in exasperation, and I can't help it, I laugh at his irritation.

"Twenty-four pack." He holds up the heavy case as proof.

"That'll do."

We make our way to the couch, Jason's smile widening. He's always loved my choice of electronics. "Man, I wish I could have a TV half this size. Remind me again why we don't watch every game over here?"

"Because you're whipped. Mel would never allow it."

"True." How is he not embarrassed by that? I'll never understand.

"I was thinking Chinese delivery. Yeah?"

"Great." He's not listening anymore as the bright colors of jerseys and turf have stolen his attention. I order without comment. If he doesn't like what I order he can piss off. Then again, knowing Jason he'll eat whatever arrives. His middle displays how picky he isn't.

The game draws on with plenty of yelling from both of us, and it's the first time I've felt like a normal person, like how I used to, since The-One-Who-Doesn't-Count. I care about the touchdowns and flags without straying to thinking about blood or weapons. I begin to wonder if there are two parts to me: the vicious killer who enjoys violence and gore, and the Regular Joe who wants nothing more than football, beer, and sex.

They won't play well together.

Jason inhales the food when it arrives, and I'm glad, as usual, I over-ordered. Between mouthfuls, I wonder if he has time to breathe. Evidently he does since he blurts out, "You know, after you guys left the other night, Amelia was horny." Interesting.

"Lucky dog," I say, wondering if she was thinking about me.

"Hell, yeah. I never get tired of pregnancy hormones." I didn't think about that explanation, but that's probably what riled her up. "She just goes insane when she's pregnant. She wants it all the time. I end up having to turn her down a lot." Is he fucking serious? Jesus, marriage is stupid. It makes grown ass men say no to sex with a hot, horny woman.

"That's a fucking shame."

He nods in agreement but doesn't add anything else of his own. Sometimes I wonder how much thinking actually goes on inside Jason's head. He's not an idiot, though he can play one when he wants to.

We continue to eat, watch tackles, and talk. Jason reveals nothing else of importance throughout the afternoon. He doesn't introduce the notion that Amelia told him she wants to ravage me, and I don't express my newfound love of torture. We chat like we always do, and I continue to feel normal.

As the third game of the day lingers on, Jason seems hesitant to leave. Normally he's gone back to his little nuclear family unit before the second game even ends.

"You're here late tonight. What's up?" I ask.

"Nothing. Can't I just spend time with my best friend?" His tone feigns annoyance, but his face reveals guilt.

"Sure, of course. I just wanted to make sure everything's okay with you. Sure you're all right?" Despite my hobby I've always been good at being Jason's friend, and I don't want that to change too much.

"Sorry. I shouldn't have snapped." His sigh is huge and it's visible throughout his whole frame. "I don't know. I mean, you know I love my wife and kids. I love them *so* much. I wouldn't trade anything for those girls. But sometimes I just get…I don't know how to describe it. I feel claustrophobic. Sometimes I have this urge to run away."

He cringes. I open my mouth to respond, but he goes on.

"I have this primal need to be stupid and dangerous. I want to make mistakes I know I can't make with a family who counts on me. I want to act young again without the restraints that weigh me down now. I know how selfish that sounds, how horrible I am."

They're normal, not horrible. But I nod.

"I just can't seem to force them away completely. I try, believe me, I try. Somehow they sneak back into my brain and burrow there every so often. Being a father and a husband is one of the best feelings in the entire world. Though sometimes I just want to run far away. It sounds worse out loud. I'm such an asshole." His whole face crinkles, and he looks like he'll collapse in on himself.

He still doesn't give me time to cut in. "Don't tell Mel, okay? I know I'll get ahold of myself. I just need to find some sort of outlet." He takes his first pause. "I'm working on it." Again Jason's body sags more as he lets out a long, slow breath.

That may be the most I've heard Jason speak in a long time.

Normally our conversations are so give and take. He has a boring home life, it seems, and doesn't have much to update or add about himself that often. Not in long spurts, at least. But when he does it's never to complain. I don't think I've heard one negative word about his family since he met Amelia. He must be struggling.

"I had no idea. I'm sorry, I'm a bad friend. I should've noticed you were having a hard time. What can I do?" Not sure how I became the asshole, but I go with it, knowing it'll help him feel better.

Jason seems more relaxed since getting it off his chest. "Nothing, man. I'm sorry I just unloaded on you. It's good just to get it out, though. I already feel better."

"Bullshit. I'm going to help conquer this early midlife crisis." He's fifteen years too young for one, anyway. Then a smile creeps across my face in a slow-but-steady march. Jason's eyes widen as my lips spread. He's nervous.

He probably should be.

"What are you thinking? You look nuts." I can't help but laugh, because crazy is exactly what I wanted. He shouldn't feel bad for feeling like any normal man would after years with the same woman, tied down by little expensive tornados of pink estrogen.

"We're going to have a guys weekend, the one after next. Don't ask Amelia. *Tell* her." His face looks doubtful, like telling versus asking Amelia is a horrible way to get what he wants. "I'm serious. Assert yourself, don't ask for permission. She'll get over it. It's better than you up and leaving when you can't handle her crazy pregnant shit a second longer. She'll be fine with it anyway. Just tell her next weekend, the one before our getaway, she can have a girls weekend to pamper herself. She'll love that shit." He starts to look excited as the idea spreads. "But when it's our turn, we're going to go up north. My uncle has a cabin he never uses. I went there not too long ago, and it's great. We will bring lots of beer and flannel shirts, we'll hunt, and watch sports. No shaving, beards are a requirement. We won't shower if we don't want to. We will pick our teeth and act like idiots. We'll be real men with no thoughts of women at home. How's that sound?"

"It's just what I need."

"Good, then it's set. That weekend we'll take your car and head up north. If Mel gives you any grief, send her my way." I'll set her straight. Though I don't think he'd like the way I'd do it. Her pussy would be sore for days. She'd have trouble walking from the sense I drilled into her.

Oh fuck, bad friend thoughts. Keep that dirty shit about Mel contained. Use those thoughts for Kristi instead.

Focus.

I'm going to need to speed up my timeline for my new plans now, because I don't think I could make it up north for a whole weekend if I'm still thinking about the waitress. Instead I should be thinking about how I did it, not how I will.

"Well, I should get home and tell Mel about the next two weekends, then. You're right, it'll go over best if I tell her to have a weekend to herself before our guys time. She loves that stuff."

"What woman doesn't?"

"You're right. You always seem to be right."

"It's taken you long enough to learn that." And with that, Jason heads home to all of his women.

chapter twenty-two;

My grin is now permanent. Someone glued it to my face while I slept, I'm pretty sure.

My plan's started. It's been set and is already in motion. It's great. *It's perfect*. I'm so fucking ready.

***

Though I won't write it down (I burned the last one I started) for fear it might be found, I've memorized every step that'll be taken. They are:

Step One: Call Kristi. Pretend to be a customer she's helped before who's starting a new business, with a fake offer for a manager's job in Philadelphia where she has no relatives or friends. (Check.)

Step Two: Conduct interview over the phone. Be convincing. Drop names she knows. Send a realistic contract on letterhead with matching business cards. (Check.)

Step Three: Drive to Philly and meet her there. Conduct a second face-to-face interview in disguise. Be even more convincing. (Check.)

Step Four: Convince her to pack up and move for said job after accepting offer. (Check.)

Step Five: In her agreement to move, receive bonus of her saying goodbye to everyone she knows. (Check.)

Step Six: Have lunch at Delta's to find out when exactly she plans to leave. (I'll do that today.)

Step Seven: Follow Kristi on her drive out of town, and intercept her before she stops at a hotel. (To be determined.)

Step Eight: Get creative with her kill. (So fucking excited.)

***

There are several reasons this plan is amazing. I've thought it through as much as I could in the hours after Jason left. I stayed up way too late pulsing with excitement, staring at the ceiling.

Some of the reasons I'll never be caught (aka why my plan rocks): One, she thinks she has a job she's moving for, so the individuals she's leaving behind here won't expect to see or hear from her in a while, if ever. Two, I used a disposable phone, purchased with cash, to make the calls, so it can't be traced back to me. Three, I drove to Philly and paid cash the entire way. Again, fairly untraceable. Four, there's no one actually waiting for her in Philadelphia, I checked, so it should be a long while before anyone notices she's missing. Five, I also have no motive. She's only met me a handful of times, she's yet to learn my name, and she didn't recognize me as Mr. Brian Johnson, so no one will think to question me. Even if they look into the bogus job, she went for the interview and came back unharmed. Plus the phone is long gone, wiped down, donated, and, as previously mentioned, untraceable.

I'm fucking brilliant. I swear I turn myself on, I'm so impressed with my ingenuity.

I think I'll strive to have better ideas for each conquest. Maybe they won't all take so much work, but each *will* be better than the last. Shiny and new plans only; nothing recycled. New means my adrenaline will amp up higher, making each more exciting.

Great goal.

With a bounce in my step and a whistle on my lips, I walk the short distance to Delta's for lunch. I go alone today, no Jason, no Eva. I want to be able to speak with Kristi unencumbered by the nuisance of conversations with a tablemate. I don't want anyone to connect me with the waitress, either.

The hostess seats me in a high-top in Kristi's section. I hadn't thought about what I'd do if I was served by someone else. I got lucky there. I guess there's always more to be considered than anticipated.

Damn.

Kristi hurries over in her usual fashion. She's a good waitress. Hopefully whoever they hire to replace her isn't awful. I'd hate to find a new lunch spot.

"Hi, doll. What can I get ya today?" Her roots are long and a lot darker than the rest of her hair, and her makeup's a little too heavy. She looks like a woman who is holding on too tight to the youth she once had, and, like sand, the tighter she grasps the faster she loses it. She'd probably look younger, prettier too, if she let go of a few of those expectations and wasted effort.

"Can I get the fettuccine Alfredo, please? With the steak added. And a side salad."

"Of course. Dressing?"

"Honey mustard."

"To drink?"

"Coke. Lots of ice."

"No problem."

She nods, looking up for the first time since starting to write my order. There is zero recognition in her eyes. She couldn't pull me out of a crowd as either myself or her new employer. Those eyes must have been a brilliant green when she was younger, but now they look dull with the hardships of working on her feet for who knows how many years. Her tits sag and her ass is wide. Despite all of that she looks like a genuinely happy person.

For now.

She'll only have time to be happy for the next few days.

Fuck me, this is going to be so much fun. I run the side of my thumb along the zipper of my pants thinking about what I'll do with her. I won't go any further than this, since I'm in public, it's just exciting to break a small rule. After my few seconds of deviancy I pull the papers from the briefcase I toted with me from work.

My intention is to pretend to read while eavesdropping on anything and everything I can glean regarding Kristi's conversations. I'm hoping I won't need to directly ask her when she's leaving. I don't want to draw any attention between her and me if I can help it, for obvious reasons. I want to play this as smart as I can, since this is stemming from a real plan versus The-One-Who-Doesn't-Count.

A bit of time goes by with nothing in the realm of helpful. Kristi chats with her customers in a friendly manner, though she obviously isn't one to divulge personal information. I'm beginning to wonder if I'll have to man up and ask her, but then I get lucky when she takes a second to catch up with the manager. I don't even need to strain much to hear what's being said. My luck is seriously helping me out today. Maybe I should buy a lottery ticket on my way home this evening.

"You hire anyone yet? I was hoping to help train before I leave tomorrow night."

Jackpot.

Tomorrow night it is. Friday and Saturday will be good to me this weekend.

"Yeah, just did yesterday. Actually, she's young. Never waitressed before, but I wanted someone fast, and she seems eager. She's nice. I'll take all the help from you I can get. She's coming in a few, so you can train her today and tomorrow." Kristi's answering smile shows how happy she is to help. She's leaving on a good note;

I don't know if that helps or hurts me, but it's too late to worry about that. Hopefully she doesn't have plans to call any of these guys when she arrives in Philadelphia, because that call will never come.

"Good. I hope she learns fast. Send her over after she's dressed." And with that, Kristi walks to the kitchen and back out with my food.

"Here you go, doll. Can I get you anything else?" Her accent isn't quite from here, I realize for the first time, and I wonder where she grew up.

"Can I get a refill on the coke?"

"Absolutely." She rushes off, tending to my needs like the good little servant she is. Will she be as excited to appease me when I have her tied down, gagged, and bleeding?

No, probably not.

I continue to listen to her conversations with little added to my bank of knowledge. Though I know she's leaving tomorrow night, I need to know when or from where. I could stake out the Grill, and follow her from here. Though, then I'd chance being seen. No thank you.

Getting frustrated, and at the end of my lunch, I have to take the punt as she comes to collect my cash for the bill.

"I heard you're leaving Delta's. What a shame," I say, but hopefully not loud enough for anyone else to hear. Flattery works with Eva. Maybe it works with Kristi, too.

"Tomorrow is my last shift. It's bittersweet. I love it here, but I got an amazing offer elsewhere." Her pride isn't concealed well as she gushes.

"Good for you. That's great."

"You should come in for dinner tomorrow. Boss is offering a free round to everyone for a kind of goodbye party before I head out from here." *Brilliant.* Who wouldn't show up for a free drink?

"I'll have to do that. Good luck with your new adventure." And I'll have fun with mine, too. "Keep the change."

"Thanks. See you tomorrow evening, doll."
I smile as she walks away. She still doesn't know my name.

chapter Twenty-Three:

I don't even remember much of what happened the rest of yesterday or this afternoon. I was pretty much going through the motions, too excited for tonight to pay much attention to anything else.

Tonight is the night.

I can't stop jiggling my foot. I've been trying to look somewhat deadpan when I've been in meetings or with coworkers, but alone I let my excitement brew, bubbling.

At Delta's I sit with Jason, Amelia, and Bee (Mel pouted to Jason until I agreed for Bee to come too. Bullied by damn Mel, I should be ashamed). I asked them out to dinner yesterday using the drinks as an excuse. I also offered to pay. That was the real clincher, more than quality time with good old Aidan; a free meal is more appetizing, I guess. Well I can't be too offended because I'm using them just as much. I didn't want to be here alone for the second time in as many days.

"So ladies, are you excited for your girly weekend?" Jason is pumping it up as much as he can. Smart man.

"Hell yes we are. I'm gonna use the shit out of Jason's money at the spa." As Bee laughs, it's contagious around the table. I like her better the more I'm around her. Plus she's willing to take my side when it comes to Amelia, and not even Jason does that.

"Oh shit." Jason tries to look worried, but I can see the cogs turning behind his eyes as he thinks about something else instead. He's a good sport.

The meals come, and we laugh while we eat. Everyone throws jokes around with gusto, the drinks fueling our enthusiasm. Bee's and Jason's laughs get louder and their jokes more outlandish with each drink they consume, but everyone has a good time. Neither strays into obnoxious mode or crosses any lines. Everyone except Amelia drinks, though I drink nearly as little. I've been the one walking to the bar for our drinks, secretly milking my own. I've come back with the same glass for myself three times without anyone noticing.

I want to be sharp tonight. I need to be on my best game, and I want to remember every second with pure clarity. This one will forever count as my first. After tonight The-One-Who-Doesn't-Count will just slowly fade away.

I keep my eye on Kristi as often as I can without drawing attention from the ladies across the booth to my preoccupation. Her shift doesn't end until an hour from now. I plan for our party to end in a half hour, so I can wait in the parking lot for those last thirty minutes.

Everything would be lost if I missed her leaving. Hence my cushion of time.

I have my TV and lights set on a timer at home in order to convince my neighbors I'm there. I've tried to think ahead. We'll see how well that goes.

I'm pulled from my internal planning when Amelia leans in, asking me a question. "Well Aidan, when are you going to take our Bee out for a real date?"

What the fuck, Mel? You bitch.

"Hey, honey, let him handle his love life for himself."

Thank you, Jason.

"Who says I'd go out with Aidan, anyway?"

Bee to the rescue, again.

"Hey now, I'm a hell of a catch." Why am I defending myself? I don't even want to take her out.

"Maybe you're not my type." Bee winks at me while Amelia stares at Jason, giggling.

"Ah, well it was good while the fantasy lasted," I say, smiling. *Thank you, Bee.* I give her a wink of my own in genuine appreciation. *And fuck you, Amelia.* I make sure to catch her eye next, glaring murderously until she breaks contact first, intimidated. She needs to learn to mind her own damn business, and she needs to learn it quickly.

Amelia refrains from embarrassing me again for the rest of dinner, but I won't forget her behavior in a hurry. She's been a snot lately, and her pregnancy isn't a good enough excuse for me. I'm not wrapped around her finger like Jason. She better start to mind her comments in my presence, or I'll she'll regret it.

As everyone stands to leave, after I've paid our considerable bill, Amelia beckons me over for a private word. I hesitate before following, not sure I want to hear what she has to say. She's pissed me off enough tonight, and I don't want to take out any of my aggression on my best friend's pregnant wife.

"I'm sorry." She looks down while I glare. "I need to learn to shut my mouth. I have this problem of not shutting up when I'm pregnant." No excuse. "But I'm working on it. I just wanted to say I'm sorry."

"Fine. Apology accepted. I can't stay mad at you for long." *Because you're fucking hot, and I don't have to live with you.* "Please knock it off. I'm a big boy and I can handle my own life. I know you want to mother me, but you have a new one on the way you can use that advice for, okay?"

"Okay. I swear I'm done." Hopefully she's sincere as she lifts her palms in surrender.

"Good. Now time to head home so you can be spoiled tomorrow." Mel claps her hands in childish glee before leaning in for a hug.

She doesn't touch my ass like last time. Apparently that was too subtle. Now that she's more intentional, there isn't anything else I can take from her actions. Her fingers find their way to the waist of my pants, her slender digits fondling the front of my belt buckle as her lips tickle my ear with her sweet breath. "Maybe you can make me dinner when Jason's out of town sometime. I hate when you're a stranger."

Before I can think of anything to say, before I can utter a single word, before I can even breathe, she turns and sways her supple hips away.

Well...*fuck*...I don't think that one can be misinterpreted. I'll have to deal with her later, though, because tonight is all about me and my plaything.

All four of us gather at the door, saying our goodbyes for the evening. Again I neglect to collect Bee's phone number despite her major brownie points tonight. We all run to our prospective cars to fight against the cold. The only difference is after I drive out of the parking lot, waving to Jason and Amelia, I simply circle the block, heading back to wait for Kristi's departure.

And I only have to wait twenty minutes before I shift back into drive, ready to follow her car full of packed belongings on the way to Philadelphia.

I'm ready for you, Kristi.

I'm so ready.

Chapter Twenty-Four.

While driving several hundred feet behind Kristi's beat-up old Pinto, I have lots of time to envision what's soon to happen. I'm giddy with anticipation, seeing red from dripping and oozing blood. I hear ear-piercing screams that go unanswered, unheard, by anyone but me. I smell incredible fear, and I smell unbearable pain. This is going to be an experience to die for. Literally.

Sorry, Kristi.

I don't have the radio on. I want to be able to run through scenarios in my head unencumbered by lyrics or beats. I don't want to be distracted. Although I'm also relishing the anticipation, it also can't hurt to create solutions to possible problems. I run through potential glitches in dutiful preparation.

All the while I ensure she won't detect my following. I stay quite a ways back, and I change lanes often enough that I'm rarely ever right behind her. I either keep a car or two between us or I'm in a different lane altogether. It's easier than I thought to go unnoticed while on the freeway. The cover of darkness may be helping as well. City streets would be harder to navigate while keeping close enough not to lose her but far enough to remain unseen. I'm thankful I chose somewhere far enough for her to "move" that she needed to make use of freeways.

I need her to pull over for dinner. I watched as she served her last shift at Delta's, and she never paused to eat. Instead she focused on training the newbie. I have to get to her before she stops and checks into a hotel. That way there will be more time before she's noticed as missing.

I can feel my senses tingling. It's as if every nerve is on high alert. I shiver in excitement. This is definitely what I'm meant to be doing.

This is where I should be.

***

After about an hour and a half of driving, Kristi exits the highway for a twenty-four-hour diner. Again I'm amazed at my luck. This is just another sign that I'm on my intended track. A car can sit here for quite a while going unnoticed. It shouldn't be too suspicious.

Kristi enters the diner, sitting by herself to eat. I don't go inside. The cold is my friend—it keeps me alert—as I jiggle her handles, checking if she's locked her doors. I'm not as lucky this time. None open. But I'm nothing if I'm not prepared. I jimmy the lock quickly, sliding into her backseat, with my killer's kit in hand, remembering to relock the door. My small zippered pack includes everything I need for my night with her.

In her backseat I'm disguised by the many packed boxes, and she shouldn't see me even if she glances in her backseat before hopping into the front. I've seen so many women check their backseat, looking for bad news in the back. But this time the extra few seconds for caution shouldn't help Kristi out.

Feeling around inside an open box, I dig for something solid and heavy. My fingers scan over blankets and clothing. Nothing is useable in this one. I reach into the second and breathe freely as my fingers encircle a crystal ashtray. As I pull it out, I can tell it's the kind I picture grandmothers owning even if they didn't smoke. It's huge, round, and thick crystal. I can feel the weight of it cold in my gloved hand, and what I can only imagine is a scary smile spreading across my face. My eyes must have a shade of resolution in them.

This will do just fine for what I need.

Thirty more minutes go by since I settled into her backseat, and then Kristi's outside her car fiddling through her keys for the correct one. I suck in a sharp breath and stifle an overly insane giggle that wants to burst through my dry lips. I hold that breath in my protesting lungs while she turns the lock. Slowly, way too slowly especially considering the temperature, she gets into her seat. Is she hesitating, or just tired?

Finally, she puts her key into the ignition and turns. This is my cue. Before she shifts into drive I lean forward and wield the ashtray. I can hear the loud CRACK that shrieks through the air as crystal finds skull. The thud is satisfying, then Kristi slumps to her right without time to think about what's happened.

Incapacitate the waitress: check.

Unintentionally get an erection: check.

Pushing Kristi from her side over to the passenger seat is easier than expected as she's hunched over, unconscious, in a bench-style seat. Though she's not parked too close to the diner, she's two spots away from an overhead light, so I rush to move as quickly as I can before anyone sees what's going on. With all the planning I've put into this, it would be a real shame to get caught because of where she parked.

I check her door is still unlocked before slinking out of the backseat and into the front. The car is still running. The radio isn't on yet nor the heat, and the gear is still in park. My timing was sensational. I turn on the heat, backing out of the parking lot, headed for the highway.

I pull out my phone and GPS the abandon farm I located along the trip days earlier. I had the foresight to scope out a location while

MARIA ANN GREEN

driving to and from her interview. I'll never make fun of anyone for over-planning something again. Elaborate is just fine with me.

The farm is about twenty miles from the diner she chose. It has huge acreage and no one around for miles. It's the perfect spot for what we'll be doing.

Kristi doesn't stir the entire drive. I begin to worry I hit her too hard and ruined my upcoming fun, but when I place my fingers next to her nose I can feel the shallow breaths in and out.

That's a relief.

As I pull into the overgrown driveway, my heart rate picks up. This is it. This unconscious bitch will soon die at my hands. Intentionally and brutally. I can feel my mind racing faster, and it's as if the thoughts are bouncing around inside my skull, going a million miles an hour. Even my blood pressure is up along with rushed heartbeats.

This is it. This is it, right now.

I pull up in front of a field along the back side of the property. Kristi's car is hidden from the view of the road, though since every property on this road is uninhabited I doubt there'll be any passersby tonight. As I shut my driver's side door, I can't tell if I hear a slight groan from Kristi or if my senses are going haywire from standing at high alert for the last couple hours.

But as I reach the passenger side I'm hit smack in the face with the realization it was a real sound from Kristi's somewhat bloodied lips. She's gained consciousness, and I'm knocked to my ass on the cold ground as she shoves me with whatever strength she can muster.

"You're going to regret that, you bitch."

In true terror fashion, Kristi screams instead of replying. She begins to run away, but her little streak of luck has run out. Since she's pushed me to the ground I'm in a prime position to hook her ankles as she tries to scramble past me, and I send her crashing

113

down as well.

"What do you want? Why are you doing this?"

Her pleading starts out frantic and hoarse, as if she's been begging for mercy for hours. She thrashes her arms wildly, searching for anything she can catch hold of in order to pull away from me.

"Convenience."

The detached look on my face must further fuel Kristi's panic because her cries morph into guttural moans void of decipherable words. She starts kicking at my hands, holding both of her feet captive, but she can't get free of my grip to kick anywhere that counts.

Her fingers search for a hold. She pulls out blades of frost-covered grass, throwing fistfuls toward me. Far from incapacitating, it only makes me laugh. Her arms swing, trying to land, and finally one does. She cracks me in the ear.

"Fuck," I groan.

I almost let go completely; I do of one ankle and she kicks me in the center of my chest with her freed foot. In the blink of an eye, I'm back on the ground and she's up, running.

I start to panic. Before I have the sense to run, I rub my eyes. Is she actually getting smaller?

"Jesus fucking Christ."

Luckily she's aging, probably has a concussion, and I'm in shape. I catch up to her, tackling her hard to the ground. This time I sit on her ankles as well as hold down her legs. Everything has a learning curve, and I've learned to also lean away. My ear is still throbbing.

"Oh my god. Oh my god. Oh...my god. I don't want to die. Please let me go."

Kristi sits up, starting to punch my shoulders with laughable inadequacy. She can't reach my face at least. She's weak from the run and even more terrified. It's doing her no favors. Her begging stops once bubbles of laughter escape my throat, and she simply begins to cry. Horrid, loud, and panicky sobs come from her shaking body.

"Shut the fuck up." But she doesn't. So I shut her up myself. One swift fist to the temple knocks Kristi out again. This time I'll restrain her before beginning my fun. Lesson learned.

chapter Twenty-Five:

Kristi's eyes flutter open, and she hesitates before making any noise. Her eyes search the surroundings for something familiar, but when she comes up short a sharp intake of breath pierces the previous fifteen minutes of silence.

"Sorry, doll." I choose the endearment she uses for so many customers she doesn't care to learn the names of. "It wasn't a dream. You're definitely here, and there's no getting away."

Her hands are tied behind her back and she's lying on top of them. Her feet are bound together as well. She's incapacitated this time, and the view is absolutely wonderful. She can't get away (though it was also an adrenaline spike, her little attempt to run was avoidable). And now I have all the time I want to do as I please. I'm not going to rush this one.

Instead of continuing to plead as she did before, Kristi just screams at the top of her lungs. She screams until she must be sore, clearly losing steam. After informing her, "be as loud as you want, there's no one for miles around. No one will hear you. No one's coming to save you," I smile, chuckling until she tires herself out.

"Are you finished?"

She doesn't answer. She doesn't nod. She doesn't move. She just continues to breathe in and out jaggedly as silent tears stream down her face. Her eyes aren't focused any longer. Her mind is somewhere off in the distance.

Well, I can bring her back to the here and now.

Leaning over, I place my face within inches of Kristi's, mine straight on to the side of her profile. My hands rest heavily on either side of her defeated shoulders. The ground prickles the skin of my palms, yet instead of irritating it energizes me. My breath bathes her colorless cheek.

"I'm going to tear you apart." Pause for dramatic effect. Though, she doesn't appreciate it. "There's nothing you can say to change my mind, unfortunately, so begging is pointless. If you want to try, though. I won't begrudge you for it." She shifts her focus momentarily to connect with me, but quickly looks away again when she finds no mercy in my face. For the second she looks into my eyes, I can see the hope there spark and just as quickly fade away again. "There isn't a specific reason I chose you, other than the fact that no one will connect me back to you."

"You're a crazy motherfucker." Kristi's head whips toward me, and she spits as she pushes the words through her frustration. Before I can get away, she head butts me. *Fuck, that hurts.* Oddly enough it's a good hurt. And luckily there's no blood. Hopefully there isn't a bruise later.

"Such harsh language from such a common woman."

"Fuck you, cocksucker."

"Tut, tut, tut." I take a moment to punish her foul mouth by slapping both of her ears simultaneously. The echo reverberates against the dead, frozen crops, sending a spike of something new and unrecognizable up my spine in a quick flash. I laugh and add, "Too bad insulting me changes nothing."

This is more fun than I imagined it could be. The bonus of toying with my prey adds exponential excitement I hadn't really been able to calculate.

Kristi grits her teeth, seething through them, but in the next breath she changes tactics. "I'll do anything."

I stand up. Start pacing. Her eyes follow me. They hold on to each movement.

"Anything?"

"Anything! What do you want? I'll give you anything. I'll do fucking anything. Please just stop now before it's too late." There's hope in her voice.

"It's already too late."

"No, it isn't. I swear I won't tell anyone. I'll leave and *never* look back." She's almost choking on her words, tripping over each. She can't get them out fast enough.

"I wasn't talking about you."

"W—what?" Confusion bathes every inch of her face.

"I didn't mean it's too late for you, though, that's also true. It's too late for turning back. Too late to stop. You're not my first, *doll*." Acid pumps through the pet name.

Kristi processes what I've said. A hundred emotions swim across her features. Each makes me happier than the last.

I take a step toward her and she finally tries to roll over. While she's trying to get up, I kick her side. Another round of screams cut the cold winter air. She's got fight in her.

And the fun continues.

***

On the ground, behind a shed, I've worked until I'm worn. After slicing flesh from muscle and breaking countless bones, I'm still not ready to stop, even though Kristi's passed out from pain. There's more blood seeping into the ground than what I thought would. Each cut I've made has been precise and far from life-threatening. I've ripped off fingernails, bitten off toes, and burned her aging skin with the small flame of a lighter.

I've gotten creative, and I'm on such a high I'm not sure I'll ever come down this time.

I cut Kristi in places that have never seen the light of sun. Her pulse is still erratically beating, and I've decided I want to watch the life drain from her eyes like I did with The-One-Who-Doesn't-Count. I want to see her take her last breath, but she's still unconscious from the sheer amount of pain inflicted in the last thirty minutes.

I need to wake her.

Leaving her naked (after cutting her clothes to bits they eventually fell away) and bound, I walk the several feet to my bag of goodies. I extract the accelerant I brought. If I can't wash away the evidence this time, I'll burn it.

The liquid is as frigid as the air as I splash it on her face. She sputters, struggling to open her heavy eyelids, but then she's awake again. As she watches, mortified, I dump the rest of the acrid liquid over her entire body. She screams as it touches each open wound. The burning must be incredible.

"Goodbye, doll. I'll see you in hell."

I strike the match and before she can suck in the breath to scream once more I flick it to her flammable body. Her eyes morph from wide to charred black as her body melts into the earth around her.

The smell is like nothing I've ever encountered before. It's horrible yet exciting. And I'm the cause. It's painful not to jack off, even surrounded by the nauseating stench, but I know I need to wait until I'm home.

Eventually all that smolders are the bones of a once-live woman. But she doesn't exist anymore, because of me.

***

The time and work it takes to dig a hole adequate for what remains of Kristi isn't frustrating in the least. I make a point to ensure it's deep enough and every piece of soil that was on top, soaked with her blood, is now below with the rest of her. The cold night bathes me in moonlight, and I whistle a happy tune.

This is so much better than I expected, what I prepared myself for.

When I've finished, as I climb back into Kristi's driver's seat, I pat my pocket, smiling. I saved something. I have a donation to remember her by forever. Every time I look at the simple necklace, I'll remember this perfect night.

Conveniently, these donations, the gifts bestowed on me after a job well done, are something I can most likely get from everyone who follows. A lot of women wear jewelry. If one of my future playmates isn't wearing any I may have to get creative, but for now it's something that isn't too incriminating and also seems somewhat universally owned.

As I drive back the way I came, along the gray and overgrown path, I flick the radio on. I can't remove the constant movement of my feet or the soaring of my heart, until I realize the one thing I didn't plan for.

What the fuck do I do with her car?

chapter Twenty-six;

Breathe.

Don't panic.

Yeah, right.

Fuck.

Why didn't I consider where to dump her car? That definitely should've been on my list of things to plan. I remembered to wear gloves at every step of the game, and I took measures to destroy any stray evidence. Why didn't I think about her car?

Because I'm a fucking idiot.

I'm pissed at my inattention to this detail. My mind's racing, anxiety dripping out from every antsy cell in my body. My nerves are on fire. I'm not sure my breath should be this quick. Or shallow.

Fuck.

Think.

Where can I leave her car, that's walking distance from mine at the diner, and that'll take at least a few days to be noticed? The restaurant is open twenty-four hours, so it may take a while for someone to complain about it there. And even if they tow it to impound there won't necessarily be an immediate investigation. People leave dead cars on the side of the highway all the time and they aren't all missing. Other all-day locations might have more cameras or security. At least the diner is a small, hometown, rickety hole-in-the-wall type. There's no guard on duty. There aren't any employees cleaning up the parking lot. And the lot looked busy even at the late hour she finished eating.

Well, I guess that'll have to do. Hopefully no one notices as I leave her car to get into my own. But even if they do, that's why I put fake license plates over my real ones for tonight. They'll be wiped down then thrown into a dumpster on the way home. At least I thought of a few important things.

I tried to think of almost everything. But this is just another experience to add to the "to-be-considered" list.

I park next to my own car, getting out, burying her keys deep into the trash. As nonchalantly as I can, I slide into my own car and slowly, politely, drive away. I don't want to peel out, rev the engine, or draw any additional attention.

My name is Mr. Invisible, and I'm doing my best to blend in.

For the first ten minutes of my drive toward home, I watch the rearview with rapt attention, keeping an eye out for any flashing lights or the possibility of someone following me. But when I realize I'm in the clear, I allow my muscles to relax.

I've done it.

Goodbye to The-One-Who-Doesn't-Count. Goodbye, Kristi. Hello, future life. Hello, future playmates.

***

With two hours ahead of me until I coast into my driveway, there's a lot to think about. I'm alone in the car with no one else to talk to, no one to share my excitement with. No one could understand, anyway.

As the lights on the freeway zoom by, I remind myself this has all been real. I haven't been dreaming, fantasizing, or watching a horror movie of someone else. I've done horrible things, and I've been thrilled doing them. Actually, more than thrilled; I've been pulsing with excitement.

Every drop of blood has enriched me. Every scream has fulfilled me. Every second has been amazing.

Somewhere along the lines a switch that used to be connected to my empathy, to my compassion, was flipped off, and now I truly feel different. There are nasty impulses I believe everyone has. Most people struggle against them. They hide the dark parts within. Not me. Not anymore.

I used to worry about what others thought of me. I used to at least attempt not to do things that are supposedly and inherently wrong. But now all I want to do is ensure I'm happy, and fuck everyone else. I must preserve my freedom. It will be necessary to continue to hide the new me. If I'm caught I can't collect donations from playdates.

I pull the car over to take a quick piss. In all of the excitement over the last few hours, I haven't taken any time to attend to my bodily functions.

While gripping my cock, I think about how I've started to use other people as objects based on my needs. I look at everyone through the lens of what they can do for me. How can I get enjoyment out of someone? What can I do with or to them to gain something for myself? And how fast can I throw them away afterward?

Back in the car I finally turn the radio on. I'm not as high anymore, and it's late; I don't want to fall asleep at the wheel. I flick it to an oldies station as mile markers stack up behind me.

***

As I pass the halfway mark, there are less cars out than before. Almost every house I strain to see is dark, and the world around is quiet. Most people are already asleep in their warm beds for the night. They tucked in their families after watching their mindless, unrealistically happy shows. They skirt through life gleaning nothing of importance from it. So many people are dumb as fuck. They do what they think is appropriate, and they try to achieve simply because it's what's expected, what's normal.

There are so many robots dragging themselves through life being told what to do.

Fuck normal. I won't be told what to expect of myself any longer. I'm much better than normal. And I have a lot more fun.

***

Little icy flakes start to spew from the clouds high above. There won't be much of a cover, but some will stick. The tire tracks from Kristi's car down the way to the farm should have a little disguise in a couple of hours. Hopefully her car isn't doused, arousing suspicion too early as it sits there covered for hours.

As I struggle to look past the flakes to the empty road, I relish the feel of my previously bloodied gloves. Looking into Kristi's eyes as I tore parts of her free was like nothing I've ever felt. I swear I was soaring through the clouds as the oxygen in my system was replaced with something much lighter.

After letting some of those feelings fade while journeying home, I'm left a little drained. Exhaustion isn't far, and though there isn't a lot of pavement left between me and my bed there's enough to need a refresher.

So I decide to stop for coffee with less than fifteen minutes left of my drive. I pull into a gas station without any worries, parking the car directly in front of a floodlight. I feel further secure because I know the fake plates are already in the trunk from my last pit stop. That guy, the killer, he's asleep now. Normal, boring Aidan is back for the moment. The bad one can rest for a while; he can wait until the next playdate.

The lights inside the building are harsh, dirty. The floor needs cleaning, and I can only imagine the grime covering the bathroom. From the aisles, I can smell a hint of whatever the last customer left behind in there.

I grab my coffee and head toward the counter with cash in hand.

"Keep the change, beautiful." I dazzle the girl, no more than eighteen, behind the counter with a wink and wide smile. Her blue eyes enlarge, and she manages to return the grin just before I walk out the door. I shake my head, wondering how tight her little pussy is.

There are possibilities everywhere. I just had no idea how to look at each before.

***

As I pull into the driveway I can see the dimmed lights in my living room are still on from the previously set timer. I sigh while shutting off my car and walk up the steps. I enter my home knowing there have been fewer times in my life I've been this satiated. I thought I'd known satisfaction, happiness, before. But it had been a farce, just a fraction of what's possible. This is it. This is how everyone should feel.

Regardless of what lead me to where I am, even if I could stop now, there's no way in hell I would. I'm having way too much fun.

***

Settled in bed, I resolve that I want to bask in the glow of Kristi's demise for a few days, but once that's worn off I'm ready to plan my next conquest.

My single donation will quickly get lonely.

chapter Twenty-Seven;

I'm so glad I decided to take care of my burning needs with the waitress before leaving for the weekend up north with Jason. There's no way I could've gotten through the entire trip while agonizing over what was going to be done. Now I can be relaxed, happy while taking time away with my best friend. The time at the cabin would've blown for both of us if I'd ruined it with agitated distraction.

Plus, bad Aidan is still sleeping, and that's probably better for the overall of the trip, too.

During the drive up, we listen to music from our college days, stopping for thick, greasy pizza halfway there. It hits the spot like nothing else can. Jason looks like he could've skipped a slice or two, though. Maybe soon I'll ask him to start going to the gym with me.

Though I know he's itching to start drinking, we only have soda with our food.

"It may put a damper on the trip if one of us gets a DUI." I tell him when he whines.

"Cheers to that." Jason raises his glass enthusiastically, sloshing a little over the side and down into his sleeve.

"Settle down. I promise we'll get there." I chuckle at his

clumsiness.

"I'm so ready. Are you?"

"Of course. Guys, beers, and wilderness. What can be better for getting away?"

"It's going to be so awesome." His cheeks puff with pressured excitement.

Jason pays for dinner without any complaints from me, and we head back to the road. The last half hour of the drive is pitch dark. The sun faded while we filled our stomachs, and the further north we get the less lights pepper the side of the road.

I continually scan the trees for beady eyes. A deer can run out so quickly, fucking everything up. While I look, I try not to see more in the shadows than what's there. Bark, leaves, needles, and an occasional small animal. Nothing else. There are no playmates, no monsters, no authorities ready to pounce. Just the darkness of night.

At one point, not far from the cabin, a bit of roadkill along my side distracts me. The blood strewn across the pavement is almost artful the way it spreads out, and the creature's head is completely detached from the rest of the body. If I was alone I may have stopped to look closer. Because decapitation is an interesting thought.

***

Pulling into the driveway of the cabin, the rest of the world feels light-years away. Somehow it still feels simpler here in the woods, in a cozy little cabin, than it does back at home. Breathing seems easier, tension melts. Away from the cities, lights, and noise, it's easier to relax.

"Well, what should we do first?"

"It's your cabin, sort of, so why don't you pick?" Indecisive bastard.

"Oh, no, no, no. This is a weekend getaway for *you*. You're the family man who needs recharging. So you, my friend, need to use those balls of yours to make a decision. What will we start with?"

I could be at home doing plenty of other things. I could be picking my next pretty lady to play with and planning a fantastic night for her. Or I could be getting sucked and fucked. Both more exciting options. Except I'm here with Jason instead, so he needs to put in more effort. I'm sure his passive stance stems from years of Amelia telling him what will and won't happen, but that shit won't fly with me right now. When I want to make the call I do, though when it should be made for me I shouldn't have to drag it out tooth and nail.

Jason's been taught he doesn't wear the pants. His face looks pinched, his brows are furrowed, and there are deep lines set into the topography of his skin. His expression depicts a man unsure.

"Ummm..."

"C'mon, man up." Tough love.

"All right, okay. Let's bring in logs for a fire then crack open the first case for drinking cribbage?" He lilts up his voice at the end as if he's asking a question instead of giving a statement.

Whatever. At least it's a start.

"Great. Let's get to it."

***

One twelve-pack gone and the second opened. Cans litter the table. Jason's ahead of me in the count, though I'm not exactly sure who's had how many. It's clear we both feel the effects by now. My lips are tingly, on their way to numb, and my speech and eyes are both heavier than normal. Jason's face is red and he's much louder than usual. He's starting to slur, too.

"You know whatsgoing on buddy?"

"Tell me. Also, fifteen." I beat Jason every time we play cribbage. I don't even know why he likes playing me anymore.

"Shit. You're pegging the shit outtame." Damn straight.

"What were you gonna say before?"

"Oh yeah. I wasgonna say that something'sgoing on with Mel." Jason drops his shoulders as if he's given up. He hangs his head, keeping his eyes on his cards.

"Trouble in paradise, Family Man?"

"No." Pause. "Maybe." Pause. "I don't know." Sigh. He's as indecisive as ever. Make up your mind, Jason.

"Out with it. Either something is wrong or it isn't." My tone is gentle, but with so many beers it'll be hard to remain as patient as I otherwise would.

"Nothing'swrong s'riously. She just seemsoff for the last few weeks. She'spregnant, so there'sthat. I don't know. She'sbossier than she used to be. And she getsmad at me way more than she used to. I feel like lessofa man because of the commentsshe makes. I know it'sprobably just hormonesso I should cut her some slack. Maybe I'mbeing too sensitive."

Or maybe she's using the little parasite inside as an excuse to be a bitch.

But what do I know?

"Yeah, it's the baby. She's just uncomfortable and stressed. It'll get better."

Or it won't. It could get worse instead.

"At least she'sfucking me a lot." That's always a good sign.

"There's always an upside. P.S. You just got skunked. I win. Again."

"Fuck me." Jason yells loud enough to bother my ears.

"No, that's Amelia's job." Jason spits the beer that was in his mouth to laugh hysterically. "Dude, it wasn't *that* funny." Except his laughter is contagious, or maybe it's the booze, but either way it isn't long before we're both sucking in breath between hearty laughs that sting my sides.

chapter Twenty-Eight

In another hour I've caught up with Jason, and half of the second case is gone. My attention is fuzzing in and out, and Jason's eyes are unfocused. We've abandoned our game, moving to the couch by the fire. The television's playing some scary movie. I'm not even sure what it is, but I've seen lots of blood and I hear that building music right before something jumps out on the screen.

"Shit." I spill my beer down the side of the couch when Jason yells in reaction to the jumpy scene.

The oozing blood on the TV reminds me of last weekend with the waitress. My mind starts to run through the things I did with her, to her. I can't help but feel akin with the bad guy in the movie. His psychological torture is awe-inspiring as he practically gets his prey to stop hoping, just begging for the end to come. But his mind games don't come close to the beauty he creates with his weapons. That's what I love to watch. There are so many things I have to experiment with in the future. Almost limitless possibilities are ready at my fingertips.

I should watch more slashers for inspiration.

Before I take any time to check with my filter, I start to speak. "Do you know what I did last weekend, Jason?"

His attention is still on the screen, my irritation flaring. I brought him up here for his own good, the least he can do is listen to me when I speak.

"Hey."

"Yessir what'sup?" His gaze moves slowly to me, and when I can see the color of his irises I can tell how glazed over they are.

Oh, fuck.

Did that almost just happen?

What the hell was I thinking? I almost just told him my secret. I almost revealed I'm a killer, and fucking love it. Jesus, what would I have done afterward? I may have had to choose between myself and my best friend.

Holy fucking shit.

Okay, I think it's time for bed. No more drinky for me. I can't chance a colossal mistake like that.

"I'm gonna hit the hay. Bedtime for Aidan."

"All right." Jason hiccups as he raises his can to me in a sort of intended salute. "Sleep tight."

"Yup," I answer without turning around and make my way up the stairs.

***

I take a few minutes to shower before making my way to bed. I can't believe I had the urge to share everything with Jason. He may not have remembered even if I'd actually slipped, but that's not a guarantee. It would've been an unacceptable and irreversible mistake. I need to watch that, better seal the vault within.

It may take some practice, but I'm new to the game, so I'm sure I'll get there. As a precaution, though, I should refrain from consuming copious amounts of liquid encouragement until the lock is secured. Well...after this weekend I'll refrain until I'm more practiced. Tomorrow doesn't count. I'll just shut the fuck up unless I've thought over what I plan to say a few times. My filter cannot fail again. I'm already up here with Jason, and I know it'll just be a huge fight if I drag my feet about drinking tomorrow.

I'll make sure to pay closer attention to what we watch.

The water on my face takes a slight edge off the weight from the beer. Just for a little bit of prevention I drink two full glasses of water on my way to the bedroom and lay the bottle of painkillers on the night table. I know I won't feel amazing tomorrow regardless, but I'd like to prevent both a migraine and throwing up.

Huddled under the somewhat scratchy comforter, I can tell I'm far from home. One of the last thoughts to float through my foggy mind is that it's nice to get away once in a while, but I do wish the bed was a bit softer underneath me and the cabin was warmer.

***

Four glowing red eyes float above me. They don't seem to be connected to a body or anything of substance. Just two pairs of horrible, crimson eyes. They sit there staring at me. They're not blinking, not moving.

But they're judging.

Slowly faces start to materialize around both sets of eyes. Each is gaunt and haunted with thin waxy, gray skin. Both float closer to my face as they continue to form, and their mouths stretch wider in silent screams of protest.

"What do you want?"

My voice sounds far away, as if it's coming from someone else. The disconnect produces even more anxiety.

"Why, don't you know?" Their heads shake in unison, disappointed I don't already understand. As they shake, flakes of decaying skin fall from each already-hollow face. What seemed to have just formed is already crumbling away.

"Why me?"

My cry sounds strangled. I can feel my entire body shaking in fear. I tremble, quaking as if I'm standing in the gallows with a noose already around my neck. I'm normally much more composed than this.

Why am I so afraid?

"We want you, Aidan." I've gathered that. But their deepening tone sends a prickle over my scalp, reminding me to bite my tongue from saying so. "We want to do to you what you did to us."

Oh fuck.

"But...B—but how can you be here?"

It's The-One-Who-Doesn't-Count and the waitress floating in front of me, threatening me. They've both come back, joining forces to take me down for what I did to them. I can see in the blacks of their eyes they know how much I enjoyed it. They can feel I lack remorse, and they're back for vengeance.

Piercing shrieks escape their toothless, hanging jaws as they leap, reaching for my throat.

Ready to kill.

chapter TWenty-Nine:

I jolt instantly from lying flat into a sitting position. I can't believe I don't have whiplash. The shrieking that I thought was only in my dream is floating up the stairs of the cabin. For a brief moment I see screaming women swimming before my eyes. But that can't be where the noise is coming from. Jason isn't like me.

The tea kettle.

Annoyance is justified. Why the fuck does Jason need hot water at—I look at the alarm—five in the fucking morning? On a Saturday? Up north?

Fucking asshole.

I throw on a robe, stomping down the stairs, displaying my frustration.

"What the fuck, man?"

"Oh, shit. I'm sorry. I didn't think the kettle would whistle. I just can't sleep when I drink more than two anymore. I'm getting too old."

"That makes two of us. Now shut the hell up so I can wake up." I turn away from him, shuffling to the downstairs bathroom, adding over my shoulder, "Slowly."

"All right. All right." In the mirror, before I slam the door, I see

Jason's shoulders shrugged up to his ears in surrender, and I hear a mumbled, "yeesh, sorry," on the other side of the wood.

After I take a good chunk of time to acclimate to the early hour, in addition to my hangover, I let Jason make me coffee in a peace gesture.

"Make it fucking strong."

"Yes, sir."

After that he's smart to wait until after I've started my second cup before attempting to speak again.

"You're not normally so grumpy in the morning. I remember you waking me at 4 AM for a party back in the day."

"Copious amounts of alcohol, plus bad dreams, plus too early of a wakeup call, equals a shitty mood. But I'm close to normal. Thanks for the coffee. Sorry I bit your head off."

"Nah, it's fine. I should've known it would whistle." I don't respond, just nod, continuing sipping from my still-steaming mug. "It's been a long time since I've gotten that drunk. I don't remember shit. Do you?"

"Barely. That means it was a good night." Especially since he can't remember our nearly fatal conversation. I barely caught myself.

"Hell yeah, it was. It's so nice to be away from the girls for a little while. It's just easier to breathe up here. Ya know?"

"Sure do."

"Thanks again for bringing me."

"What are friends for?" Maybe someday I'll tell him my secret and he can pay me back for this trip with his assistance mopping up blood.

Or maybe not.

Half a pot of coffee later we make cereal and toast for breakfast, but after eating and washing the dishes it's still only seven in the morning. I hadn't anticipated being awake for at least a few more hours.

"Well, what do we do now?"

"I was about to ask you the same thing." *Oh, Jason, be a fucking man.* I narrow my eyes to glare at him, showing him how I feel versus telling him again.

"Okay, okay. How about we...go hunting?" Again he forms it as a question, so instead of answering I just raise my eyebrows then stare. "Hunting. Let's go hunting." This time it's a statement. Better.

"Good. We'll shoot shit." He has no idea how much I like this plan. I feel a tingle deep in my bones at the idea of killing even an animal. I can't get creative, but I can still steal a life. The memory will be my donation.

***

Pulling into Jason's driveway late on Sunday morning feels like entering New York City after leaving Amish Country. Admittedly the weekend isn't over, and I'll get to relax at home before heading back to work Monday, but the two worlds of here and there are starkly different. The contrast is apparent, and though both have their positives, tomorrow morning will be harder to face than Mondays past.

Maybe I should aim toward living up north in the country permanently. It's so much quieter there and I wouldn't have to answer to anybody. There are definitely remote finance positions. It's a possibility to ponder over, at least. Thinking about our hunting, drinking, appreciation of the wilderness, the covering darkness, the quiet solitude—it is a possibility to ponder more than just a little.

"Thanks for coming up with me."

"No, thank you for taking me." I try to wave my hand in dismissal, but he cuts me off. "Hey...seriously, your idea for mine and Mel's separate weekends was just what we needed. She was so relaxed after her pampering, and I'm pretty sure our boys' time was just what I needed to refocus and appreciate my family more. You're a good friend." Jason averts his eyes while his voice drops a notch, displaying how humble and genuine he intends to sound. But he can only remain serious for so long. He can't help himself to add, "Always one-upping me. I'll have to think of an amazing Christmas gift." He nudges me in the ribs while I agree he should spend a fortune on me.

I help him bring his bags into the house and share a quick hello with Amelia. "Hey, beautiful."

Jason huffs, "That's my line," and pretends to scowl. He'll never see me as a threat. He turns to Mel and concedes, "Well you are beautiful." And he plants a sloppy kiss on the corner of Mel's mouth. As he turns to drag his bags down the hall I catch her sneaking her sleeve up to wipe away his saliva.

"Glad you both made it back home safely."

Amelia's wearing a tight pink sweater that barely keeps the mounds of her growing tits in check. Her dark jeans are snug from waist to ass to ankle. Fuck me, I wasn't kidding when I said she looked beautiful. Though I don't think they *need* a fourth, pregnancy in the early stages sure does Amelia good. "Thanks for taking him up." She whispers.

She leans in to hug me after I drop Jason's other bag, and she pats my jacket pocket as she leans away. She was brief and almost stiff, which is preferable to her last few embraces that went beyond friendly, seeing as Jason is right here this time.

"See you tomorrow, bud." I wave to them both and make a hasty retreat to my car, anxious for a few hours of solitude before the week begins. I never felt like weekends were too short before, but now with their new uses to me I could go for a few Saturdays in a row. In fact, I wouldn't mind taking an early retirement to make my new hobby a full-time gig.

That'd be amazing.

chapter Thirty;

On the short drive home, all I have time to consider is what I'll order for take-out dinner. The house looks normal when I enter, throwing down my bags. I toss my keys into the bowl and close the front door behind me. But as I dip into my jacket pocket for my wallet to throw into the bowl as well, my fingers wrap around a piece of paper.

What's this?

As I pull it out to examine, a sinking feeling moves heavily into my gut. The folded piece of notebook paper between my fingers looks suspicious. I eye it, wondering if it will bite me.

I unfold the page several times to reveal a handwritten note. There's only one person who could've put this here. I'm simultaneously intrigued and worried, but I can't stop myself from reading the loops and curls of a woman's handwriting.

Oh shit.

Aidan,

I didn't want Jason to get mad because I went behind both of your backs, so I had to find a way to tell you privately. Please don't tell him. I know you hate it when I meddle, but I just know I'm right in this. Bee will be waiting for you at Hanson's at 8 PM for your first date. I put the reservation in your name. Don't be mad. Just trust me.

All my love,
Amelia

P.s. Wear your navy blazer, that's by far your best one.

Well, she's managed to be both bossy and out of her fucking mind at the same time. What a talent she possesses.

I know I'm stomping around my kitchen, but I can't seem to stop. I need to let off some of this frustration before I break something expensive I won't want to replace. She didn't even give me Bee's number to call and cancel. What the fuck am I going to do? What a cowardly bitch. And she pulls this stunt after I just coordinated a weekend for her.

I'll have to find a way to get payback. She better watch over her shoulder. But for now I'll be having dinner at Hanson's instead of ordering takeout like I wanted.

Bitch.

I continue to seethe in the shower, cursing Amelia's name. Expletives pour out like fire under my breath, and the more names I let out the better I feel. At least Bee is entertaining company, though we've never had a conversation one-on-one. This has potential to be an awkward evening. What a damper on such a nice weekend.

I refuse to wear the blazer Amelia demanded of me. She may have forced this dinner, but she won't pick out my clothes as well, and if she ever says one word to me about that jacket again she'll regret it.

***

Fucking Mel.
Fucking bossy, nosey, bitchy Amelia.

I still can't let it go even on the twenty-five-minute drive to the restaurant. Why did she have to pick a place so far away? The food isn't even that good there, and the drinks are way overpriced. But I do plan to drink, regardless of whether it makes Bee uncomfortable. Maybe the first will calm my anger and I'll be better company.

As I arrive at Hanson's, swinging the door open a little too hard, I charge up to the hostess and see the widening of intimidation in her eyes. Okay, knock it down a notch.

I smile, trying to make up for my tantrum of an entrance, and switch to charming instead.

"Eight o'clock reservation for Aidan Sheppard, please."

The thin girl, of no older than nineteen, recovers, embracing my charisma. She rocks on her heels as she returns my smile with an added hint of lust behind her glossed lips. "Let me see, oh yes, your date is already here. Let me show you to the table. Can I take your jacket?" I hand her my winter tweed, waiting as she places it with the other outerwear, trying hard not to tap my foot in impatience.

I just want to get this meal started so I can get it over with.

"My name is Mandy, but Candy will be your waitress tonight. Can I get you anything to drink?" Mandy and Candy. Jesus fucking Christ, our future is doomed. Their IQs are probably just above idiotic. But I bet they suck cock like champs with those names. Mandy does look like a pleaser with the way she sways her round ass while walking in front of me.

"Jack and coke please. Double."

"Of course. And here's your booth. It looks like your date made a trip to the ladies' room. I'll get your drink while you wait." She hesitates awkwardly by the table for a moment, watching as I sit before she moves away.

I drum my fingers on the table, waiting for the appearance of Bee. I should've just stayed home and stood her up. I could've feigned ignorance, pretending as if I never found the note.

Damn it. Why didn't I fucking think of that earlier?

I jump as a finger taps my shoulder from behind. Apparently Bee is back from the bathroom. I hope she washed her hands before touching me. Standing, I turn around to greet my date.

And I lose all ability to speak.

I know my mouth is wide open since my jaw has dropped, but I can't seem to make my brain tell my muscles to move. My eyes go from the top of her head down to her toes and back up again, pausing at the good bits on each pass.

"Hello, Aidan. I'm glad you decided to come."

I suck in a breath after holding it too long, struggling to find an answer.

All I come up with is, "Hello, Amelia."

chapter Thirty-One;

Mind-blowing boredom.

It's Monday and it's as dull as ever as I attempt to keep my thoughts of last night as far from my consciousness as possible. I haven't processed it yet, so I don't know how I feel. I'll work on it later. Maybe much later.

This shit just doesn't seem to happen to other people, I swear.

I think I may start to hate Mondays just like the rest of the world soon.

Jason is still in a happy-go-lucky mood, due to the cabin I'm assuming, and Eva has been as boisterous as ever. If I had to guess, I'd bet she's pitching her terrible ideas soon. She's so confident she'll soar straight to the top. I'd beg to differ. Luckily, she's too selfish to say I had her back when she brings them to the table; she doesn't want any name mentioned but her own. But just in case I'm wrong and she does move up with this, then at least she'll feel as if I was helpful. It's a win-win for me, which I'm okay with.

Speak of the devil. I can see Eva twitching her hips down the hallway toward me now. She's side-by-side with a higher up who looks a bit intimidated (or embarrassed, I can't quite tell, though either way his eyes are averted as his pace is picking up) by her too-loud laughter at something he's said. I bet it wasn't even funny.

He veers off toward the kitchen a few paces before my open door and Eva keeps moving forward. I know she's coming to see me. I've yet to see her pop her head into Jason's office unless he's requested her presence, so there's no one else she'd be walking toward.

Damn.

I start the conversation, knowing the faster it begins the faster it ends. "How's it going, Eva?" Why does she insist on coming to my office so often? She's such a pain in the ass, and her stupid face is more frustrating than ever.

Go away, annoying hag; no one likes you, just go away.

"I'm absolutely wonderful." Her cheeks rise as her smile widens. She looks like the Cheshire Cat, on crack.

I chuckle insincerely and reply, "Well that's great, especially for a Monday." I'd rather she were crying from a deep depression, leading her to quit work, isolating herself far away from ever crossing my path.

And I'd prefer this every day of the week, not just on a Monday.

Eva's crazy smile remains. She leans forward, giving me a better glimpse at the tight collar of her sweater—too bad it isn't dipping to show off more of the heat she packs underneath it—and she lowers her voice. "Take me out to dinner tonight." Again she doesn't ask. She commands. "Or else."

Or else what, bitch?

She's insane, and she thinks she owns the world.

"7 o'clock. Delta's." At least if she's going to be throwing out demands I can return the favor, refraining from asking for agreement.

"See you there," she says seductively, after nodding. Without another comment she turns on her high heels, walking back toward her side of the building. Her hair bounces as she trots down the hall.

As much as I despise her, I can't help but appreciate the view of her walking away. If I didn't want to kill her, I'd gladly fuck her silly.

And I *really* don't want to spend my evening with her. I see more than enough of her here. I should've protested, even if it fucked with my win-win. Too late now, though. I guess I'll just grin and bear it through dinner, hoping she gets thrown out on her ass soon.

***

After thinking more about the situation, it's clear I need to help Eva's downfall along. So I make my way to Dan's office for a private chat.

"What can I do for you?" the aging VP asks.

He's smiling, carefree. We've always gotten along. I close the door before answering. My face pulls taut, and I do my best impression of embarrassed.

"Can I speak to you confidentially?"

"Of course. What is it?" He tenses every muscle, instantly concerned, and leans forward, encouraging my honesty. Well, what he'll take for honesty.

"Will this stay between us?"

"I promise."

"I don't want anyone else involved. HR doesn't need to know. I just wanted you to be aware." I'm hysterically laughing inside. This is so perfect. He's so intrigued. I don't think I could build it up any more.

"Please, you can trust me." At this point I think he may bend over backwards for the pain to leave my face.

"It's Eva, sir."

"What's she done?" He exhales loudly after finishing.

This time I almost let the laughter break loose. He assumed guilt on her part. Priceless.

"She...just goes too far."

"How so?" Dan's brows are furrowing, and he looks close to bursting with stress.

I start with a sigh, reflecting his. "She goes too far. She's too sexual. I've asked her to stop. Several times. Yet she just keeps pushing my boundaries, my buttons." Pause for dramatic effect. Look down awkwardly. Fidget with hands. I employ every tactic I can think of. Finally, when I look up again to continue, I know I have this in the bag. But I dig the knife in deeper. "She calls me names that aren't appropriate for work. She uses any excuse to touch me. I hate to admit it, as a man, but she makes me incredibly uncomfortable."

Dan opens his mouth, breathes in, changes his mind, and closes it again. Before speaking he stands up, pacing back and fourth behind his desk. Finally, he tries once more.

"And I can't persuade you to put this on record?" He sits back down heavily.

"It would only make me feel worse here."

"We don't want that."

He slams his fist hard on his desk. He's pissed. *Perfect.*

"I'm sorry." I stand to leave. "I shouldn't have said anything. Forget I did."

One...

Two...

Three.

And that's all it takes.

"Absolutely not." He shoots up. I turn back. "Do *not* feel guilty. I just wish I had known sooner. I'd like to do more."

"Please don't say anything to her. Hopefully she'll stop on her own."

"I wouldn't bet on it."

I'm a devious mastermind.

"If she continues, please let me know. I promised I would keep this between us, and I will. I always keep my promises. But if she crosses the line I need to know."

I silently nod with a frown. I refrain from making eye contact and turn to the door again. I think better of it and quietly add, "Thank you."

As I open his door Eva walks by, butting her nose into the wrong conversation at the best time. "Just the man I wanted to see. My little Aidan. I need your help in my office." She puts her arm through mine, smiling at Dan.

I'm having a fit inside and shake a little keeping it in. He must assume the tremor is based somewhere in unease, because he adds, "Remember what I said. I *need* to know."

As she pulls me away, I turn to Dan with "help me" written in my eyes.

***

The rest of the workday goes by without distraction.

Jason chats with me a few times, but he shows no indication of knowing Amelia met me for dinner. He's blissfully ignorant, and if it's up to me he'll stay that way.

Before long, I make my way home to get ready for dinner with the reigning queen of all bitches. I need to put my game face on tonight. If I can focus, I know I can charm her until her panties are moist.

After slapping liberal amounts of cologne on, I take one last assessing look in the mirror and steel myself before heading out.

Here goes nothing.

Chapter Thirty-Two;

The drive is quick, and it leaves me wishing I had more time to mentally prepare myself for Eva's domineering presence, but I'm just not *that* lucky. When I enter, I scan the thick crowd, but turn up empty, so instead I request a table for two.

As I stand waiting for the hostess to seat me, I hear the doors open behind me and feel the gust of winter air on my back. Before I can turn around, I sense the presence of someone standing way too close to me. My bubble is being popped, and I don't appreciate the close proximity of strangers.

"Do you mind?" I try to sound even-keeled.

"Not at all, Handsome." Eva leans closer to my face and slings her sinewy arm over my shoulder for an awkward half hug from behind and slightly to my left. I can already smell the liquor on her. She's started early tonight, and evidently drunk driving laws don't apply to her.

"I'll show you to your seats." Saved by the hostess.

Eva again tucks her arm through mine as we make our way to the table in a surprisingly full crowd for a Monday night. Her eyes roam around the room in a slow and deliberate appraisal. I worry when I realize she's looking to see if anyone from work is here.

Eva waves her hand to the hostess as a request for her dismissal the moment we get to our table.

Rude bitch.

"Now what shall we have tonight?" Her eyes aren't entirely focused. She's struggling to appear sober. "How about a few drinks?"

"After you." I'll just follow her lead, doing my best to get out of here unscathed. If I can.

When our waiter arrives it's obvious he's busy. His words come out quick and staccato. "You folks ready to order?"

As I open my mouth to answer, since he has eye contact with me, Eva, oblivious to the rest of the world, interrupts. "I'll have the sampler appetizer platter and a sex on the beach." What a weird order. She turns to me, winking, which I pretend to miss as I turn back to the waiter.

"And for you, sir?" His smirk is slight, but I can tell he's laughing at her.

"Cheeseburger with a Jack and coke, please. Thank you." At least one of us has manners.

"I'll get those orders right in, and I'll be back with your drinks."

Eva skips all preamble, bolder when she drinks. "As of tomorrow we're riding success to the top at work." I knew she was ready to pitch her shit.

"I can't wait to ride your coattails, beautiful." I almost choke on the last word, but she doesn't notice. I manage to get it out because I know she'll be putty for me when doling out enough compliments.

"Oh, stop." Though her words say stop her body language says the opposite. She's eating it up. "I figured we'd celebrate tonight." Her need to be in control pours off her like body odor. Too bad that doesn't work for me. At all.

"Can do, boss." Eva's crackhead look is back. Her Cheshire smile is fucking creepy. When I see it, all I can think is, *We're all mad here.*

She makes a sound that mimics a cat's purr just before our waiter arrives with our drinks. "A sex on the beach for the lady." Her puts down her drink with extra care. He must know she's trouble. "And a Jack and coke for the sir." He smiles for a nanosecond before nearly running away to his many other tables.

"So, what should we talk about?" *Honestly, bitch?* She's the one who forced me here and she can't come up with a topic of conversation? Lord help me through this dinner, and make it quick, because if I have to sit here too long Eva will be the next to give me a donation.

"Anything your heart desires. We're celebrating your ideas," I say.

"That's the stuff I like to hear." Eva nudges my leg with her foot, and I ignore it. I will not fuck her. I will not kill her. I will *not* fuck her or kill her.

Our food arrives in the nick of time, and I busy myself with eating while she prattles on about who the fuck knows what. I try to listen, but I just want to go home.

I can't look at her without wanting to put a dent in the middle of her pretty features.

Eva orders two more drinks and she's past sloshed by the time we're finished eating. I only had the one, to which she's been oblivious.

"So, are you ready to take me home?" Goddamn it.

"Uh...What?"

"You heard me. I want you to take me home, and I want you to do dirty things to me."

Holy shit.

"Eva, I'd love to." Her smile widens before she starts biting her lower lip, and I go on. "And please don't get me wrong, but I can't."

Her face falls comically slowly as it sinks in I've turned her down, and I have to suppress the urge to laugh in her face. She blinks once, twice, three times before responding.

"You're saying you don't want to have sex with me?"

"No. That's not what I'm saying." I don't elaborate. I'd fuck her despite her treacherous work ethic and bitchy attitude. I'd gladly stick it to her roughly. I just know I can't. I'm smarter than that. It would go horribly wrong sooner or later, and I'm not willing to risk my career for a cunt like Eva.

"Then what exactly are you saying?" She speaks in a disgusted sneer. Clearly she doesn't handle rejection well.

"You're my boss. And you've had a few to drink. I just don't feel right about it. I don't want to take advantage of you, and I don't want to jeopardize our working relationship. I'm sorry." No, I'm *not* sorry. This is a little more fun than it should be. She should know better than to ask.

Her features smooth out a little with new determination. "You don't need to be a gentleman. I'm a big girl. I'm saying yes, and I'm asking nicely." Okay, she just needs to give it up. She looks more desperate the more she begs, and desperation looks awful on her.

"I'm so sorry. Please don't be upset. You're fucking beautiful. But my answer is still no."

She huffs and puffs, and for a second I'm genuinely worried she's going to throw a tantrum or cause a scene. But instead she stands up, grabs her coat, and smiles. Placing both palms on the tabletop, she leans toward my face, stopping inches from my nose.

"Fuck you." Her voice has a menacing edge that would be intimidating to someone else, especially if it wasn't laced with a drunken slur.

Before she straightens up, I try to look genuine as I apologize once more. "I truly am sorry."

"You should be." She stands again, grabs my drink, and throws it in my face.

Are you fucking serious?

I struggle to stay calm. I'd love to bash her head into the floor continuously. But all I do is grab my napkin and clean myself off. I don't give her the satisfaction of a reaction.

Unstable whore.

Eva starts to walk away, but after a couple steps she throws one last comment over her shoulder. "Take care of the check, asshole." Another command. What an entitled twat. Hopefully her memories of tonight will be hazy by tomorrow morning.

The waiter doesn't look surprised when he returns with the bill and I'm alone.

"She's awful." His observation is true, and it's refreshing he shares it so candidly.

"Abso-fucking-lutely." He smiles, and when I look at the receipt I see he's comped her meal. As a thank you I tip him by doubling the total. Anyone who hates Eva is a friend of mine.

***

On Tuesday, I walk in the building with Jason after pulling up next to him while he was getting out of his car.

"How was your night?"

"It was shit, actually." He chuckles before elaborating. "Olivia puked right in my lap. She's got the flu, which means the other two will have it by tomorrow. I hate when they get sick. I feel helpless, and I just want to be able to make them better."

"You're a good man." If I had some little bundle of trouble blow chunks in my lap I'd be a lot more worried about cleaning it up than making her feel better.

"I guess I am." He smiles a genuine smile, and I have a slight pang somewhere deep in my stomach.

"That's fucking gross she hurled right on you, though." I'd have dropped her to prevent something like that. And that's why I can never have children. Those defensive reflexes aren't looked upon favorably by child services.

"Uh yeah, you don't have to tell me that. It worked to my advantage, though."

"Really?"

"Yeah, Amelia cleaned it up, and then she cleaned me up in the shower after putting the girls to bed." I feel something else entirely a bit deeper in my stomach with that comment.

"Lucky. See you later." I nearly sprint the last few feet into my office in order to end the conversation, having no desire to hear any more details.

After wasting time checking voice mails and staring into space, I boot up my computer to the tune of a new email from Jason. Our emails are monitored, though, so I know it isn't anything further about last night and his sex-capades. I open it without worry.

From: Jason Moore
To: Aidan Sheppard
Subject: Missing in Action

Aid,

Thought you'd be interested. Our lovely boss is out today. Apparently she's sick too. Looks like today will be an easy day.

Cheers,
Jase

Well, Eva must still be feeling the effects of her few too many. *Good.* Just makes my life easier not to have to face her today. I type a quick response to Jason, joining in the excitement.

After that's done I finish my few tasks that need completing today, which doesn't take long. And with ample time to drift off into my own thoughts, I regretfully recall Sunday night at Hanson's.

chapter Thirty-Three:

I'm so shocked to see Amelia instead of Bee it takes me a while to come up with a coherent sentence after my hello.

"I'm sorry I tricked you. And I'm even sorrier I kept pushing Bee on you. I know it seemed like I was being a bitch. Though, I had my reasons. At first I thought you two would be good together, so I shoved her at you. Then this plan came to me, and I knew it would work. So my motives changed for the selfish. Don't get me wrong, she's a nice girl, but I realized my needs were more important. I had to get you to meet me." She pauses after babbling, waiting for me to reply. When I don't, she continues. "Jason thinks I'm getting my hair done, so we have a few hours."

Instead of commenting on the obvious details or even asking why she set this up, I pick up on the one thing that comes to mind. "But won't he notice your hair is the same?"

Amelia's laughter peals through the air like soft wind chimes. "In all these years together, he has never noticed any difference in my hair. Remember that time I cut off a foot after Sophia was born, and it was to my chin?" I nod. "He didn't notice for two weeks. So we're fine." She chooses to end with the reminder we're sneaking behind my best friend's, her husband's, widening back.

Finally I find the right words, but they feel like sandpaper as they scrape across my tongue. "Why are we here, Amelia?"

She looks nervous.

"I don't love Jason anymore."

And just like that she can never unsay it. I can never unhear it.

Mel's watching her fingers twist as she wrings her hands next to her silverware.

"Fuck." The word is so deflated it comes out breathy.

"I know." She doesn't continue. I can tell she needs to talk about this, but I have no idea why she chose me, considering who I am to Jason.

"When did this happen?" I ask as if it was one event, one thing, that caused her to stop loving him.

"It's been a while. I haven't felt the same in the last few years." She peers up from her hands to meet my questioning stare.

I can't help but say it again. "Fuck."

I'm so eloquent tonight.

"Yeah, I know I'm a horrible person." Her eyes start to look a bit too shiny, and I realize she's on the brink of crying.

"No you're not." Please don't cry. *Please.*

"We just grew apart. I don't know exactly when it started, or what caused it, but I just can't get it back. And believe me, I've tried. It's too far gone. I was going to ask him for a divorce the day before I found out I was pregnant again. But I realized I was late, and then it was positive, and now it's too late."

One tear falls down her cheek, hitting the table. She doesn't move to wipe it away. She just leaves it. No other drops follow. She blinks a few times and the gloss is gone.

"I'm so sorry, Mel." I reach across the expanse of space between us, hesitantly, to touch her hands. As soon as I do, she opens her palm to grasp my hand tightly. Hers are softer than any woman's hands I've ever held, and they're warm.

"I just had to tell someone." She squeezes my hand in an effort to show me she trusts me. She didn't tell a girlfriend. She told someone she knew would understand. She told someone who doesn't believe much in the idea of love.

"So what are you going to do?"

"Honestly?" Again she looks nervous.

"Of course." I smile to coax the next confession out of her.

"I'm going to have the baby, and after that I'm either going to leave him, or I'm going to cheat on him."

"Fuck me." Seriously, I need a new word.

"Well, that's the idea."

***

A loud knock on the glass next to my open door brings me out of my memory.

"Lunch?" Jason's loud voice sounds almost as if he's yelling in comparison to the silence that surrounded me moments before.

"Sure, give me an hour? I need to finish a few things first." I don't mention it isn't work I need to finish.

"Sounds good." He walks loudly down to the copier.

After he's left, I allow myself to remember the rest of the night. I still need to finish processing.

***

"Wait...what are you saying, Amelia?"

I know what she said, and I know what it should mean, but the idea just doesn't make sense in my head. She *can't* have meant what it sounded like. I heard wrong. I must have.

"I'm saying, if you're interested, I want to have an affair with you."

Her words sound clinical. They aren't sexy. She doesn't coat them in emotion or pleading. She's making a simple proposition, inquiring if I'm interested. She knows me better than I thought she did. Amelia is more emotional than this instinctively, and she's suppressing it to appeal to me.

Fucking brilliant.

"And if I say no?" I need to know everything she's thinking.

"If you say no, then we'll never talk about this again. I won't say a word, and I trust you won't either. I'll leave Jason a while after baby number four is born, and we will all live our lives as if this night never happened."

My eyes are wide, I know, but I can't get them to close at all. My lips are pressed into a thin line, and I can feel the creases pressed into the skin of my forehead.

"If you say yes, then until I leave Jason we will have as much sex as you can handle. Then I'll still get a divorce down the road." She fidgets, but continues. "And Jason will still never know. The only detail that changes is you."

Me.

"You decide if you're in or out. Either way, I can't stay with him, Aidan. It's going to end one way or another. You can't prevent it, and it won't hurt Jason any less if you say no to me. The ball's in your court."

"Can I take a couple days to think about it?"

I want to say yes. Fucking fuck, I want to say yes and screw her brains out on this table right now, but I need to think this through. Jason is my best friend, one of my only true friends. But what Mel said makes a lot of sense, too. Will this complicate my new hobby? Surely not. I need to think about this from every angle.

I need time.

"Of course." Thankfully, she's willing to give it to me.

Her smile is radiant, and she squeezes my hand once more before letting it go. As I pull away reluctantly, she traces her finger down the length of my palm. The touch sends a shiver throughout my entire body.

"I promise I won't say anything regardless of what I decide."

How could I?

"Thank you, and I trust you. If I didn't, I wouldn't be here."

"Let's have some food?"

"Absolutely, I'm starving." Amelia's eyes twinkle as she looks at me.

How the hell did I get here? What a complicated clusterfuck.

Fuck me.

chapter Thirty-Four;

It's been two days and I still haven't decided. I know I need to. Soon. But I'm still baffled, and that's making it incredibly hard to think about what I want to do. I've given myself a deadline of tomorrow night to let her know if I'm in or out.

In the meantime, I need to start scratching my own itch. I want to do my dirty deed again. I'm ready for it. All I need is a playmate and a plan. So, basically everything. Tonight I'll come up with one or the other, get it started, and tomorrow I'll think about what to do (or not do) with Amelia. One thing at a time, I guess.

Somehow I think my best ideas come when I just stop trying to come up with an answer, when I relax. I don't know why, but they do. So I let my mind wander, stopping the pressure on myself.

I hop into the shower once I get home from an Eva-free day at work. Lunch with Jason went fine. I'm feeling less and less guilty when I'm with him as he talks about Amelia. But when he mentions anything sexual about her, my feelings of jealous rage get more pronounced. Everything is give and take, meaning I have to find the balance I'm happy to live with.

As the hot water pounds into my skin, I think about what my next murderous move should be. Though planning has worked fine for me so far, maybe this time I should be more spontaneous with the actual method of killing. Just bring a hoard of tools and pick at random whichever catches my fancy in the moment.

Yes. That's tantalizing.

I'm on a roll, because suddenly I've got the next piece, too. I look up just to make sure a light bulb hasn't materialized above my head with this outpouring of ideas. I'm going to pick up a hitchhiker, sedate or subdue her, bring her into the woods, and have so much fun.

I sigh. My life is just perfect. So perfect.

***

At work on Wednesday, Eva stomps by me without a greeting. I'm surprised she can walk so heavily on heels so thin without breaking her ankle. Guess she does remember my rejection, and she still isn't too happy about it. Her choice to ignore me doesn't cause any heartbreak. Oh well, I'll let her cool down some, and then I'll kill her with kindness to get back in her good graces.

Jason and I keep ourselves busy on a newly assigned project from an adjacent department. We have no reason to interact with Eva, which is good for us. Every time I see her walk by the conference room Jason and I are holed up in, she looks angrier. Her interactions with others in the office look awkward as she snaps at everyone.

What a cunt.

People are going to assume she's on the rag, and maybe she is, but I doubt it's the only thing causing her bitchiness. She doesn't handle rejection well at all.

Just after lunchtime I watch out of the corner of my eye as she prepares to enter her pitch meeting. She stands outside the doors adjusting her blouse, then her skirt, and going back to fix both once more. She's nervous. And she should be, because if I'm right they're going to fucking hate every single one of her ideas.

Finally, she enters the office after almost five minutes of incessant fidgeting.

"They're gonna eat her alive." I don't mean to mumble it out loud but nonetheless it pops out from my mouth, and Jason cocks his head to the side.

"What'd you say?" His eyes dart from me to the doors Eva just walked through.

"Oh, nothing." I smile with an evil squint to my eyes. "Nothing at all."

Not even fifteen minutes after she walked into the office, Eva is walking back out. Her pitch should've taken at least an hour. *Interesting.* Maybe that means she fell hard on her ass.

She walks quickly past our conference room, manages to glare at me while passing, and heads straight past her office to the shitty old elevator. It would just make my day if it fell to the lobby floor, crushing her inside.

No less than two minutes later, my phone pings with an incoming email.

"I never should've added work's email to my phone." I sigh loud and exaggeratedly as I pull it out of my pocket.

"Yeah, tell me about it. Mel flips the hell out when it goes off at home. She says work is for work and home is for home. The two shouldn't mix." Smart woman. "But she doesn't get it since home is her place of work. What's it say?" Jason leans toward my phone to read as I do.

From: Management
To: Everyone
Subject: Half day

To Eva's team,

Eva will be out the rest of the afternoon. If you have any questions please feel free to contact any of the other departments' supervisors. Thank you.

Sincerely,
Management

"Hmmmm." I struggle to keep the laughter absent from my voice. "Two days in a row. She must've caught something nasty."

"Yeah, probably." After Jason turns away, I roll my eyes. Sick my ass.

Sometimes I wonder if he actually is as clueless as he plays at.

***

Leaving work, I know tonight I need to finally make my decision about Mel's proposition. I'm fairly sure what I want to tell her, but I need to be positive.

As the days have worn on since she asked, I've slowly leaned toward my answer. I'm not sure why it took me so long to give in to it. I know I've already started down a selfish road with my new hobby, and though I never want to lose Jason as a friend, he'll never find out I want to try Amelia on for size. If I'm getting exactly what I want in the realm of carnage and animalistic desires, why not in the sexual realm as well?

Let's face it, her body is amazing, and I'd regret it looking back if I missed the opportunity to get my dick inside her hot, wet slit. Okay, so it's decided. I'm going to agree to have an affair with Jason's wife.

Fucking hell.

I pull out my phone and wipe the perspiration accumulating on my forehead at the hairline. As my fingers shake I type in my one-word answer and hit send to Amelia's phone number. It's funny I'm nervous about this when I didn't bat an eye at the idea of the waitress.

Yes is all I send.

chapter Thirty-Five:

Early Thursday morning I hit "door close" desperately as I stand inside the elevator. Eva's walking across the lobby, but the fucking piece of shit won't react in time to my frantic punching of the likely broken button.

They need to fix this monstrosity, because it just fucked me.

"Good morning. Feeling better today?" All I get is crickets, and it's making me uncomfortable. So I add, "Since you left sick yesterday, I mean." Better to play nice.

"I am." Her tone is cold, curt.

She's still pissed.

We ride the rest of the slow ascent in silence. It's a horribly awkward, pregnant silence. The tension's palpable. I wish I could just smack some sense into her. It would be so much easier if I could just say, "Hey, I think you're hot, but frankly you're a bitch. *And* you're my boss. I'm sure a short-lived affair together isn't worth losing my job over." But I have a feeling that wouldn't go over any better than my gentler letdown. She just wants to be mad, and there's nothing I can do about it other than ride it out.

As the doors finally jerk open on our floor, Eva pushes me aside to exit first as if she's in a class above mine. Looking around to make sure no one's near enough to hear her, she utters in a nasty tone,

"See you at the meeting, asshole."

Well, that wasn't nice.

Instead of further jeopardizing my standing, I decide to take the high road. "Can't wait. Let me know if you need anything at all, I'd be happy to help." She doesn't answer. She just whisks away, shaking her head more than her ass down the hallway.

I need to resist all urges to push her buttons. It's too easy.

***

As odd as it sounds, ten minutes before the department meeting I'm getting excited. I know, who wants to sit in a boring meeting when it goes way too long about information we already know and barely care about? But maybe something will be said about Eva's pitch, and, if so, I bet it won't be good.

Oh god, *maybe she'll quit.*

I stand up and crack my knuckles loudly. The anticipation alone will make it better than a normal boring meeting.

I lean my head into Jason's office and knock on the outer frame. "You ready?"

"Oh crap, that's now isn't it?" He rushes to save whatever he's doing and stow away his papers until later.

"How do you forget every month?"

"I don't know. You'd think I'd learn. Time just gets away from me."

"You just work too hard."

We walk toward the largest conference room on our floor, and halfway there are joined by several colleagues. Sarah is short and slight with mousy brown hair, but she's funny. I think she lost her filter several marriages ago. She's only in her mid-thirties and on her fourth husband. Ben is taller than both Jason and me, but he's the dullest man you'll ever meet. I swear he thinks skipping rocks should be a competitive sport. Last to join us outside the conference room is Lisa. She's forgettable. She's average height, average build, and average looking. She doesn't talk a lot. Sometimes I forget she works here.

"So what was up with Eva's disappearing act yesterday?" Sarah whispers louder than I would, considering the bitch herself could walk into the room at any moment.

"Shhh, dummy." Thank you, Jason.

"I bet we find out sooner rather than later." I just have to fuel the fire, at least when I can.

"What do you know?" Sarah's definitely a gossip, and I've piqued her interest.

"I'm not totally sure. I'll let you know if anything comes of it."

Keep her intrigued enough to keep an eye on Eva.

"You're bad."

She swipes her hand toward me, scolding me for being naughty. I just smile and nod.

I'm glad I didn't say anything else because Eva storms in then, just before her two superiors. And as more stragglers wander in, the group is all ready to start. Eva sits in the chair farthest away from me instead of opting for the head of the table as she usually does. Maybe she'll knock herself down a few pegs as a result of my politer than necessary decline.

"Let's get started, shall we?" Frank, the senior most person here and VP of the company, rarely comes to our meetings. He's here today, though.

The next most senior attendee, Dan, usually runs the show, but not today. Dan looks content to take a backseat, while in contrast Frank's features are pinched as if he smells something foul.

The meeting drones on without much to note for a while, but then things start to spice up. When Eva opens her mouth to begin she gets no more out than, "Yes," before Frank cuts her off with his own continued ramblings. I try so hard not to smile, but when I catch Sarah's eye and she's covered her own smirk with her papers, the corners of my mouth spite me, turning up.

Unfortunately, Eva looks to me when I still have laughter written on my face. She glares, and I swear, though I hate the saying, if looks could kill I'd be dead in my chair. I think I may have seen a spark or two of flames behind her pupils. I wonder if that's how I look just before I collect a donation from a playmate.

Fire in the eyes.

Frank continues on, and on, and on. It's hard to remain focused. When he asks for updates from everyone he starts with Dan, but then surprisingly, instead of Eva, next he asks me.

"Aidan, how's everything going in your world?" I don't miss a beat in my readiness to reply, and I make sure not to look shocked.

"Everything's good. I've been ahead on most of—" before I can finish my sentence Eva decides she can't contain her frustration any longer.

"Well, Frank, our department has been a well-oiled machine, as usual. Everyone works so hard under my guidance. Well...almost everyone." Eva has the nerve to look pointedly at me for her last comment. *Oh fuck no.* I work harder than anyone else here.

"Right," is all Frank says in response. He's not having her attitude either.

Dan looks to me again with apologetic eyes and in a gentle tone adds, "I'm sorry, Aidan, I believe it was your turn to speak."

Ha.

I finish my short little spiel as waves of excitement and pleasure wash over me. The grin I wear is plastered tightly across my face. I'm so glad I'm not the only one who has seen her shitty ways now. Frank and Dan remain attentive to me throughout.

Fuck that evil bitch.

When I finish, I watch Eva make an even bigger mistake next. "Fucker."

Her mumble is louder than she probably intended, because out of my peripheral vision I see Dan's eyes pop wide, and I hear Frank scribble notes before moving onto the rest of the updates around the room. She looks unaware that anyone heard her.

Everyone else's statements are received without comment by Eva, and it's clear I was her only target. Dan and Frank speed through the rest of the meeting without letting her talk again.

Dan jokes, "Class dismissed," and everyone stands.

Though rustling papers and shuffling bodies make background noise, it isn't enough to drown out Frank's request to Eva. "Please meet me in my office in thirty minutes."

Chapter Thirty-Six:

Eva makes no reply to Frank.

She appears completely surprised, which is so stupid after the obvious spectacle she's made in the last hour. Frank walks away before her body language morphs from stunned to enraged. She stands in the middle of the double doorway and we all have to maneuver around her.

I'm the second to last out, followed by Jason. When I think I've cleared her I feel a sudden tug on the back of my blazer. Then I hear a rip.

No fucking way.

"Where do you think you're going?" Eva's words are a hiss.

"Why don't you cool down, Eva?" Jason sounds surprisingly assertive as he stands beside me in camaraderie.

"Stay out of this, Jason. It has nothing to do with you." In an unladylike fashion, Eva spits with her last few words.

"All the same. I think I'll stay to witness anything you have to say if you feel the need to continue." Fuck yeah, Jason my boy. I knew I've kept him around so long for a reason.

"Thanks." I'd elaborate, but Eva looks angrier than ever, so I opt for a pat on his shoulder.

"Okay, fine. All I wanted to say…" She struggles for words which don't contain an expletive or a threat. She clears the rasp from her voice, stalling for a moment, before continuing. "All I wanted to say is if you think you're still going to ride my coattails to the top, you're sorely mistaken. I won't be taking you anywhere with me, and when I'm able you'll be out the door."

So she couldn't resist the threat, but A-plus for effort.

"We'll see." I choose to remain aloof to hold onto my control, and hopefully further unglue her.

Jason and I turn to walk away before she adds anything else incriminating.

When we're outside our adjoining offices, and out of Eva's earshot, Jason finally asks what he must be burning to know. "What the fuck was that all about, dude?"

"I think it was the last straw against her."

"What does that mean? What's going on? You have to tell me." His eyes are determined.

"Okay, I'll tell you, but you have to promise to keep it quiet." I trust him despite the fact he shouldn't trust me anymore.

"Cross my heart." He even makes the motion.

"Are we thirteen-year-old girls?" I can't help it, I crack up at his ridiculous choice of phrase. As usual, he can break tension when it's needed. He nods for me to continue with a smirk on his face. "Well, Eva forced me to take her out to dinner Monday night, and when I wouldn't sleep with her afterward she threw a fit. She still hasn't let it go, and today's performance was embarrassing."

"Incredibly. Did she seriously just do all of that over a rejection?" Jason doesn't look as if he's quite ready to believe my explanation, but when I don't offer another he's eventually convinced. "Wow."

"She's one fucked-up cookie."

"Shit." Jase still looks dazed by the information, but then realizes one last thing before we part ways to our own desks. "You sure have a way with women, man. Everyone wants to get in your pants."

I bark out one burst of laughter.

Oh little do you know, Jason, how encompassing the word *everyone* is.

***

Forty-five minutes after the end of the meeting (fifteen after Eva was supposed to begin her meeting with Frank) a company-wide email goes out, but I think someone hit send too soon, because the entire scene hasn't finished playing out yet.

I open my email but only have time to read the subject before I hear a lot of yelling near the elevator. It never hurts to dream, and today my dreams are coming true. Eva has a box of her possessions next to her heels on the floor; her face is more flushed than I've ever seen it, even when she was plastered and pissed off on Monday night.

"Idiots. You're going to regret this!"

"Eva, please save some dignity. You just weren't the right fit for us." Frank is trying to be diplomatic, but I bet he's struggling to keep a hold on his temper. I know I would be.

"Oh, fuck off, Frankie. You ignorant assholes have no idea what you're losing. I could've doubled this company's profits. Expanded. Who knows what else." Eva's head is shaking harder as her volume increases, and I think she might be on the verge of a heart attack or maybe an aneurism.

Please let it be an aneurism.

Frank steps around her to push the down button for the elevator. Once he steps back to face Eva—I'm surprised he put his back to her—he speaks as calmly as before. "I'm sorry you're taking this so personal. We appreciate all you've done for us. We wish you the best and much success in your future. That future just won't be with us." I have to give it to Frank; his performance is amazing.

I wish I could clap.

By now almost everyone in the office is peering at the scene unfolding. I've never seen so many curious eyes at once and all pointed in the same direction. Jason and I are both standing in our doorways, his eyes as animated as mine.

"You're going to be crawling on your hands and knees in a week's time begging me to come back." *Wow,* she's full of herself. I wish I could yell that no one will miss her.

"I assure you, our decision is final." Frank's tone takes on a harsher edge. He had to get fed up eventually.

"Go fuck yourself." The doors to the death trap open and Eva kicks her box inside. Before entering she flips Frank, and everyone watching, her perfectly manicured middle finger. She sputters out one final, and classy, "Fuck you all. Cocksucking motherfuckers."

As the doors close to take Eva down to the lobby one last time, Frank finally raises his voice. "I'm incredibly sorry for her inappropriate behavior. Anyone who'd like lunch on management tomorrow afternoon, please help yourself to Delta's. If you show them your badge your meal will be on our tab. But for now let's finish out this work day with more class than we were just shown, shall we?" Chuckles go around and Frank smiles before strolling back to his office. He took her outburst in stride.

"Holy shit, did that just happen?" Jason's face is priceless.

"Yes, sir, it just did."

When I sit back in my chair I take a moment to read the entire email now since Eva's wrath isn't a distraction.

From: Management
To: Everyone
Subject: Supervisory position opening

To Eva's team,

Eva will no longer be working with us, starting immediately. The position is now open. For the time being Dan has graciously agreed to fill both his and her place for the interim period. We will begin interviews on Monday. If you'd like to be considered please submit your updated resumes to Dan by Friday evening.

Sincerely,
Management

Thank you, management.

Job well done, Frank. Well done, Eva, for digging your own grave. And while I give out congratulations, well done me for helping her along.

My computer chirps again as I receive an email from Jason.

From: Jason Moore
To: Aidan Sheppard
Subject: Re: Supervisory Position opening

I'm going to try for it. Do you think I have a shot? Are you going to apply too?

Cheers,
Jase

I smile. With what I know is going to happen to Jason in the future he definitely deserves a good thing now. Or at least hope for a good thing. A baby is great and all, for him at least, but the happiness won't last long when he realizes he has to change shitty diapers alone after Mel leaves.

From: Aidan Sheppard
To: Jason Moore
Subject: Re: Re: Supervisory Position opening

Hell yes I'm going to apply. May the best man win. I'm actually rooting for both of us. Co-supervisors?

Sincerely,
Aid

I can hear Jason's laughter in response to his opening of my email.

May the best man win.

chapter Thirty-Seven:

I've never been in a better mood leaving work than I am right now. Wednesdays might only mean the week is half over, but this one ushers in an amazing second half. Eva's ass is gone. For good. I never thought this happy day would come so soon.

Dan even cornered me before leaving to check in. He'd asked if I was okay. He suggested with Eva gone hopefully I'd be more comfortable at work. He hinted it added to the list of missteps which sent her packing. And he even thanked me for being so candid with him. "The harassment's done," he'd added, even offering for the company to replace my blazer she ripped.

Score.

It's time for a celebration. Time for a trip to the grocery store for steak and beer.

TV, good eats, booze, and room to put my feet up should make for a relaxing night. The drive to the store goes quicker than the one home from work, and in minutes I'm inside the warm building with a basket in tow.

Focused, I make a beeline for the butcher, wanting something red, something thick, something juicy, large. I go for the biggest single sirloin available, tossing it into my basket with a satisfied feeling building inside. Not much could make this already great day better than a fat steak on the grill.

After I've grabbed the meat, I head to my next of three destinations in the store. I'm out of dry rub, and that's a necessity. I have the charcoal and grilling provisions, so after this it's just beer.

In the spice isle I feel out of place next to a tiny white-haired woman with more wrinkles than years, I'm sure. She reaches for cinnamon and vanilla extract, and then nudges past me down the aisle. Her little voice sounds odd as she mumbles, "Dick. Shoulda helped me reach for the vanilla." But even her misplaced anger can't bring me down. Instead it makes me laugh. I throw the rub into my basket on top of the steak, heading to the back where the beer sits on the shelf.

As I reach for a twelve-pack, I hear a familiar female voice say my name. I know it, but I can't place it.

"Hey, stranger." Bee stands next to me, reaching for her own wine coolers.

"That's a chick's drink." This clearly isn't what she expected as her laughter comes out in a burst. If she had had anything in her mouth it would be on the floor.

"Well I'm a chick, Aidan, or am I too fat these days to tell?" *Whoa.* I know better than to call any woman fat or even hint at it out loud. Can't even agree, either. Bee doesn't look offended, though.

"Have a hot date tonight?" Better to just change the subject.

"Yep. I have a date with the entire cast of my favorite shows. Them and my couch. Oh, and these drinks." She holds up her coolers in a sort of salute before adding them to her half-full basket. "And apparently I'm just a big slut juggling so many dates."

Now it's my turn to belch out surprised laughter.

We start walking toward the checkout lanes. After getting my laughter under control, I respond with the only thing that comes to mind. "Oh my god, you're such a girl."

"That's what I keep telling you." I'm incredibly shocked. The more I'm around Bee, the more I seem to like her. She may not be the best-looking woman I've ever met, but she's fun.

"I know you turned me down before, but any chance you'd like to get together Friday? Without the Moore bullies?" I ask. *Holy shit.* I can't believe I just asked her out. It kind of popped out of my mouth before my brain knew what was happening.

Bee's smile strains a little before falling away. "Aidan...I—I don't know."

"I'm really not your type, huh?" It shouldn't bother me.

"That's not necessarily it. I'm not *your* type."

"I'm just asking you to hang out. No pressure. You have full control of the evening." Why am I so adamant about this? If she says no again I'll just drop it.

She *is* good company, though.

We enter the same checkout lane, our conversation on pause while the pimply faced adolescent boy moves way too slow. Isn't he getting paid to do this? At the end of the conveyer we're each on one side, bagging our items. Bee hasn't answered yet, so despite myself I add, "Well?"

"Okay fine, but you asked for it. Come over to my place Friday night, and bring comfortable clothes. I'll cook, you bring the drinks."

"Deal." Somehow my plans with Bee give my mood an additional boost.

Go fucking figure.

We leave the store and both start walking to our cars on opposite ends of the parking lot, after waving goodbye. My heartbeat picks up when I realize I have no idea where she lives. "Hey, I need your address." I shout loud enough for her to hear.

"Get it from Jason." Again she waves, getting into her car. I finish the brief walk to my own, and after buckling up I see she's already gone.

As I drive the few minutes home, I think about Bee. She gave me a test. I'm smart enough to know that. She probably figured if I didn't actually want to get together I could feign ignorance, saying I forgot to get her address or couldn't get ahold of it. She's thinking if I want to see her then I have to put in a little bit of effort. Well, okay then. I'll pass the test.

I pull out my phone when I get home to send a message to Jason.

I type before I throw charcoal into the grill. **Hey Jase, can I get Bee's address?** And I hit send.

After the steak is on and coated with seasoning, I feel my phone vibrate in my pocket.

Jason's reply is curious, but he can wait until tomorrow for any answers. **Why?! She's a block and a half down from us. 1518. Is it a date??** He's probably as shocked at my interest as I am, but I never answer his question, instead pocketing my phone again.

***

Late Friday afternoon, I realize how little I've thought about my next plan. Some unsuspecting hitchhiker awaits me, and I've neglected considering her at all in the last couple of days. I've been preoccupied with Amelia, Eva, and now Bee too. The women in my life are such a handful.

On top of the estrogen to consider, I've gotten my resume together to apply, along with half of my department, for Eva's vacated position. I put it in Dan's inbox five minutes ago, and I noticed mine went on top of Jason's. Hopefully the competition isn't a problem. I don't anticipate it will be, but I guess you just never know. Money can do weird things to friendships. Only time will tell.

"Want to go downstairs for coffee? I need a break."

Jason seems all too eager to oblige. Seems he can't wait for the weekend to start, either.

"Yes, please." He nearly jumps from behind his desk, bounding toward me. "My turn to buy?"

"I think so. Don't care, though. I just need the pick-me-up." After an eventful week, and somewhat sleepless nights, the statement couldn't be truer. I've lain awake thinking about Amelia's body, all of Eva's shit, and Bee's jokes.

"Me too. This day is just dragging its ass, isn't it?"

"Perfectly put." I wonder what's making Jason as run-down as me. I don't want to think he's up all hours of the night playing games under the sheets with Mel. I know it's irrational, since she's his wife and all, but now that our arrangement is agreed upon I'm the only one I want to picture having sex with her. Actually, I haven't heard from her since I told her my answer. She just replied, Good. Wait for me to arrange. And so I'm still waiting, days later.

Jason orders and pays in the lobby, and we head back up for the hour left until the weekend officially starts. As we move up slowly, I add a to-do on my checklist for this weekend. After tonight with Bee, I'll put more thought into the hitchhiker. So far it's only an idea, and it needs more planning before execution (pun intended).

"So, I haven't had a chance to ask about your date with Bee."

Damn, I thought he'd forgotten. Jason makes the statement to the space in front of him as he looks straight ahead, walking from the elevator to our offices.

"I ran into her Wednesday night, and I asked her. So we're hanging out. That's all." I shrug. There's nothing else to say, so I stop. I felt like asking her, so I asked. I keep my eyesight forward as well.

"I'm just surprised is all." We reach our doors and stand outside to finish our conversation. I have no idea why, but his shock offends me.

Why should he be surprised I want to go out with her? *Fuck.* Even I was surprised at my own choice, so Jason should be allowed the same reaction. When I first met her, I never thought I'd be going to her house, either.

"Yeah, I know. Turns out, she's just a fun person to be around. Don't worry, we won't be having sex." I lean against the doorframe, relaxed. Jason's eyebrows shoot up his forehead, comically and quickly, when I inform him there are no plans to jump to the physical with Bee.

"What will you even be doing then? It's you. You're going to her house..." Jason just trails off, waiting for me to fill in the blanks.

"Actually, I have no idea. She's making dinner, and I'm bringing beer. That's all I know. Oh, and she told me to bring comfortable clothes...no idea why. I'm sure I'll find out."

"No sex? Just hanging out. In comfortable clothes..."

Jason looks doubtful, and I can't blame him. I never wait with women to have sex since there's never any intention of forming a relationship. And I don't have female friends, either. This is definitely a new one for me.

"You got it." Tired of the inquisition, I start to turn to go to my desk, but Jase interrupts with more curiosity.

Enough, man.

"I want to hear about it on Sunday. My place for football?" His tone is hopeful.

"Sure, but I'm only watching the noon game." Yet another entire Sunday spent in front of a television. I can't deal with that. Not this weekend. I love football, but I'm just not in the mood. Plus I have such little desire to watch Mel and Jason interacting as a couple right in front of me.

"Why, going out with Bee again?" Now Jason's trying to rile me up. He jabs toward me with his elbow, yet I don't let it get to me. It'll never work on me as well as it does on him.

"No. I just have shit to do this weekend, and tonight's accounted for. My house is a fucking mess. It's been forever since I cleaned. Unless you want to be my maid? Then I'll stay longer."

I raise my coffee, taking a sip. It's beautifully rich and will get me through to the weekend. Jason hates cleaning, so I know to him it's a valid excuse, but what I need is time alone to think about my next playdate.

"Uh, not a chance. One game it is." Jason finally drops the conversation, letting me finish a little work before heading home.

Chapter Thirty-Eight:

I have no idea why I'm nervous, but I can't get myself to knock or ring Bee's bell. I've been standing here for a while. I don't know how many minutes have passed. I never get nervous anymore. I'm a grown man. *This is stupid.* I don't want it to be awkward. I want...I don't know what I want. I just don't want this evening to go poorly.

What the fuck has happened to me?

Looking down at my loose-fitting sweatpants sitting on the points of my hips and my old alma mater hoodie, I'm second-guessing my choice to actually *wear* my comfortable clothes instead of just bringing them along to change into. The Jack, coke, and beers feel heavy in the brown paper bag, and now I think it might just be better to quickly run home and change. Maybe switch out my drinks to a lighter beer, too.

I look like an idiot.

As I turn around to head back to my car, the lavender door, now behind me, opens with a whoosh. *Shit.* Now I have to stay, looking like a moron who's planning to get trashed. I wish I'd thought more about what I looked like before rushing over here.

Fuck.

"So are you going to turn around and come in, or did you just plan to stand on the doorstep all night long?"

Bee's voice surrounds me like warm honey, and shockingly it soothes my anxiety. I have no idea what's going on with me right now, but at least I have the nerve to turn around. As I do, I'm greeted by a genuine smile.

"I was debating running home to change into more attractive clothes. I look like a college student. I should've just brought these." I gesture to my classy attire. "But I didn't want you to think I was changing my mind. And while I was still debating with myself you caught me." I suck in a breath from saying so much so quickly. "So here we are."

Wow. So smooth. I just word-vomited all over her.

This night may not go as well as I'd hoped. Maybe I *should* just give up and leave.

Instead of looking confused or worried, Bee's features soften, and she giggles. It's a sound that should be coming out of a model. It's light and airy and surprisingly attractive. It almost sounds like music.

"Get your ass in here." Okay, I need to be more aloof, more like my regular self. This is getting ridiculous. *Breathe.* Despite how I appear at the moment, I swear I'm not, and never have been, an awkward teenage girl.

I follow Bee into her entryway, taking a second to look around. It's odd, intriguing, that her décor is similar to mine. The lines are clean and the colors are bold neutrals. To someone else it may feel cold, but to me it just feels like home. Sharp but comforting. I should have her over sometime to see what she thinks of the similarities.

"Okay, I'm going to be more suave the rest of the night. Promise." God, I hope I will. I chide myself for my behavior thus far as I follow her to the living room. Here she has colorful paintings displayed, highlighted with professional lighting.

"Please don't." Her smile is radiant, and for the first time I notice how flawless her skin is. "I like this weird side of you. *Much* more relatable." Her cheeks rise with the upturn of her mouth, and her eyes sparkle with the laughter in her voice. Though, yes, she's a bit overweight, I realize you'd never tell if all you saw was her shoulders and up. There isn't a blemish or bump on the entire landscape of her face, and that flawlessness is sexier than any bimbo caked in makeup.

Okay, what's happening to me?

"So what are our plans for this evening? I've been dying of anticipation."

I actually have been intrigued. Most women I ask out want to be treated to an expensive meal, wined and dined. Plus they want to put out afterward. So they wear expensive clothes and lots of makeup to impress. But not Bee. She asked me over to cook for me. All she asked was that I bring the alcohol. Little expense on my part, and she's putting in the effort, too. She didn't wear a cocktail dress too short for public or curl her hair for hours. She's in yoga pants and a long-sleeved t-shirt. It eases my mind about wearing my sweats instead of toting them in a duffle bag.

Her hair is up in a messy sort of bun, and though she's been wearing makeup every other time we've crossed paths, this looks better. I feel like I can see who she is underneath the exterior she presents. I can see the real her. No mask. There's something in her eyes I can't quite name, don't know how to place, but it feels familiar, almost kindred. I see a flash of it, and then it's gone. When she's dolled up, whatever that is, it's camouflaged.

"Dinner will be ready later. First we'll need to work up our appetites." Her grin is laced with innuendo and mischievousness.

"Not touching that one." Again her laugh surprises me in its allure.

"C'mon, I'll show you what I have in mind." If I weren't one for surprises, this would be killing me, but I'm enjoying it instead. "Follow me." And I do.

Bee takes me to a large den, just off the living room. I can tell it's her office, though I still have no idea what she does for work.

Actually, I don't know a whole lot about her yet, and now that's my goal for tonight, to learn more about who Bee is beneath the surface. What she hasn't told me, whatever she may be hiding.

"You're going to help me paint my office." Her smile boasts a successful prank, like she's tricked me into this. Okay, I'll go along with it. No problem, I won't give into this idea she has about me, that I'll just run away or disappoint.

"I'm game. Where's the roller?" Her eyes give away a hint of surprise at my willingness, but she quickly recovers.

"Right there." She points to the pile of painting supplies. "And don't you dare think of getting any on me. I know self-defense, and I'm not afraid to use it. I'm stronger than I look."

"Well, well, well. Aren't we a little proud of ourselves?"

"Fuck yes, I am. If you haven't noticed, I'm freaking awesome." She turns her back to start the painting process ahead of us.

I laugh at her.

"I wonder if your head will fit in the room with us while we paint."

"Only just." Her retort is quick, and she continues to refresh me with her wit. "And after dinner I was planning a video game dance-off. Can you handle my moves?"

She starts doing the moonwalk and almost knocks the full can of paint onto her carpet.

"On a full stomach, even," I say.

***

After a layer of elephant gray is slapped on the walls, we sit down at the marble island to eat an amazing meal. If she cooks like this for herself every day, it makes sense to me now how she's a few pounds heavier than my typical date.

"I don't think I've ever eaten food this good. Did you go to culinary school?"

In the office I learned a few facts about the increasingly

interesting Bee Iverson. She's a freelance writer as well as a ground investor in several well-off businesses around town. Witty and smart, with a bank account to back her up. She has two siblings, a brother and a sister, and she told me more about them than she's revealed of herself. The more I learn, the more curious I get. Frustratingly, she hasn't asked a whole lot about me other than surface questions. I wonder if she's keeping a wall up to protect herself from the big bad version of me. The less she knows about me, the less connected she gets, and the easier it will be when I leave.

"Nope. My mom's an amazing cook. She taught me everything I know. Melanie, that's my mom's name, her cooking is still better than mine. As I get more practice, so does she. I'll never catch up."

"I'd like to try something of hers sometime then, since apparently it can top the best I've ever had." Bee's head whips in my direction, and some of her bangs fall into her eyes. She didn't expect that one. *Neither did I.*

"Maybe…" Noncommittal response as she turns back to her plate.

"My parents passed away a few years ago. I wish my mom had taught me to create food masterpieces like this." If she isn't going to ask me anything of importance then I'll just take the leap and share without prodding.

"I'm sorry." Chip, chip, chip at the wall. Her posture is more relaxed than it has been all evening. Maybe I'm on to something.

"No need. They lived long lives. I don't have any siblings, though, like you. Only child over here."

"Oh, so you were a spoiled brat, huh? Makes a lot of sense." Her smile is coy as she finishes the last bites on her plate, and I think I'm starting to get somewhere.

"You got me. Spoiled rotten. That's why I don't mind finishing the last of what's left without offering any to the cook." I walk to the stove and take the remainders without waiting for permission.

"How about those drinks before we start the competition?"

"Crack 'em open. You'll need it to even come close to me."

"Well see about that, sucker," she says.

I finish my last crumbs and clean off the counter while she brings the drinks to the living room. Since when do I pick up for anyone? Rolling my eyes at myself, I follow after her like a puppy.

***

I'm breathing heavily as Bee takes her turn to dance. We've played several rounds of the competition, and I'm losing. By a lot.

Her hair is falling out of its holder, and we're both sweating. But this is the most fun I've ever had with a woman outside of the bedroom. I've never tried to get to know any female, not really. And I've certainly never participated in activities with them not leading specifically to sex unless forced somehow. This is all new to me, and I have no idea if it's going anywhere. But I'm willing to wait it out to see, which is something I've never thought before.

"This is how I've already lost 30 pounds. These games are my bitch." I can't help but laugh at her dance moves to the obnoxious music.

I hear my phone chirp, but Bee's too engrossed in the game to notice. I make an excuse to go to the bathroom, so I can read the message in private. She acknowledges my leave, but keeps dancing, and I shake my head the whole way to the bathroom.

When I look at my inbox I see the message is from Mel.

My eyes widen as I read, **Sunday. After the game. Your place.**

I guess I've gotten my arrangement.

Shit.

chapter Thirty-Nine:

My legs are heavy, sticking in whatever I'm walking through. It's holding me down. Won't let me get away. But I *need* to get away. There's someone behind me. I can't remember who, but it's someone bad, that much I know.

"Freeze. Police."

Yep. That would be bad.

When I turn around I see thousands of officers in uniform, chasing me. Running fast.

They're gaining.

I shouldn't have looked. They have medieval weapons instead of guns and batons.

"Put your hands up."

I don't.

"Or we'll shoot."

Go ahead. My life is over already.

They know.

They'll get me.

I'll hang.

I turn once more and see familiar faces. Faces that can't be real. Faces buried below the earth, or under water. Faces that aren't faces anymore.

One cop gets close enough to zap me, and I fall to the floor, pissing myself. She's got her flashlight in my eyes, and the only thing I can think is, "How'd they find out it was me?"

***

The sun is an asshole this morning. A real bastard.

My dreaming unconscious isn't much better, either.

I stayed at Bee's way too late playing games and talking, and now I'm paying the price while my shades and curtains are wide open. But it was hard to leave her place. She basically had to push me out around two in the morning so she could go to bed. I can't think of the last time I talked with a woman just to learn about her.

Maybe never.

We have another date set for this upcoming Friday. And though I'll never tell Jason, even when he begs me to spill, I'm pretty excited about it. Again I'm not exactly sure why, but I'm done questioning; I'm just going with it.

Though, there's one thing exciting me more than anything else. More exciting than dates, more exciting than sex. When I got home, while surfing on the high of an emotionally fulfilling night, I made the decision to look for the hitchhiker *tonight*. I'll hopefully put my one free weekend day to good use. A Saturday wedged between two other packed days. They're filled by intriguing women, neither of whom I'd have guessed I'd be even a little involved with if you'd have asked me a few weeks ago.

And this middle day will have an event altogether different from the preceding and the following. Though it will still involve an interesting woman.

I have the daylight hours to pack my kit, followed by driving around town. I'll stay busy "completing errands," while really trying to scope out streets and highways more likely to have a possible hitchhiker.

I heave out of bed to brush my teeth since I can't stay still any

186

longer. It's time to start my day off right. I'll get ready, eat, and then pack.

At least I don't look tired. The handsome devil looking back in the mirror at me is happy, confident. Dates and playdates do wonders for my skin and hair. My smile fades, though, as I wonder how hard it will actually be to find a hitchhiker on a specific day and in a set time frame like this. I hadn't thought too much about that, though I hadn't anticipated only having one day for this fun-filled project, either. I could draw it out and go driving around for a few nights, looking for my chance.

And I will if I *have* to.

But I want it now if I can have it. I don't want to wait. I want to feel the high tonight. The high nothing else can, or will, ever reach. I want to soak my hands in the blood of my next pretty little lady.

I know I've seen hitchhikers around before. Maybe I'll just get lucky? But what if I don't? What can I do instead? I've seen lots of homeless people holding signs, asking for handouts from suckers willing to part with their hard-earned money. A bum may be a surer bet since I see them around often enough, if I want it to be tonight. Need it to be.

Okay, plan revised. Homeless woman tonight. Hitchhiker whenever I spot one another night. I'll make her spontaneous.

Yes, that'll work. No more need to run errands until dark. It'll be a lot easier to find someone on the corner than it would've been to find someone with their thumb up waiting for a ride. There are plenty of homeless near the shelter.

And with that, my nerves are again alight with anticipation while the new decision settles into place. I hope this never gets old, and I never lose this wonderful feeling. It's as if everything inside is sparking and bouncing around. I feel every single nerve in my body. If I could bottle this to sell it, I'd be a billionaire.

***

After picking jeans and a t-shirt at random, I make my way around the house, preparing my kit for tonight. My bag already contains rope, duct tape, knives, the usual paraphernalia. But in addition, I head to my toolbox for inspiration, adding a hammer, a drill, a screwdriver, pliers, and a box cutter.

The tingling in my spine shoots from the center of my back in both directions, to my tailbone and all the way to my scalp. The creative things I can do with these items—it's so thrilling. I'm giddy.

I want more unexpected items, too. Knives are obvious. Tools are less so, but they're still nothing brilliant. I want something more surprising, something creative, devious. Something unexpected.

I walk around my house with no destination in mind, looking for anything that'll catch my eye, but I'm coming up empty. *Damn.* This thinking outside the box isn't going too well. I want something new and fresh, something that'll be painful. Something harsh.

In frustration, I start to stomp rather than walk. My bare feet slap the hardwood floors louder with each step, and the soles begin to sting. I need something else. My kit doesn't feel finished. I know that much, even if I don't know what's missing.

In anger, I throw the bag on an end table, knocking all the previously stable contents off. I cringe as something shatters.

Breaking things may have been unnecessary, even if the outburst felt good for a second. I seem to build more pent-up rage since collecting donations. Maybe eruptions like this are good every once in a while now. I feel looser afterward.

I bend to clean the mess, knowing I need to act gingerly. I heard the porcelain bowl break. The pieces are sharp, jagged. It'd hurt to slip with this in hand.

A light bulb sparks.

This would be great for tonight. So I drop it into the bag. With one irregular piece added, I feel a little better. It's great, but it still doesn't feel complete yet. I finish cleaning the mess I've made, and restart my trip around the house in search for what's missing.

Lazily, I add a pair of scissors, bleach, another strong-smelling cleaner, a meat tenderizer, and a crème brûlée torch.

I'm almost there now.

And suddenly, I know the last piece I need.

With something in mind, I head down to the basement. The last weapon is the least expected in the bunch. Tonight is going to be *so* amazing. Reaching into my kit of wonder to pick out a weapon at random will be new and totally incredible.

The basement is cold, like most basements are, but right now I don't feel the temperature change. Heading to an old box that's been packed away for years, I steady my pace, refusing to run like the overexcited child inside wants me to. When I get to the box, I have to blow off the dust on top before I can peel back the tape. Some of the dirt blows back in my face, which starts me coughing.

I guess I should clean down here more often.

Opening the box, I'm so happy I thought of this. It'll make an appearance in many of my packed kits from now on. I pull out an old sculpture made for and given to my parents. When they passed it made its way to me, and I never cared for the supposed aesthetic, so into a box and down to the basement it went.

But now I love it.

I rotate the abstract cold metal piece in my hands, looking at it from all angles. The size of a football, it almost looks like a crown with sharp, spiked edges rising from its solid base. And along that base are feet of bike chain wrapped around in layers, slightly rusted over time. Various metals were used in shades of copper, steel, iron, and so on. Each side has patterns etched into the metal with no real semblance of design. It looks medieval, and I was always a bit scared of it as a kid.

This is perfect.

Now my pack is ready.

***

As I watch the sun set, I realize I haven't had dinner. In fact, I could barely eat all day. I've been too excited, too entranced by visions of tools painted red, to pay attention to the rumble in my stomach. I should eat before leaving, though. I wouldn't want to get faint with the torch at the ready.

After making a sandwich and inhaling it, I stop at the bathroom on my way out. I don't want to have to stop for either tonight. Once my pants are zipped back up, I nearly sprint out the door. At least I remember to lock it.

My timers are set at odd intervals in different rooms to appear I'm home again tonight. My TV is on as well and it's a little too loud, not high enough to be annoying, but just enough to be heard. Little precautions, hoping some neighbor glances outside to see I'm "home."

I'm not driving more than two minutes before a freezing mist starts. This will either serve me well, or it'll make my intentions impossible. I'm hoping for the former. The sky is cloudy, and the moon isn't showing much except to peek out for a second or two at a time.

I get near the shelter relatively quickly but drive by without stopping. I don't want to pick anyone up right outside even though I have a new set of fake license plates on the car. So I creep down a block and to the back of the building, hoping to find a straggler *alone* outside after supper.

At first I think I've struck out, ready to drive around for a while before making another pass, but then out of the shadows I spot someone with long, ratted hair under layers of coats walking toward my slow-moving car.

Bingo.

chapter forty:

I pull to a stop next to the curb, but don't put it in park. Instead I roll, inviting her to follow. She does. It's darker, farther away from where we spotted each other. I stop again when she knocks on my window and this time finally switch to park. I roll it down, trying hard not to smile at the prickling on my scalp.

"Have any change?" Her words come out garbled, slurred.

"Sure." I make to dig into my pocket. "When's the last time you ate?"

Don't need to ask the last time she drank.

"Yesterday." Her teeth are brown, several missing. She's underweight. This isn't her first night without a roof over her head.

"Hop in, I'll take you through a drive-through, and then you can keep the change."

Luring the hungry in with the promise of food. How terrible. And terribly smart as well, *thank you.*

"You're not gonna try anything funny, are you?" Smart girl.

"I've been down on my luck before, too; just trying to help out. If you don't want dinner, that's okay. I'll move on." A cleverer, or more sober, person would notice I never actually answered her question. But she doesn't.

The threat of losing my offer works. She jumps to reply. "Okay,

okay. How about McDonald's?" She smiles broadly, showing more rot and gums than I wanted to see. It's hard not to cringe. A foul, pungent odor enters with her, but I'm too excited to mind. Hopefully it doesn't linger after she's out.

"How long have you been on the streets?" Interest from me should mean trust and relaxation on her part.

While she answers with a longwinded sob story, I offer her my soda. Her taste buds must be damaged from the hardships of living outside, because she doesn't taste the huge dose of crushed sleeping pills dissolved inside. She carries the conversation on for about ten more minutes before her head starts to bob, and she's out before I even pass the drive-through she wanted.

"Tsk, tsk. How rude of you nodding off in the middle of the conversation. You should learn to pay better attention to the person offering you a warm meal." I chide the unconscious passenger next to me.

I finally let my face contort, stretching into the grin that's been waiting to be set free, as I drive along the highway toward a thick patch of woods in the middle of nowhere.

***

When Homeless comes to, she's already been tied securely with thick rope in a standing spread eagle between two closely growing trees.

"What the fuck's going on?"

I walk a circle around her and the pair of trees, relinquishing nothing. Withholding a reply, I tap a knife along the bark as I move. She flinches with each scraping sound of metal to wood, but she doesn't speak again. Instead she pulls at her wrists until her irritated skin reddens, begging for her to stop.

She wants so bad to get free.

This one should prove to be *exceptionally* fun.

"What's your name? You didn't mention it earlier." She makes eye contact with me as I pass back in front of her, and she doesn't look away.

"Does it matter?"

She grunts after asking, offering no moniker. Her struggles against the ropes must be painful. Even in the darkness I can see tiny drops of blood trickle down her arms from the friction. My cock stirs, and my pupils dilate.

"Not really, no. Just curious."

I change from circling my prey to pacing in front of her, keeping my eyes on her face, watching every little change in expression. This will never get old.

"Thought so." She's a woman of few words, but she doesn't stop moving. Her limbs continue looking for a weak spot in the material binding her. She won't find one. As much as she tries to hide it, there's a need to break free deep within Homeless. She wants to run.

She wants to live.

But she won't. Not if I have anything to say about it.

"You were just in the wrong place at the wrong time." I stop in front of her and place the point of the knife on her cheek. I drag it slowly down her jaw, stopping along her collarbone. Goosebumps raise everywhere the metal grazes.

"Nothing new. Have been my whole life." Her conversational skills in the face of death are exceptionally collected.

I don't answer right away. I watch as her breathing becomes more labored. She's finally starting to panic. The pulse in her throat is pounding against the thin layer of skin. I can see her struggling against a scream.

I stop observing, finding my voice again. "Well, then at least this end was expected." With my last words her eyes scrunch tight, and her lips form a hard, solid line. But she can't will the pain away. She'll still feel every bit, even with her eyes closed.

It's just too bad for her it won't be quick.

I drop the knife back into the kit without using it. Tonight I'll let my creative side out to play. I bend over and grab the first three items to touch my pulsing fingers. As each comes into view, I stack them neatly on a stump in plain view of us both.

First out is the drill.

Second the bleach.

Third the art piece.

Homeless sucks in her breath, sharply, after all three are staged. She must have looked. I can tell she's determined not to scream, and I decide it's my goal to break her resolve. I can only kill her after she screams.

My blood pumps forcefully under my skin, and I'm surprised it can be contained. There are sparks flying with each surge of it out of my heart. Its feels on fire, like I'm burning from the inside, but it doesn't hurt.

It feels incredible.

I point to the three items, taunting, "Eeny, meeny, miny, moe...," before throwing my head back to laugh. My jests don't faze Homeless enough. Her eyes and lips stay tight. She's unwavering, but I'll crack her. I know I will. I *have* to break her spirit before I cut it from her.

Ready to hear screaming, I start with the drill, running it close to her ear so she can hear the force of its spinning, so she can feel the air whipping from its bit.

Then I strike.

I'm amazed at how easily it plows through the flesh of her stomach. She grits her teeth, moaning, but nothing coherent escapes, still no screams yet. So I move to a more sensitive area with the drill.

I take the walk around to her back as slowly as I can force myself to. I want the terror to build. Though, I don't manufacture a monologue for her, I just set back to work once I reach my destination. Words don't seem to work on this one. The psychological is pointless. Torture must be the shining star of this masterpiece.

I smile as the pleading begins, after pulling down the waistband of her pants.

"Please don't. Please. Please..." Her shaking becomes frantic as the drill starts to spin once more.

"Ah, she does care what happens to her." I hold the drill in my armpit, clapping loudly with my leather-covered hands. The sound is sharp.

Her body lurches with her sudden sobbing. *She's crumbling.*

"This is too much fun."

Her sobs become silent, but the movements from them continue to rip through her. I lean close enough to her that my zipper touches the bare skin of her ass, and my lips are millimeters from her ear.

"Scream for me, baby. It won't stop until after you've screamed."

All sound catches in her throat, and she groans in desperation after the rush of air surges out. Without getting what I want, I press the dripping metal of the bit to her back entrance. I let it enter before turning the power button on. Once it's at full speed, I finally have the satisfaction of her beautiful screams. They're loud, panicked, and incredibly nourishing. Somehow I can see the vibrations of each pass through the cold night air around us. They're brighter than the stars above. And then each noise is colored. Her deep cries are as red as her blood, but the higher squeaks turn to blue and green. A rainbow of screaming flows like paint on a canvas.

I've never been so thrilled in my entire life.

***

After the drill, I douse each wound with bleach to elicit blinding burning. Her screams continue, morphing into low, hoarse pleading. The second round is as amazing as the first. I never knew what a range of sounds one person could make until tonight.

Once her head is limp against her shoulder, I replace the bleach on the stump, trading it for my final device in tonight's showcase. After slapping her cheeks to make sure she's still awake, I say the last words she's ever going to hear.

"Buck up, kid, this life is shit anyway."

Poetic, I know.

Before she has any time to answer, I start to bash her head repeatedly with the sculpture. Her face puffs up, blood pouring from her scalp. She's dead after the first couple of blows, but I can't stop myself. The metal spikes bend after a while, and I'm not sure this can be used as a weapon after tonight. I continue for several minutes, only stopping when I nearly pass out from an overloaded system.

After sitting on the ground for a few minutes, my composure returns. I cut her down, using the rest of the bleach to douse her.

Burying her is slow, and I relish the time to relive every second of tonight's playtime. Each woman I've played with has been special, each unique. The-One-Who-Doesn't-Count was dreamy and all instinct. I didn't realize what I was doing. The next, the true first, was calculated and scheming with a huge amount of planning before the fun took place. And tonight was a brutal show of my ability to conquer a challenge, to elicit the reactions I wanted.

I strip her clothes and throw them into the hole first. After dousing them in some of the cleaner, I light them and watch as they turn to ash. Flames crackle until they burn out, and all that's left is beautiful black soot. I have the odd urge to roll around in it, barely resisting.

But then I remember. I'm supposed to have something. I'm supposed to be given something. Something special. So I can remember. Where is my donation? I don't see any jewelry on Miss Homeless, and I start to feel a panic rising to my throat, and like bile it stings.

What should I do? I want a donation. I *need* a donation.

I need her to have jewelry. *Fuck*, I should've considered someone homeless wouldn't have jewelry.

But before I have a full-blown freak-out, something shiny sparkles in the brief moment of moonlight between cloud cover. There must have been something in her pocket too solid to burn in the temporary flames. I reach in to pull out what caught my eye. It's a single cuff link now smudged with soot. It's silver, and it's simple.

It's so perfect.

I can breathe again as the fog that was starting to move in clears.

I can't stop myself from bouncing once in elation. Since I have what I need, I kick Homeless into the hole and start covering her with the earth I just dug up. I smile, thinking it's fitting I didn't know her name. It's been a pattern so far. First The-One-Who-Doesn't-Count, and now this one. I knew Kristi's name in between. So the next must also divulge hers.

chapter Forty-One;

After I got home from the woods last night, and before I went to bed, I took a quick trip down to the basement in search of something specific. It took a couple boxes, but on my third try I found what I was looking for.

My mother's old wooden jewelry box now contains the pieces of jewelry donated to me. It's lined with black velvet that's aged with time. It was an old piece given to her long before I was born. Now I'm exceptionally glad I kept all of my parents' belongings for the second time in as many days.

I left her jewelry in the box and added my own tie clips and cuff links. Everything of my mother's, and everything of mine, the donations included, was cleaned meticulously. Only I know what two gems are special. The box's new place on the dresser, just inside my walk-in closet, is perfect.

I can look inside any time I want.

***

In my all-consuming excitement of last night, I almost forgot what's going to happen this afternoon.

I'm going to fuck Amelia, holy shit.

After years of fantasizing, of imagining, I'll actually get to touch her bare skin, burying myself deep inside her. This is going to happen, and I'm going to relish every second.

A slight pang of guilt strikes deep in my gut, but it hits softer and leaves quicker than the last few. It's getting easier, and Jason will never know. Besides, even if I'd said no, it wouldn't have prevented Mel from leaving him in the future. At least she'll be sleeping with a friend while pregnant with his fourth kid instead of some stranger. At least I'm clean.

At least I can rationalize.

I flash to Bee's face after Jason's. And after a moment I let it go as well. We haven't even hinted at exclusivity; hell, we've only been on one date. For now this is my choice, and I'm still eager.

I wonder how Amelia will act during the football game with everyone all under the same roof. Will she try to ignore me? Will she corner me for a stolen moment? I don't even know how I'll act or which is preferred. Obvious or suspicious behavior will hopefully be avoided at the very least. If I have one goal today it's to be calm, normal. *Normal.* I wouldn't go as far as to hope I appear trustworthy, because, well, I'm not, but I just want to act like my usual self.

Well...my usual, non-psycho-killer self, at least. That half that's usual. I do have this double personality thing going well right now, which is helpful. I can be nervous to spend the evening with a woman who intrigues me one night, then the next night I flip a switch and can viciously murder another woman, bathing in her screams. Those two sides are a little opposing.

If I had to guess, I'd bet those two sides won't play nice together *forever.* I'm thinking one will eventually win out, taking over. But only time will tell; for now, they're both intact.

I continue to sit in my pajamas on the couch, watching as the morning minutes tick by. Each time the numbers change, I get closer to the moment when I'll have to leave for the Moore house.

I'm not nervous like I was while standing on Bee's doorstep (was it only a day and a half ago?), but there's a certain twinge of unease. I dig deeper, finding a little guilt is present, and I can't tell if it's for Jason or for Bee. Or maybe a little of both. I'm more unsure about what will happen.

I have to drag myself to the bedroom in search of daytime clothing. I'm not excited to don denim, a belt, or shoes with laces.

Fuck it.

I'm not getting dressed. I'll show up in my old, worn flannel pants topped by my same sweatshirt from Friday, because I've no idea what I should wear otherwise. I'm not dressing to impress, anyway; she already made the proposition, and I already accepted. No cat and mouse left to play. I skip the coat and jog to the car, wondering if this is how Jason's felt since landing Mel.

I'm ready to find out what's in store.

No more waiting.

***

"Get in here, it's freezing." Jason has the front door open before I even reach it. Maybe I should've grabbed my jacket.

"How's it going?" *How's your wife?*

"Same ol', same ol'." He slams the door behind me, unintentionally, with help from the wind.

"That good, huh?"

Jason lets out his hearty, belly-deep laugh as we walk to the living room. It gets louder as his belly gets bigger.

"Mel's upstairs with the girls, so we're on our own for food today. I was thinking delivery?" My stomach sinks just a fraction. I hope she comes down to interact with us at least a little. Maybe she's afraid of giving anything away, thinking it's better just to hide.

Maybe she knows best.

"Delivery's great. How about lots of wings?" Jason drops his weight on the couch and it groans in protest. He'll break it one day, and I wonder if he'll take it as a sign to lose a little weight. I sit down without the dramatic effect.

"It's like you can read my mind." Jason makes the call to order while pulling out the cash. He lays it on the table in front of me as a cue to answer the door when it arrives.

***

Over an hour later, my stomach growls as I answer the door.

"Here."

I shove the cash into the young kid's hand, slamming the door in his face. I wish Jason hadn't included such a generous tip, because it took way too long to get here, and it's already close to halftime. Mel still hasn't made an appearance, either. My irritability is starting to show. Jason's already made several sideways glances at my sighs and huffs.

"Winner, winner, chicken dinner...well, lunch." I don't grab plates. We can just eat out of the to-go boxes.

"Good, maybe now you'll get your panties out of the twist they're in."

"Definitely." I make a show of licking my lips in anticipation of the food. Better he thinks my hunger is all that's bothering me.

As we eat, the second quarter ends, and Jason takes a breath between bites to dive into what I know he's been dying to approach. "So, how was your date on Friday?" There's excitement in his voice.

"Oh boy, you had a *real* date? With who?" Amelia's wide eyes come around the corner, and they display far more jealousy than curiosity. *Shit.* Of fucking course this is the time she'd finally come downstairs.

"Bee had me over. On Friday." I watch my wings instead of her reaction.

"I didn't tell you, honey? I swore I had." Good job, Jason. Fucked me with that one. It would've been better if she'd known before right now. But it's not like he has any idea what's going on behind his back, so I guess I'll let this one slide.

"No, you definitely didn't. Well, that's great. How'd it go?" Amelia's expression is soft, inquisitive, happy. Though she let the darkness show for a second when our eyes locked, she hid it quickly. It's a little freaky how good of an actress she is. I never knew.

"Good." I *do not* want to talk about this.

"That's it? That's all you're going to give me? It was good. Unacceptable. What did you guys do? Why did you need comfortable clothes? Please, you're killing me here." Jason's enthusiasm is overwhelming. But luckily Mel interrupts before I can respond.

"Leave the man alone. It's his business." And she returns upstairs without another glance toward either of us.

"Don't listen to her. Tell me everything." Jason's smile is wide and hopeful. His eyes are lit up like a Christmas tree.

"Not a chance. Look, the game's back on."

I turn up the volume, trying to ignore his shocked pouting.

"You'll cave."

Jason's grumpy concession is a relief. The less I divulge to him, the less he'll relay to Mel. I can guarantee she wants to hear about Bee and me as much as I want to hear about her and Jason.

Seems fair.

chapter Forty-Two:

Amelia leaves sometime in the third quarter with a believable explanation of late lunch with a friend and shopping afterward. She reports to Jason she won't be home until dinner. That will leave about two hours together.

I can do a lot with two hours.

My phone's on silent, and I remember to leave it in my pocket. Everything would be ruined if Jason saw a text on my screen from Amelia.

The game's a blowout and I make my excuse to leave with three minutes left of play. "Well, the house isn't going to clean itself." I stand up, heading toward the front door, careful not to walk too quickly.

"You sure you have to do it today? I'll get dinner if you stay." Jason's pleas border on pathetic, but I'm impermeable to it.

"It's been a month. Imagine your house after a month. But like I said, you can feel free to do it for me while I stay here with the game." Jason's cringe says it all. I've won the battle.

"Yeah, okay. See you tomorrow."

"Tomorrow." I wave and run through the chill to my car.

I wait until I pull into my own driveway to look at my phone. My stomach sinks when there isn't a single message. Maybe Mel changed her mind. Maybe she lost her nerve or just decided she couldn't go through with it after she heard about Bee.

Fucking shit.

Guess I'll be watching football instead. Shoving my phone back into my pocket, I throw my car door open in anger. Instead of swinging to its full extent, it hits something soft; the contact is followed by a gasp. My head whips toward the sound.

Or she didn't change her mind.

Amelia's standing next to my car holding the door open. Her eyes are filled with enough lust to spill over. No, she definitely didn't decide to skip this. Her eyes scream ready.

"I thought you were backing out. Where's your car?" I get out of mine, standing up close to her. Her skin smells sweet, and her eyelashes flutter.

She points several houses down the street where her little silver car sits, still and quiet. I hadn't seen it there. I close my door, walking toward the house. She follows.

"Not in the slightest. Just didn't want to look suspicious."

"Sneaky. You've thought this through." I don't turn around to see her face as I unlock the door in front of us. I hesitate after the bolt is turned, resting my hand on the metal of the knob. The solid door is the last thing stopping us before taking this somewhere we can't turn back from. I don't want to ask what I'm about to, I'm not even positive I care about the answer, but then it's falling out of my mouth anyway. "Are you sure?"

"I've thought about this for years. I've thought about *you* for years."

And that's all I needed to hear.

I turn the handle, walking inside with Amelia on my heels. She closes the door behind her then pushes her chest tightly to my back. Suddenly I'm glad I didn't wear a jacket, and I appreciate how much thinner pajama pants are than jeans. I can feel all of her curves pressed into me.

This will be worth it. There are no thoughts of Jason or Bee left in my head. They've flown far away. Right now all I can think about is her behind me and the stiffness in front of me.

I reach behind, grabbing Mel's wrists. Instead of pulling her to my front, I wrap them tightly around my middle, and she nuzzles my back. I'm not going for intimate, though, so I slide her slender fingers down my waistband. I moan as her skin touches mine, and when she gasps I chuckle. She squeezes before letting go. My dick is rock-hard throbbing, so the release of pressure is tantalizing.

Amelia slowly walks around me, dropping little bits of clothing along the circle. When we're face-to-face, she smiles with half of her mouth and walks closer. Her heels are off. Her jacket is gone, and her shirt is open, exposing the most delicate lace bra I've ever seen.

She leans into my body with hers, coming close to my ear. As she brushes her lips against the lobe, I flash to Saturday night in the woods when I whispered to Homeless from behind. My cock stirs again, and Mel murmurs, "I've been dreaming for so long about when you'd finally fuck me. Won't you fuck me, please?" Oh man.

This is my kind of afternoon.

I growl out a, "Yes," before pushing her backwards toward my bedroom.

Her hands are down my pants once again, and mine are inside her bra. I don't think before I act, and I rip her bra in half at the front.

"Oops."

"Good thing I actually went shopping." Her words are spaced between biting my lip.

Once I have her knees backed up to the edge of my bed, I push her down on it. We aren't making love here. I'm not planning to play sweet. She squeals in surprise, but doesn't stay put. She scrambles to her knees, yanking me down with her.

"Get ready, big boy. I'm going to make you forget your own name."

"Don't make promises you can't keep."

Mel hops off the bed. She only has her g-string left on, and *fuck*, her body is better than it ever looked in clothes. I prop myself up on my elbows as she kneels down. My pants are ripped from my hips and thrown to the corner of the room. She sucks my dick into her mouth faster than I can inhale.

She wasn't kidding.

I have no idea what's coming out of my mouth, and I'm not even sure it's English, but I don't give a shit. She brings me to the edge, then backs off before she goes too far.

"Don't think it'll be so easy for you. I want mine, too." She shimmies out of her panties, kicking them aside.

"Well hop on, then." And she does as she's told.

I can't keep my hands off her smooth legs. There isn't an ounce of cellulite on this woman, and she knows exactly what she's doing. Her thrusts meet mine with perfect timing and equal intensity. My mouth moves from her nipples to her neck, but never to her mouth.

That seems wrong, somehow too far.

Before long, Amelia throws her long hair back, screaming in pleasure. She continues moving, moaning, for several moments before looking down to smile at me.

"My turn." I grab both of her hips, bucking her off. Her face displays confusion, but I don't leave her waiting long.

I rush at her, shoving her face first toward the wall, but not letting her collide with it. I kick her feet apart and run my fingers along her smooth skin. She's still wet and throbbing for more. I aim to deliver.

Holding her wrists above her head and against the wall with my right hand, I enter her from behind. My left hand moves between her breasts and the wall, squeezing her nipples harder than she probably prefers. But right now is about me. She already had her time. I bite her shoulder, though I make sure not to bite hard enough to make a mark. That'd be hard for her to explain later. Soon I'm on the precipice, and wrapped in her pleasure I let myself fall over the edge.

When I catch my breath I pull out, letting her turn around. We're both flush, covered in a sheen of sweat.

"So have your years of dreams set the bar too high?"

In other words, was it good enough to have a repeat performance later?

"Absolutely not. I think I saw stars for a minute. This needs to happen again."

Amelia then gathers her clothes, walking to the bathroom to freshen up. I hear the shower starting while I throw my pajama pants back on. No need for a shirt any longer, especially since I'm still hot as hell. I flop down on the couch and think of Jason doing the same earlier. Then I wince.

Well, shit. What's done is done, and the new, improved Aidan does what he wants without looking back.

I turn on the TV to watch something other than football, surfing a few channels while the water still runs. The news is on, and I leave it there while I head to the kitchen in search of something to snack on. I didn't have lunch too long ago, and I still want a real dinner later, but I worked up an appetite. I deserve a little treat.

With chips in hand, I move back to the couch. Amelia walks into the room fresh and clean, looking the same as she did before ever stepping foot inside.

She leans over to kiss my cheek and requests, "Let's not wait too long to do this again."

"Absolutely," is all I reply. I don't get up or walk her to the door, but I do say goodbye.

***

After Amelia leaves with a wide grin still on her face, I redirect my attention back to the TV, and what I see sends my heartbeat racing. I dump the chips on the floor as I jump to my feet.

No, no, no, no, *NO.*

The volume isn't loud, so I don't hear what's being said, but I see a picture of The-One-Who-Doesn't-Count and the giant block letters MISSING. I turn it up to learn her name was Kate Masten, and no one has any clue of her whereabouts. The police are requesting any tips to be called in.

Breathe in.

Breathe out.

Repeat slowly.

I count to ten, forcing my heart to slow. There's still no connection to me. Hopefully her body is never found, or at least not until the water has washed away every trace of evidence.

My secret must remain safe.

chapter Forty-Three;

I still can't sleep. My eyes haven't closed longer than a blink since I flipped to the news. I have my interview in the morning (this morning), and I'm first in line to give my pitch for Eva's position. I need to be on my game, but it's only an hour and a half before I'm supposed to leave for work. I might as well get up to get ready. I'll need a shower and a whole lot of coffee to make a workday possible.

In the hot water, my senses start to come to attention. I curse myself again for not sleeping. It didn't solve anything. I watched the news for hours yesterday after Amelia left. I watched way too late, and even when I finally turned it off I continued to think about what I'd seen. I worried, chided myself, worried more, and then started the process over again.

And again.

I couldn't look away. I felt pushed to keep watching to see if any new information about The-One-Who-Doesn't-Count was revealed. Nothing ever was. But I watched and watched regardless. I learned she had no family. Her roommate, a plain-looking girl named Ashley, is the one who reported her missing, but not until several days after she'd spent her last night with me. She regularly spent a few nights away without checking in. Not much else was disclosed. They know she's missing and she was last seen at the bar. That's pretty much it.

All of that should relax me. It's nothing to go on for the police, and so far from connected to me it's almost laughable. Almost.

I waited for the anchor to say something along the lines of, "Aidan Sheppard killed her. The police are in pursuit of him now." Though it never came. To the authorities, and everyone but me, it all remains a total mystery.

Knowing didn't do much for my anxiety. I had two oversized glasses of Jack to calm down, and then I repeated a mantra over and over until I could relax enough to lie still in bed. *You have no connection to her. None at all. You'll never get caught*, went round and round my head for a few hours.

That's what helped the most. When I thought logically, took my fear out of the equation, I could see there wasn't a single soul who could connect me to her. Even the evidence *should* be gone by now and will be further degraded by the time she's found. If she's ever found. Which she probably won't be if she hasn't been by now.

I finish my shower, brush my teeth, and get dressed. I don't need to rush, but I leave myself twenty minutes to make and drink two cups of coffee. I take the third with me as I head to work.

The timing of the news report could've been a little better.

***

I exit the interview feeling okay about it. I didn't do terribly. I didn't do amazing, either. I won't be surprised if I don't get it. It will sting if I miss out again, but every single coworker interviewing today is a thousand times better than Eva. None of these people are stealing what should be mine. I didn't help them and later have credit stolen from my ideas and work. I used to deserve the spot, I used to work harder, though now I've landed some new objectives in life, and I'm not quite as focused as I used to be.

I'm not even completely sure how much I want it.

Going back to my office, I finally feel okay again. I hadn't from the moment I saw The-One-Who-Doesn't-Count on television. It was as if her ghost was coming back for me, to torture me. But I've let the nervousness leech out of my system now. I've been careful each time. And I make a final concession to myself to up my cover-up tactics even more from now on.

I poke my head into Jason's office to wish him luck before returning to my own.

"Go get 'em."

"Thanks. May the best man win."

I nod, heading to my computer for a boring day of numbers and spreadsheets. The thought makes my eyes droop a little. This all used to be fulfilling. Not so much anymore.

Just before sitting down in my too-comfortable chair I backtrack, deciding another cup of coffee from downstairs is needed.

***

Before I know it, Friday afternoon arrives, and my spirits are high again while leaving. I'm not sure where the whole week went, but now it's the weekend again. I'm okay with that. Tonight I have a second date with Bee. Or…is it a date? I don't know if she considers us to be dating. I don't even know if I do. Either way, we're spending the evening together, and I'm excited about it again. Tonight it's my turn to make the plans, so I'm doing something different than what she put together last week.

I'll be picking her up, and each activity is a surprise. I have no idea if she likes surprises, but don't most people? We won't be spending any time at either of our houses, either. I'm proving a point. I know she's already tested me, so to stay ahead of the curve I'll ace one test before she even poses it. I'm showing her I'm happy to be with her in public, and I don't intend to hide whatever it is we're doing (though, I'm still not entirely sure what that is). Either way, I'm racking up brownie points.

Our plans don't begin until midnight, so I have a lot of time to kill between now and then. I've already debated getting a haircut, cleaning my house, and doing laundry, but none of those options are striking me. The weekends have become wonderful lately, and I don't want to do anything today that's not begging me to be done.

I settle on getting dinner and heading where the wind blows me until it's time to go to Bee's.

I choose Randy Red for dinner. Even though it's a bit out of the way, they have the best chicken between here and Vermont. I have no qualms about sitting alone for dinner, so it's a table for one. I don't rush, but I don't stay long, because I've gotten a little bored. There isn't a TV or game to watch while waiting.

Leaving the restaurant, it's already dark.

Fucking winter nights.

I still feel unfinished, so instead of heading home I drive to the mall in search of a new shirt. My first date with Bee was in sweats, and I think I can do better. I pick out dark jeans, a replacement watch for the one I still can't find, black chucks, and a charcoal gray, long-sleeved thermal shirt before heading up to the register.

"How are you tonight?"

The cashier is overweight, sweaty, and she has lipstick on her teeth. Her words are slow and almost sound as if she's done some rehab after a stroke. *Unappealing.*

"Fine. And you?" Three polite words in return and her eyes light up like Christmas. She widens her red, smeared smile.

"Wonderful. Buying these for anything special?"

None of your business.

"Nope."

After cutting off her line of questioning, we finish the transaction in silence until she bids me a good evening. There are so many people in the world that'd serve me better tied to the back of my car, bumping down a dirt road.

chapter forty-four.

I jog to my car in the bitter air, wishing for warmer weather. Just before I reach my driver's side door I hear a cough, and, startled, I look around for whoever it came from. A tall, emaciated, dye-job redhead saunters near my car. She'd been standing against the building in the deeper shadows, but if I'd have looked closer I would've seen her lit cigarette.

The little orange bud glows brighter then almost goes out, and repeats the process.

"Hey, sugar. Have a fun night planned?" As she comes close enough to study I can see she's a hooker. I take a moment to look her up and down, which she clearly appreciates. Her boots are knee-high and incredibly worn in. She must wear them every night. Her skirt is covered in sequins and if it were half an inch shorter I'd be able to see her (literal) moneymaker. Her jacket is zipped down halfway, and she has nothing on underneath. She has no curves, and her facial features look hollow.

She definitely does some sort of drug in her spare time. Or several.

She saunters close enough to touch me but thinks better of it. Instead, she sizes me up and must like what she sees. Her mouth is practically watering. I guarantee she's seeing dollar signs across my face.

Instead of turning her down, I consider an exciting possibility, and I think quickly before answering her. "I don't take ladies home who have a man waiting for them afterward. Pimps and I don't get along." I want to make sure she doesn't have anyone who will report her missing. Not that a pimp necessarily would, but since the news I'm covering my bases better. I continue to face her, not opening my door.

"Well lucky for you, I'm an independent entrepreneur."

Big words, with lots of syllables.

"How do I know you're not just saying that to get the job?"

"I guess you'll just have to trust me."

Wrong answer.

"Sorry, not good enough. I'm not the trusting type."

I turn to get into my car. I can be patient if it means not getting caught.

"Wait." Her voice seems desperate as she tosses her cigarette to the ground to stamp it out. If she did have a pimp she wouldn't be worried about finding another taker. "I *am* on my own. You don't see anyone around, do you? No cars are running with the muscle waiting for me to return. Here, you can look at my phone, even. No one to report to. It's just me." She hands me a phone that's seen better days, held together by duct tape and hope. I scroll through her contacts for show, because I already believe her. She has a few female names and about 20 Johns with numbers, identifying features, or streets for last names. There's no one else listed.

I hand it back to her slowly, pretending to still be doubtful. It's entertaining she's trying to convince me. "I don't know…"

"How about half off?" Coupon shopping now, are we?

Price reduction on all tits, ass, and pussy; blue aisle special, the next two minutes only.

"I have a date tonight…I could get it for free." Her face falls and she takes a half step back. Maybe I should've accepted her offer.

But she has one trick left when she looks back into my eyes, practically purring, "Oh, yeah? Well I bet you've never had anything as good as this." She gestures down her body. "It's what I do for a living, and I'm fucking *amazing* at it."

"You're a good salesperson." She steps forward again, reaching for the crotch of my pants, rubbing it over the material for a few seconds. Her breath smells of stale cigarettes. I interrupt her. "Hop in." And she bounces away toward the passenger door.

My mind starts to race. I know what I'll be doing for most of the time before my date. I have a new toy to play with for the next couple of hours, only she thinks we'll be playing a different game than what I have in mind. I stop short. Where should I take her to play? I've had an idea brewing for my next playdate, what I want to do with her, but I don't know where to do it.

"Where should we go?" Maybe her suggestion will have what I need.

"Your place?" I shake my head no. I'm not carrying another body out of there. My house is off limits for all playdates. "A hotel?" I shake again. A hotel would notice a dead body as soon as housekeeping turned up in the morning. Plus the room would be under my name. No way. "Ummmm well I have a place, though—"

I cut her off before she can dismiss the thought. "Perfect." I throw the gear into drive and move out of the parking space before she has time to decline. Once we're driving away from the mall, I ask for directions. She leads me to an incredibly run-down part of town with houses barely larger than my living room.

Instead of feeling guilty or sorry for her circumstances, I'm excited. *Something new.*

As I pull in front of the house, I have a moment of panic as I realize I don't have a set of fake license plates on. It's dark and no other cars have driven past us in the last five or so minutes, but still, *shit.* So when hooker gets out of the car I grab two fake plates from under my seat, the only set of magnetic ones I have, and walk around both sides of the car to slap them on. They aren't straight, and anyone could pull them off with a flick of the wrist, but in this time crunch it's going to have to work. After I've finished I breathe easier. She's stopped in the middle of the sidewalk to light another cigarette, and I pull my hood over my head, reaching into my pockets to fish out my gloves. Once they're on I tighten them at the wrists.

I smile. *There are good things about the winter, too.*

When I look up she's walking slowly and deliberately, in what I assume is supposed to be a seductive or suggestive walk toward her front door. She didn't notice the exchange on my car. She's oblivious and anxious for the money. I'm sure she has ideas of calling a dealer after I leave. Too bad she won't have the chance.

I rush up behind her as quietly as I can. As she puts in her key to unlock the door she turns around, and I'm waiting as if I never stopped to hide my identity.

"You ready for the best you've ever had, sugar?"

"You have no idea."

chapter forty-five;

Once inside, I can tell she lives alone. It's basically a studio, which she keeps pretty clean for the neighborhood she's in.

"What do ya wanna do first?" She's ready to begin and ready to be done. I wonder what she thinks about when she's fucking her Johns. Does she go over her to-dos, her grocery list? Is she thinking about how she'll spend their money? Either way, she won't have much time to think with me. I plan to go faster than normal tonight, too. I have shit to do after this.

"Can we take a bath together and fuck in the tub? I've always wanted to do that. I've never had anyone to do it with." A look of surprise flickers over her gaunt features, but she recovers.

"Sounds hot. I'll start the water." She walks to the bathroom, undressing as she goes.

As the tub is filling, I strip down to nothing and then wait for the scene to be ready. She gets into the water and playfully splashes me. I play along and laugh with her, but in actuality I'm ready to do what my body has been ready for since she asked for a *fun night*.

The electricity running through me like a current is starting to feel normal, expected even, before, during, and shortly after a kill. Everything inside of me is so alive.

As Hooker gets into the tub, beckoning me over, I think to ask her a question before jumping into what I want to do most. "What's your name, honey?"

"It's Tristan. What's yours?" Interesting, I bet that's her real name, too. I was expecting an answer of something like Bambi, or Cinnamon.

"I'm Aidan."

And with the intimate reveal, time is up for Tristan the hooker. *It's time to play.* But this time I'm taking a different approach. I've strived to make each experience unique so far, and this one will continue with the tradition.

With sheer excitement threatening to burst from inside me, I push it down to continue. Sitting down next to the edge of the tub, I lean her head back toward the water, and she wraps her wrists around her knees for support. I turn to grab the cup from the sink, starting to wet her hair.

This is intimate, so unlike any of the other kills. She still feels safe. I'm nurturing her first, building her comfort before taking it and everything else away from her.

I squirt shampoo into her wet hair, starting to massage her scalp. The suds give off a pleasant aroma, and she mews little sounds of pleasure. I bet it's been a long time since anyone has done something like this for her. She doesn't look well-loved.

I use the cup a few times to rinse the suds, and then I ask her to lie farther back.

This is it.

She keeps her eyes closed as she leans back into the water. *Goodbye, Tristan.* I strike like a venomous snake. My fingers wrap around her throat, pushing her head under water. Her eyes pop open in fear and shock. They're blurry beneath the patches of leftover shampoo, but I can still see the panic in them. She was completely blindsided, and my laughter bubbles up and out of my mouth in loud bursts.

She flails her limbs, getting water over most of the surfaces in the bathroom, but she isn't strong enough to get out from under my grasp. Her tiny frame and drug habit have both done her a disservice here. My fingers tighten as her time ticks away. She must feel every second pound in her struggling lungs.

She tries to scream, but only bubbles pop the surface. I can see the blood rushing to her face as she struggles to hold her breath as long as she can. Unless she can hold it forever, it won't be long enough.

Finally she sucks in the water and quickly she's drowned.

The struggle after opening her lungs to water isn't as long as they make it look in the movies. It only takes one gulp to flood the system. But under clean bathwater, one is enough to see it happen. One is wonderful.

One is fucking amazing.

***

I switch into clean-up mode, acting quickly. Draining the tub, I rinse her body as well as the tub with cleaner. Then I refill the tub once more, letting her float. I mop up every surface in the bathroom and clean the mops as well. The sting of cleaners, bleach, in my nostrils has come to mean something incredibly different than it used to. I don't want any of my skin cells that may have flaked off into the water to be a problem. Once I'm confident in my work, I get dressed.

I walk to the door, then remember something key. *A donation.* After running back to the bathroom, I stop to look in the serene tub. She has no worries anymore. No problems. She had nothing. She is *nothing* any longer. I shake my head to clear it. I need a donation from her. I can't believe I almost forgot. Opening the medicine cabinet, I spot a pair of little diamond earrings and tuck them deep into a zippered pocket.

There. Exactly what I needed. The donations are what last forever.

Finally ready, I head out the door, locking it from the inside first, making sure to leave the lights on. Hopefully with her bad choices in life, her premature death won't come as a surprise to those she knows or even the police.

Well, that's three now under your belt. I want to raise my arm to pat myself on the back.

Looking at my phone, I realize I'm late. I should be arriving at Bee's now, and it's at least a fifteen-minute drive from here. She's going to be pissed.

"Hey." But apparently that's not the worst of my problems.

The baritone's shout almost makes me jump out of my skin. My heart falls to my feet. Please let me have imagined it. But I know I didn't. So I pretend I didn't hear, walking faster to my car.

I need to get out of here.

"Hey, you."

Maybe he'll think I'm deaf. If I can just get to my door...

"I'm talking to you." And a meaty hand falls on my shoulder.

Fuck. Fuck, fuck, FUCK.

I don't want to turn. No one was supposed to see me here. I want to die. I want to disappear. I want to run. But I can't. I have to turn. So I do.

"Yeah?"

"You dropped this." And the giant of a man, six and a half feet and as wide as Jason, hands me my wallet. I dropped my fucking wallet.

More air leaves my lungs than I knew could be stored there, exhaling my relief with it.

"Thanks."

"Yeah." He doesn't even make eye contact. He's already walking away as he replies.

Holy fucking shit.

Completely unacceptable of me.

What if he hadn't given it back? What if my wallet had been outside Tristan's house when she was found lifeless, strangled, in her bathtub? How could I have been so careless? I'll have to think more about this later. How to correct it. How to prevent it. How to be punished for it.

Once I'm back in the car, I can't stop shaking. I quickly text Bee, letting her know I'm on my way, but despite my wanting to rush I know I won't speed. There's no need to draw any attention to myself. I change into my new outfit in the front seat before driving away from Tristan's place and toward Bee's.

chapter forty-six;

Before heading up to Bee's door, I pull the fakes off my car, tossing them into my trunk. I'm feeling a little worthless after my mistake earlier. But I also still have my playdate pride. The mixture of worry and excitement is something new.

Another thought mixes in with my own crap about earlier. Maybe I *should've* brought Bee a gift. That's what normal dates do, though the thought is too late, not helping me with my empty hands walking up to her place.

I knock timidly, waiting for it to open.

"I thought you might have changed your mind." She sounds stern.

"Something came up, but I took care of it."

"I know." Her eye contact is steady, deliberate. She couldn't...

"You know?" My blood pressure spikes instantly, and I feel dizzy.

My eyes are trained on her, hard, looking for every movement or any silent indication of what she meant. She can't know anything about what I've been doing tonight. *She can't.* She pauses, shakes her head, and looks to the sky.

"Sorry. Meant bet...I bet."

If she knew, there's no way she'd have opened the door. I struggle but decide to let it go.

"Hurry up and get out here. We have lots to do tonight."

"You're awfully bossy for someone who turned up twenty minutes after you said you would. Off doing *horrible* things, I'm sure." Again she's taking the upper hand, to be the one in control.

"I'll make it up to you." I flash her my widest and brightest smile. It works as she melts into the palm of my hand. She moves outside, locking her door. "You ready for the best date of your life?" Is it a date? Well, shit, I guess I just made it one if it wasn't already...unless she says otherwise.

"You better not build it up too much or I'll have to give you shit when it sucks." She didn't correct me.

Guess it's officially a date.

We get into my car and drive toward my first destination.

***

"Midnight, black-light bowling? No way." She bounces on her heels as she peeks around the few couples in front of us in line to pay. She tries not to say anything more, but I can tell she's holding a compliment back. Eventually she caves, "This is pretty awesome. I love dark games like this."

I had the suggestion from Jason. He told me she's mentioned to Amelia once how much she enjoys bowling. I think she played competitively when she was younger.

"A little birdie told me it might be a good idea." Her eyes light up even brighter, and I'm surprised by the swell of pride filling my chest.

Evidently, making just a pinch of effort to find out what would go over well is impressive. I wonder how badly her dates have gone in the past, and I have to swipe away a nasty scowl wanting to plant itself on my face. Has anyone ever bothered to find out about her as a person? I mean, she's a little overweight, but she's fucking cool, which has definitely made her more attractive. Maybe she could give me a list of people who've hurt her before.

That's something to consider.

This dating thing is more confusing than I thought it would be, though. I don't know what I want from her or what she wants of me. It's all so new. Getting to know someone and hoping they like you too is a lot of fucking work. Just getting laid never took this much effort. I never cared enough to truly try, either, and now I find myself nervous I'll fuck it all up.

"Okay, this almost makes up for being late. What were you doing, anyway?" Oh shit. She pulls me from my thoughts as we move closer to the register.

A lump forms in my throat, making it hard to answer at first. Why doesn't a lie come forth as easily as it does for Jason or Eva, or anyone else? I almost want to tell her what I was actually doing, but *obviously* I can't. *That's fucking insane.* She'd run out of here screaming for the police, and I'd be lynched. No, I can't tell her. I can't tell *anyone.* Instead I need to come up with an excuse, a lie, and it's proving harder than it normally does. It's harder than it should be.

I've already wasted enough time.

I know Bee can see my hesitation, and her eyebrows rise as a look of suspicion spreads across her face. I blurt out the first thing that comes to mind. "I can't tell you, dummy. It's a surprise."

Well, I guess that settles it. I need to buy her a gift after all. But now I need to do it while I'm out with her, without her noticing.

Goddamn it.

Maybe I should've just told her. Might have been easier.

"Really?" I nod. And again Bee looks as if she may burst with excitement. If I can continue making her look like that, I want more than friendship. Because every time she lights up, something inside me starts to wiggle a little.

She claps her hands together, trying to stifle her glee as we move to the desk. "A lane for an hour, please."

The twenty-something cashier looks high as he gathers our shoes and takes my cash. I'd need to be stoned if I worked here, too.

We gather our ugly shoes, making our way to the dark lane, grabbing our glowing balls along the way. The black lights make everyone look tan, even a little mysterious. The odd lighting provides shadows and a dim sense of adventure I hadn't anticipated. I wonder what it would look and feel like to have sex in the corner of the alley with the flashing strobes, loud music, and purple lighting. Blood flows at the idea. No wonder these were so popular back in the seventies.

"Ladies first." She's going to kick my ass, which I bet she'll love.

"I hope you left your pride in the car. Because, kid, I'm going to *murder* you." Oh, she'll love this alright. Determined, cocky, ready to kill. She sounds like me with a playmate.

"I bet you the first round of drinks I can keep up for at least five frames."

"You're on. It will be *so* fun to torture you." Her devilish grin is made creepier by the lighting and her evil laughter, but I can't keep my own hysterics quiet at her attempt to look sinister. She has no idea what real darkness looks like in someone. Though, she sure looks adorable pretending.

***

After Bee kicks my ass bowling, I bring back two rounds to the lane for our second game, which I lose even worse than the first. Her happiness is clear, making the evening even more fun than I'd anticipated. She keeps throwing out jokes absurdly appropriate for what I was off doing before without any idea how funny murder and torture can be.

"You know, you're not what I expected, Sheppard." Her honesty catches me off guard. We've been cracking jokes and poking jabs at each other for the last hour, so it's unexpected.

"Did you expect me to be an asshole?" If she's going to lay it out, let's get everything on the table. Well, everything that wouldn't warrant a call to 911.

"Pretty much." She turns to throw yet another strike. I walk to the lane while she remains rooted to the spot. There's a sparkle in her eyes that reminds me of the one I saw at her house. It's secretive, sinister. And then again, like before, it vanishes. It could have been lighting. "There's a lot more to you than I saw at first. I'm glad I was wrong."

"You sure were." I wink at her. Then I move in even closer until my face is an inch away. I can feel the warmth from her lips as they still in front of mine. I run my fingers from her shoulders to her wrists, looking straight into her eyes the entire time. She struggles to keep her eyes open as I utter just above a whisper, "I don't fit into a neat little box. I'm not like anyone you've been out with before. And gladly I can say the same for you. Just try to give us a chance."

Us? I meant to say "give me a chance," but "us" slipped out.

Bee sucks in a sharp breath, and instead of indulging her by pressing my lips to hers, I step to the side then over to the lane. I throw a strike, too, and turn to see her staring off into space in the same position I left her.

I wish I could hear what's going through her mind.

I walk up behind her, this time letting my lips graze the bottom of her ear lobe. "Your turn, bowling queen. You seem a bit distracted all of a sudden, but if you want to slaughter me for the last game you better step it up." I lean back and chuckle.

Bee spins on her heel, showing me how well she can play under pressure. She does kill me, and worse than either of the games before, just to spite me I think.

***

We take a cab from the bowling alley to our next destination, since we've both had a few drinks. There's no way I'm trashing my car or looking like an idiot for insisting I can drive.

"Where are we going next?" Bee was disappointed when I handed the driver our next address on a slip of paper instead of saying it out loud.

"You'll just have to wait and see." I've never planned a surprise for anyone, probably not since I was a kid. I've been missing out, because this is fun.

"How the heck am I going to top this for our third date?" she asks, and I just smile.

I guess I don't have to ask if we'll be seeing each other again after tonight. That is, unless I do something stupid like blurt out what made me late. Then she'd likely change her mind about wanting another date.

"You're pretty smart. I bet you'll think of something." She returns my smile of confidence, and for the first time, something changes in the air around us. Something electric charges, and I can almost see a current between us even though we aren't touching.

My line of sight moves from her eyes down to her lips, and I have an urge stronger than anything I've felt before; it's more powerful even than urges I've had to kill. I've never wanted to kiss anyone more than I want to right now.

But before I can react, the cabbie slams on the breaks, sending us both toward the plastic partition. "Fucking idiots," he mumbles under his breath. Bee cracks up, throwing her head back, while I let out a long, annoyed sigh.

Moment ruined.

***

After the odd incident in the cab we don't have one like it again, making me wonder if I was the only one who felt it. Maybe I imagined the whole thing. Either way, we continue chatting like nothing happened, her cleverness on par with earlier.

The cab drops us off at the casino, and I hold her hand walking in. She doesn't pull away, and her grip is strong. When we get inside, our first stop is for another set of drinks, which she gets this time.

"Are you trying to liquor me up?" Bee lets out a soft little hiccup after finishing her girly drink.

"You idiot, you bought this round." I shake my head in feigned disappointment while one corner of my mouth remains turned up.

"Oh, yeah. Well, I'm trying to get *you* drunk, then." This time a louder hiccup escapes between her lips as she nods, widening her eyes, trying to look dirty. The effect is lost with the squeak at the end of her hiccup. It's a high-pitched little sound that's the most endearing thing I've ever heard.

Jesus fucking Christ, I'm losing it.

"Then you're in for an expensive night, because I'm not a cheap date. I can hold my drink." Which is a good thing. I don't need to get drunk enough to spill my guts like I almost did with Jason at the cabin. And if I were to dive too far into the pool of alcohol, I just might let those dirty secrets out to Bee. There's something about her that's been making me want to be totally honest. Like a fucking moron.

Maybe I should turn tail to run, because that's a terrifying thought.

"Well, shit." She starts to double over with laughter as we stroll between the slot machines, looking for the best one to play.

We put money into machines here or there, but neither of us is on a streak yet. We weave through the drunks and grandparents, searching for our big win. I rub her shoulders each time she picks one to sit in front of and play on. She continues to giggle with the sweet sound as well as throw insults and smart-ass comments my way. A few times I catch myself looking at her a bit too long.

After losing at the blackjack table, we walk around once more through the haze of cigarette smoke. Another swell of something I can't describe starts deep in my gut and rises up. I reach for Bee's hand, and we move along through the maze of machines and noise, holding onto our cold drinks, with our other fingers intertwined.

I haven't held hands with a girl since I was in middle school.

And now I've done it twice tonight.

chapter forty-seven;

As the cab's fare continues to rise, I walk Bee to her door at the end of our evening.

"The sun will be up soon."

I have no idea how to finish out this date. I don't think I've ever walked a woman to her door, not even in high school. I guess I've pretty much always been an asshole. And the path I chose is looking a little less surprising from this angle.

"You kept me out all night, my mom'll be furious." She winks at me and twirls her hair. Again the unknown part stirs inside.

"Just sneak in quietly or she won't let me take you out again." I sound and feel like a complete dumbass, but she's eating it up, which makes it worth the stupidity.

"Oh, I think she will." Then without warning she leans in for a kiss.

It starts out hesitant, then works into something more. Before long, her hands are around my neck and mine are tangled in her long hair. It's passionate, but it never crosses the line to dirty. There's something sweet somewhere in there, and that's not something I'm used to.

Though, I think, maybe, I *could* get used to it.

Just before she breaks away, the kiss speeds up. She bites my lip hard, and then I'm out of breath. Not what I expected. When she finally does pull away to lean back, I see a determined but glazed look in her eyes before she blinks it away.

"Wow," is all I manage to breathe out.

And, "Yeah," is all she responds with.

This new territory is so foreign to me I forget to say goodnight as she opens her door and walks inside. She remembers, though, just before closing her door. I stand there a few moments longer, a little dazed, before heading back to the taxi.

"Home, please." And I give him the address. I'll go get my car from the bowling alley in the morning. As we drive, I realize I never bought a gift for Bee like I'd meant to, as part of the excuse for why I'd been late; in all the fun, I forgot.

Once in bed, I can't stop thinking about the two sides to my current life. I'm one person with Bee, Jason, and the people at work, and a completely different one with Amelia and my playthings. There is some part of me wishing to be both with Bee, but that stupid yearning needs to be erased. I can't be too honest with her. I have no idea what will happen when these two sides of me try to integrate, but I can't imagine it will end without trouble.

***

I stand on an island. There's black swirling water everywhere I look. White caps burst at my shins. Only they aren't white. They're puss-colored, smelling rank. Beady eyes stalk my movements just below the surface. The sun is covered in inky splotches. Or maybe it's the moon.

I can't tell.

There's moaning hitting my ears, but I'm alone, so I don't understand who it's coming from. I can see every side of this island. It's no more than a hundred square feet. No one else is here. I raise my hand to my lips to check, and it isn't me crying out.

Then the pain starts.

A burning, searing pain pounds through every inch of my skin, coming in quick pulses. I can't run from it. And I can't make it stop. I watch as red lines streak across my skin as it's cut from the inside. It's all coming from the inside. My stomach rips open, and dozens of playmates fall out. Clean and naked.

They continue their groaning.

They try to run but have nowhere to go. I ignore the pain still tearing me apart and run after my playthings. I laugh as they cry. My own pain fades as I hurt each one. Screams fill the air as I collect donation after donation.

***

And I roll off my bed, wakened when my forehead smacks the hard floor.

Fucking hell.

***

Saturday is mostly comprised of sleeping and walking around without clothes on. I remain exhausted from staying up until morning with Bee. Despite the date being worth it, I need to allow my body the rest of the weekend to fully relax.

In the afternoon, I remember what's hidden, waiting for me in my jacket pocket. When I add the tiny earrings to my collection, a new thrill runs through me. It's not as exciting as planning, or playing, but it's there nonetheless. It'll be what gets me through the downtime between playdates.

After dropping the diamonds in with the rest of the jewelry, my dick has a mind of its own, and it comes out to play.

***

Jason comes over Sunday for television, mandatory male bonding time. We eat, yelling at the TV, and everything with him remains normal. I try not to think about Amelia when he's over.

I don't hear from her the entire weekend, but I do share several texts with Bee. Each puts a dorky smile on my face, and I continue to wonder what exactly we're doing and how she brings these completely foreign emotions out of me.

On Sunday night I jerk off, again, to thoughts of each of my adventures, and visions of both Bee and Amelia sneak their way in as well. It used to be surprising that the ideas of sex and violence mix so easily when I let my guard down, but I've come to accept everything I feel now. Especially the dark. I did kill The-One-Who-Doesn't-Count after fucking her, and each kill has gotten me hard at some point. Though, I have no desire to hurt Bee or Amelia. Thankfully, it seems my wants to hurt and fuck don't *always* go hand in hand.

I concede I'm a confusing fucker as I lie down for bed to end the weekend.

***

At work on Monday, Dan announces the decision for Eva's replacement will be announced in no sooner than two weeks, maybe three. He reports they want to observe us and weigh each candidate thoroughly to prevent making a mistake like last time.

Smart. Too bad they didn't do it before to save themselves months of lost time.

This also forces everyone to be as productive as possible. Some will take it far enough to be a kiss ass, others will just try to make friends with everyone. I won't. I plan to act no differently. I think it's worthless to try to be something I'm not when I'll still be myself as a supervisor. They liked both my personality and work ethic enough to hire me, and to continue my employment since then. It's genuine, and by far the best course of action. Jason has vowed to take my lead and continue with his normal behavior. We'll see if he sticks to it.

Dan also announces he'll remain in both his and Eva's positions for the interim.

"Sounds like a lot of work for just one salary."

Jason sleepily nods his head in agreement. I refuse to ask if his fatigue stems from a happy or not-so-happy excuse. Despite my continuing (and possibly improving) engagement with Bee, I still don't want to hear about his sex life with Amelia, not until my entanglement with her has ended.

Jason and I are in the kitchen, digging around for a snack. It isn't quite lunchtime, but we both decided we needed a pick-me-up. I scrounge up a granola bar and settle on stale coffee since I'm just too lazy to go down to the lobby. Jason continues looking while I face the elevator across from the kitchen to eat.

I never would've guessed what I'd see next.

The elevator doors open just as Jason stands next to me to eat the fruit he decided on. A few coworkers from other departments walk out unaware of who was in the elevator behind them. After the rest have dispersed, Eva sneaks out. She has her hair up, sunglasses on, and is hiding her prominent figure under a large winter coat, but holy hell it's definitely Eva.

chapter Forty-Eight

Jason and I exchange glances, both perking up. This will be better than any dose of caffeine, guaranteed.

"Holy shit, is it seriously her?" As Jason asks, Eva strips the sunglasses off and his question is answered.

"Fuck me." There's little else to say.

I hope she embarrasses herself even more. I'd love to see her cry.

"You can say that again. This should be a shit show." There is as much amusement in Jason's tone as there is on my face.

"Fuck me." I do say it again because there's nothing else to add.

Both Jason and I walk to the entrance of the kitchen to watch as another uncomfortable scene is about to unfold. It's like we're in high school again, and we're the cool kids lucky enough to watch the fight in the hallway between classes. We'll get to brag about it later to those unfortunate enough to have been in the bathroom at the time.

Eva walks quickly to Dan's office, trying to avoid being noticed before she's able to make it to his door. No one drags her away, though plenty are already gawking. She knocks loud and short before opening his door. I guarantee he doesn't have time to say a damn word before she enters.

In two short seconds, before she can get more than a step and a half into his office, Dan is forcing her out.

"What the hell are you doing here?" And he held it together so well last time. Leave it to Eva to break everyone's last straw.

"I came back to start back in my position. I can see where I went wrong, and I'll strive to do better in the future." Holy fuck, she's batshit crazy. After the scene she made last time, after getting kicked out, has she diluted herself into believing she'd *ever* be welcome back? No way. Not even at half the salary.

"No."

Dan spits the single syllable out as if it's scorching his mouth. He looks like he can't get her away from him fast enough. All of his features are pinched. I hope he doesn't have a coronary right here. She'd probably walk over him into his office and barricade herself inside if he did.

"I understand the errors I made before, and I think it would benefit us both if you gave me my job back." She must have had a psychotic break. I elbow Jason, making sure he's as absorbed in this ridiculous scene.

"Are you crazy?" Dan almost chokes as he starts to yell. "I wouldn't hire you back if you were the only one in the world left qualified for the position." She looks wounded, as if she expected her ploy to work. "Now turn around, go back to your car, and stay the fuck away from here. *Forever.*" By the last word he's hissing.

"But, Dan..." Eva drops down, holding her hands, clasped together, in front of her face. Holy fucking shit. She's actually begging, on her knees, for her job. I look to Jason and neither of us can say anything. Eyes bulged, jaws dropped, we simultaneously turn back to watch her continued humiliation of herself. "I beg you, Dan," *obviously*, "take me back, and you won't regret it. You need me as much as I need you. Please, Dan..."

He cuts her off before she can continue. "You have five seconds before I call security."

She huffs, but wisely doesn't retort. Instead, she retreats to the elevator with her tail between her legs, her shoulders hunched. With the boldness of her endeavor, I'm shocked she gave up so quickly. But she's leaving. As the elevator doors open and she steps inside, she finally sees how many of her old peers and subordinates have witnessed the whole embarrassing scene.

"Fuck off." She screeches just before the rickety doors slam closed, effectively cutting her off.

"Show's over. Back to work, folks." Dan is calm once again when he returns to business as usual. It ended almost as quickly as it began, but it was incredibly weird regardless. Worth its weight in gold, those few moments.

Why had Eva thought anything so stupid would work? Did she have amnesia? Or maybe she thought Dan and the rest of us were the ones with amnesia instead.

"That is one crazy bitch." Jason's whisper contains a chuckle of astonishment.

"You can say that again." I mirror his previous retort.

"One crazy bitch." We both shake with laughter walking back to our offices.

***

I have no plans for the evening as Jason and I leave the building for our respective homes at the end of the workday. The event with Eva is almost forgotten with all of the numbers and reports we've dealt with all afternoon.

That is, it *was* forgotten until I see her. She's sitting in her car parked directly behind mine in the lot.

"What the fuck?" Jason follows my gaze, seeing her as well.

"What's she still doing here?" His face mirrors the confusion in his voice.

"My thoughts exactly."

She isn't on her phone, or reading, or doing anything to occupy her attention. She's just sitting in her car, looking at the spot where

Jason and I stand. Has she been here all day? Has she been watching the lobby doors for hours? What a creepy bitch.

And I know creepy.

"Maybe she forgot something?"

He's definitely trying to give her the benefit of the doubt.

"Who the hell knows, but I think it's time to get out of here." If I keep seeing her, I'll want to add her to my list of playmates, and that can't happen. I have a connection to her, and I even had a motive.

"You're right. She's starting to look a little nuts." We walk to our respective cars, and when I get into mine I hear my phone beep. For a second I debate waiting to read it until I get home, because Miss Crazy Pants is feet behind me, but then I wonder if it might be Bee or Amelia, and I take it out instead.

It's only from Jason, and I decide I could've waited after reading, **Good luck with that. She's staring daggers into the back of your head. Psycho.** Though I'd have preferred a text from one of my wonderful women, I couldn't agree more with Jason. Time to get out of here.

I start the car, pulling out of the emptying lot as the snow falls lightly from the cloudy sky. Jason is ahead of me waving frantically, trying to get my attention.

"What the hell does he want?" I look down to my ringing phone. He's calling. "What, dude?" I do have a life outside our friendship.

"Turn around. She's following you." I glance in my rearview mirror to see Eva holding a look of severe determination.

"Fuck." I breathe the word out in a cloud of frustration and helplessness.

"Like I said, good luck with that." Jason starts laughing before hanging up without a goodbye.

As I drive through town, Eva continues to follow me. I try to stop looking in my mirrors, but every few seconds I find myself checking to see if she's left yet. She hasn't. In hopes of losing her, I drive to the store to do some shopping. I spend tons of time meandering through aisles, picking up everything I need or may need. I try on clothes, and even chat with a few clerks about electronics I don't need.

An hour later, I leave with high hopes Eva has given up and driven home to stew in her own embarrassment and anger. But I don't have much luck. My stomach sinks down to my groin as I see a horrifying Cheshire grin above Eva's steering wheel in the parking spot next to mine.

I have two choices right now. I could flip shit, trying to scare her away, or I can refrain from any and all contact. Both have potential to work, and they also have equal opportunities to backfire. Eva is nothing if unpredictable. I should take the safer route. I shouldn't encourage her.

I'd like nothing more than to knock on her window, screaming profanity and threats once she rolls it down. But that'd give her the upper hand, which is the last thing I want. No, I need to be smarter. I won't show my annoyance; in fact, I won't give her any display of emotion. Just like the bully in school, she'll get bored if I continue to ignore her.

So with this resolve, instead of telling her to fuck off, I simply avert my gaze, hopping into my own car without any acknowledgment of her presence. It takes a lot of effort not to drag her by the hair from her car to mine and shove her into my trunk for a rough ride toward the middle of nowhere. But I resist.

I pull away as if I've no idea she does the same behind me. I don't make any evasive moves, because they wouldn't do shit. As my former boss, she knows where I live. I drive as I would any other day.

I decide to do every errand I can. I head from store to store with my shadow in tow. I linger at the grocery store, remembering running into Bee last time, and then I stock up on ingredients I've neglected on quick runs. I trot through the hardware store, saying hello to everyone, and I go to dinner alone, even adding on dessert.

She never once comes inside the stores, either out of laziness or fear she'd lose me inside, I'm unsure which. She just sits in her car letting it run next to or near mine, waiting to continue following me. By late evening I've run out of places to go, so I eventually drive home with Eva as a constant behind me.

Getting out at home, it takes a lot of willpower to refrain from flipping her the middle finger as I go back and forth between the car and the house with the loot I've purchased. She's parked right in front of my house, across the street, with her driver's side facing my front windows.

The curtains will be drawn tonight.

A small current of unease ripples throughout my system. It starts between my shoulder blades, moving up to my scalp in the time it takes me to blink twice. Nausea quickly follows. If Eva stalks me for any length of time, it's going to make a playdate incredibly hard to orchestrate. Impossible, really. What the fuck am I going to do if she never goes away?

I have to run to the bathroom, and I barely make it to the toilet before I puke.

This is bad. This is so bad.

Wiping my mouth, I grab the landline and dial Jason's house number. Maybe he'll have some idea to get rid of this crazy bitch.

chapter Forty-Nine:

As I hang up I huff, because Jason had nothing brilliant to offer me. His only suggestion was to notify the police (fuck that) but he added they probably won't even do anything anyway since she hasn't threatened me. Stalking is hard to prove. Truthfully, even if she had made a threat, unless I sincerely believed myself to be in jeopardy, I'd be hesitant to make that phone call. With three—nope, wait, with four if you add The-One-Who-Doesn't-Count—murders to my name so far, it doesn't seem like a wise decision. I don't need any attention from the authorities.

So I'm back to square one with no ideas and a crazy fucking cunt outside my house stalking me. My heart leaps at a thought. I haven't checked in an hour. Maybe she's come to her senses, realized how psycho she's being, and given up to go home. I peel the charcoal curtains back then hunch over with disappointment. Damn batty bitch is still there. The exhaust from her tail pipe plumes clouds in the cold.

Well, at least she'll be paying a ton for gas to stalk me in the winter. But that's a shitty consolation prize.

I stomp to my bedroom with thoughts of blood and gore in her future, all of which are only fantasies, I know, but they help calm me down. I shower, trying to let the water wash some of my worries away.

Surely she can't keep this up forever. It's only been half a day, anyway. Maybe I'm overreacting in my angst. She has to give up eventually. I've seen her work ethic, and it isn't all too determined, so she's sure to stop this before long.

Fuck.

As I head from the bathroom, my shower done, toward my bed for some mindless television then sleep, I can't shake the bitterness soaking into my system. She better fucking knock it off soon or I may not be able to control my irrational rage, and then we'll both be in trouble.

Settled into bed, I grab my phone to charge it for the night. Despite my pissy attitude, a waiting text from Bee puts a smile on my face. **I'm busy with a deadline tomorrow, but how about Wednesday night I try to beat your planning extraordinaire?** I type back a quick positive. At least I have something to look forward to.

I flip to the news after replacing my phone on the nightstand and freeze as the face of The-One-Who-Doesn't-Count fills the screen again.

Fucking shit fuck.

I can't seem to get a break today.

The police are boasting new evidence, but they won't reveal what it is. They say they're close. But what could it be? Is there a link back to me? I may not have to worry too long about Eva hindering my life, because prison will be considerably worse.

I count to ten to calm myself.

This isn't the time to lose it. I won't dig my own grave.

I continue watching the report, changing my tune as I learn they're just blowing smoke. They don't have anything concrete. If they even suspected me, there would be knocking at my door. All they have is a missing girl, and they don't even have her body. The authorities are begging for any information, which makes me smile knowing not a soul other than myself has any to give.

Again my phone goes off. Picturing Bee's sparkling eyes, I grab it ready to come up with a witty retort. But it isn't from Bee, and for the first time I'm torn about the two women I'm juggling. Tomorrow? The only word she sent is filled with more promise than I knew three syllables could hold. Full of uncertainty, I send her a positive response.

Shaking my head, I sink into my plush covers, trying to block out all of the confusion I've lead myself into.

Shit.

***

At work the following morning, I'm second-guessing my decision. Agreeing to see Mel today could be stupid. With Eva still following me, this could end up fuel for her fire and come back to bite me harder in the ass than I'm prepared for.

I never want Jason to find out how I've betrayed him.

Ever.

I open up my email and compose an explanation of my situation for Amelia, worded in a way that's asking for advice instead of mentioning our rendezvous. If she has any ideas we can move forward, but if not I need to cancel. Since she has as much to lose as I do, it's only fair to let her in about what's going on.

"You know she's outside again. Did she stay in front of your house all night?" Jason's large shoulders lean into my office as I look up from the email I just sent his wife.

"I don't even think she slept. Bitch is determined."

There's clear animosity in my voice. Jason looks empathetic.

"I don't envy you right now."

Well, I don't envy you either since your wife is having an affair and planning to leave you…but I leave that part unsaid.

"Do you think I should tell Dan?"

I figure the more people aware of the situation, the less damage she can do, and thus the less power she has over me. I don't want her to have a single drop of power, but that's pretty much impossible with the list of secrets I carry.

"Shit, I didn't even think of that. Yeah, maybe you should."

I grab a scrap of paper to list everyone I need to talk to about my unfortunate tail.

"I'll have to warn Bee tomorrow, too." I'm thinking out loud now. I look back up to an amused look on Jason's chubby face.

"Still happening, huh?"

Yeah, her and your wife, dick.

"As a matter of fact, yeah it is. So what?"

Jason upturns his palms in surrender to the ice in my voice.

"No offense, I swear. No judgment. I'm happy for you." He pauses before adding, "I like her. She's pretty cool."

"Good. I like her too."

Jason's smirk widens as he realizes I've confessed an emotion I don't think I ever have before. I've always admitted to lust, horniness, want, desire, but I don't do the dating thing, so this is a new revelation.

Jason walks back to his own office giggling, and I stand to follow him out.

"Good luck telling Dan."

"Fuck, this is embarrassing."

I hope it blows over quickly and my admittance to everyone ends up unnecessary.

"Better to tell him now, though, rather than have to explain it after she's tried sabotaging you."

He's right. I hate it, but he's right.

"True. You've sold me." And I start the walk of shame with my head hung.

chapter Fifty;

After my meeting with Dan I'm feeling better. It was horrible having to confess about the crazy glue doing her best to stick it to me, but now my head is held high once more. He's seen firsthand how unstable she is, and he promised to assist me in any way he can. He was pretty kind about it all.

Thank fucking god for that.

I return to my desk and open my email. I have two waiting. One is from Amelia, and the other from Bee. I sigh as I open the first.

From: Amelia Moore
To: Aidan Sheppard
Subject: Tuesday

I'm sorry you have to deal with such a sucky problem. She's nuts. But, I don't think you have anything to worry about for tonight. Your plans can remain the same, I think. As long as you're still in, seems safe to me.

Sincerely,
Mel

I wonder what her plans are. She may have a disguise in mind. The thought is intoxicating, and I almost forget I have a second email to read. I get lost for a few minutes in visions of dark corners and veiled identities.

But I'm pulled from those fantasies when the face beneath the wig and sunglasses morphs into Bee's. And I'm thoroughly shocked when I realize I'd rather be having sex with her tonight. I'd prefer her in a dark corner whispering softly in my ear.

Well shit, so much for not wanting anything serious with anyone. This is the most serious I've ever felt with anyone other than playmates.

Double shit.

From: Bee Iverson
To: Aidan Sheppard
Subject: Date Night

Hi,
I'm procrastinating on my writing, and I just wanted to take a second to say hey. Okay, dorky, I know. Anyway, looking forward to tomorrow.

See you soon,
B

I choose to leave Amelia's email unanswered; there isn't much to say. But I do respond to Bee's with a quick hello in return and an agreement of excitement for our third date.

It's followed by another *what the fuck's happening to me?* moment.

Looks like I have another few days of juggling the women in my life, which unfortunately now includes Eva.

Not the most appealing ménage à quatre there ever was.

245

***

At seven, while I'm lounging on my couch after dinner, trying to pretend Eva isn't outside my house again, I wonder if Mel has gotten distracted or had something come up to prevent our chance to meet tonight. I wouldn't be heartbroken if that's the case, and I don't plan to text her to check in.

It is what it is.

Of course, my phone buzzes in my pocket after I've decided my night will be spent at home. I dig it out and read Amelia's message. **One hour. Z.**

I answer with two letters. **OK**

***

Eva followed me to Spot Z, as expected, but at least she stayed outside. She probably assumes I'm just trolling for drunk snatch. Hopefully Amelia is smart enough not to take Jason's car. If she's trying to conceal her identity then it would be stupid to show up in his vehicle. I should have coached her more.

I leave my house half an hour after Mel texts me in order to put plenty of time between our arrivals. With this fucking stalker, I can't be too careful. Eva may be crazy, but she isn't as stupid as I'd like. She's cunning, so I seriously need to watch my back with her behind it at all times. Goddammit, she's making everything so much more complicated. I wish I could just collect her donation. It'd be so satisfying to kill her and get it over with.

It was incredibly weird walking to the bar with a car creeping along slowly behind me. Eva's determined, and though she's obvious, she doesn't seem to be quitting any time soon.

I sit in the back of the bar where little light reaches except for the occasional flicker from the dance floor. The rhythmic beats of the music are loud and fast. This was a good place for Mel to choose, I'll give her that.

A song into my third drink, I see a familiar silhouette slink across the dance floor toward my secluded booth. It's Amelia, but she's covered her hair with a short blonde wig, naughty librarian glasses, and a dress that's sluttier than any I've ever seen on her. My earlier indifference sways as my blood pumps downward. Her tits are almost popping out of the top of the sheer dress as it rides up her thighs with each step.

I watch as she picks a female partner at random on the dance floor and starts to work her curves into those of the stranger. Her intentions work as my dick reacts quickly. It actually hurts, it's so hard.

I can't tear my eyes away as Mel runs her fingers down the sides of her willing participant. She grazes the woman's breasts, grinding into her from behind. The woman flings her head back as she places her hands over Amelia's as encouragement. As the first song blends into a second, the stranger pulls Mel's hands around to her front and holds them to her chest.

Amelia doesn't protest, but instead she starts to massage the tits she's been encouraged to touch. She's clearly enjoying this show as much as I am. I have no idea if she experimented before she met Jason, but if she didn't the chance is now.

I suck in a deep breath as Mel lets one of her hands start to travel downward while the other continues to work the woman's cleavage. From my seat, I can see her fingers dip down into the low-cut top. I watch in a trance, completely unable to look away. Amelia's wandering hand moves past the navel and travels past the final destination to her dance partner's thigh instead.

Fuck, what a tease.

I don't stop watching, though.

Her dexterous fingers work up the creamy thigh unencumbered by pants or tights. Lucky the stranger has only boots beneath her skirt. Amelia's hands move from the outer side of the woman's thigh toward the inner portion as she moves continuously upward.

In the next second her hand has disappeared up the skirt and the stranger's head is back against Mel's ample chest.

I can't wait any longer. I stand up and let go of fantasies of fucking back in the isolated booth. I have new ideas now. I walk up to the willing woman, wink at Amelia's smile, and lean into the other woman's ear. I can smell the drinks she's already had. This is a sure bet.

"Do you two want to come to my place?"

She barely opens her eyes before nodding. Amelia voices for them both, "Give us a second." She spins the stranger to face her, leaving one hand up her skirt, and hopefully buried deep between wet pussy lips. She uses her other hand to pull the woman's face toward hers and in a second two tongues intertwine before me.

"Now." I'm going to be involved.

I pull Mel by the elbow and lead all three of us outside. A few taxis are waiting, and I snag one to take us the few blocks to my house.

Eva follows the taxi and parks across the street once again.

I intentionally leave the curtains open so she can enjoy the show.

***

I can't keep track of whose mouth is where, and I've never been so lost in an experience. There are constant moans, so many noises of pleasure. I'm never unattended. There's plenty to do, and even more to watch.

Amelia is as enthusiastic as I am, and it's so fucking hot.

"Fuck me harder."

I learned in the cab the stranger's name is Liz. She's a brunette. Young and horny. I didn't need to know much else. She told me her name with one hand wrapped tightly around my hard dick and the other rubbing Mel's clit. Now she's begging for my cock to be deeper inside of her.

I strive to appease her request.

Amelia never gets jealous, which is a bit of a shock, and I can't get enough. I refrain from coming for over an hour. Watching her buried in Liz's cunt is one of the best things I've ever seen. She even lets me in the back door while she's face-first eating pussy.

I think I may have died and gone to heaven.

chapter Fifty-One.

I use a day of PTO at work on Wednesday. After a cab took Liz and Amelia home hours later, I couldn't sleep. I was way too worked up, and I decided to reward myself from a night well done. Besides, it's been about six months since I've taken a day off that wasn't already a freebie holiday.

Amelia hit me with a new development while Liz was freshening up in the bathroom just before the two left.

She lost the frisky look and took on a more serious one to tell me, "I just wanted to let you know I decided to leave Jason before the baby's born." She paused then to let it sink in. She may have been waiting for a response, I don't know; I was a little dazed thinking about Jason's response to the inevitable news. When she didn't get one, she continued. "I want to give him time to adjust to everything before the addition of another baby. I don't know when yet, but I just thought you'd want to know." Again I had no response, but I didn't need one because Liz returned to the room and the two women left together from my house.

I looked outside as their cab left and caught Eva's murderous glare. I smiled in return.

I waved to her even though I shouldn't have egged her on, I know, I just couldn't help it. *Hope you enjoyed the show, bitch,* was all I could think. I had the urge to write it on a piece of paper and hold it up for her to read. It felt like too much acknowledgment.

I shouldn't even have waved. In retrospect, it wasn't the best way to ignore the bully, but what's done is done.

***

With my day off, I move slowly. And after finally getting out of bed I think about Eva, hoping she was revolted by last night and left. I check outside; she didn't. Doesn't she need a bathroom, a shower, food? I bet the car is getting disgusting.

But the idea of her stewing in her own filth is somewhat satisfying.

Knowing Eva'll be close behind tonight, no matter where we go, I text Bee to let her in on what's in store. I'd so hoped the cunt would be gone by now, and since she isn't I have to fess up. I'd rather tell Bee in person, but she needs to be warned. I want to give her the opportunity to change her mind or our plans if needed.

I shake my head at what I'm forced to type by the manipulative, crazy lady outside. **Just so you know I have a legitimate stalker right now. I'm not kidding. She'll probably follow us on our date. I won't blame you if you want to back out, but I hope you don't.**

I shouldn't have added the last part, but I did anyway. Call me selfish.

Thankfully Bee responds in her typical fashion. **Don't worry, I'll protect us both. My place at 6. Should I set a plate for the stalker too?** We're still on. I stop myself from doing some sort of weird happy dance and just tell her two settings is enough.

I can't believe I'm losing my mind over a chick. One I haven't even fucked, *or killed.*

***

On Bee's doorstep, I have a bottle of wine and a bouquet of flowers in hand. I couldn't feel cheesier, but I was happy buying them, and even Eva couldn't dampen my mood as she tagged behind each stop along the way.

After I knock, Bee answers quickly as if she'd been waiting behind the door ready for me, and as I look her up and down I swear she looks thinner. She *is* thinner. She's been working her ass off to lose weight, *literally*.

She looks amazing. Though all I'd seen of her when we first met was the extra pounds, now they seem to be melting away (both figuratively and actually) as I get to know her. Her figure not only seems smaller, it's more proportionate and curves in every spot I love. She has an hourglass shape that's getting more defined, and I never noticed before how great her tits are.

No sense in trying to play it cool anymore. It's time to be as honest as I can. I hate to admit it even to myself, but I'm starting to fall for this mysteriously charming woman. "You look beautiful." My voice comes out in more of an exhale than a substantial statement.

"Well, well. You're pretty handsome yourself." I glance down at my outfit and feel a bit homely compared to her. Maybe I should've dressed nicer. Her tight black dress is hugging her perfectly, and it dips lower than anything else she's worn before, showing off a wonderful amount of cleavage. "Well, get inside, dummy. You're letting all the hot air out." She chuckles, waving her arm frantically, begging me to come in.

I trip over myself to get inside and collide into her warm body. For a second I let my frame press against hers before I take a step back.

"Sorry, sorry."

Who the fuck am I around her?

"If I didn't know better, I'd think you were trying to cop a feel. Then again, your hands are full..." Instead of denying it, I wink at her. Some of my suave demeanor is rekindled. I *refuse* to be a slobbering idiot.

"Oh, yeah. These are for you." I thrust both the flowers and the wine at her unceremoniously, but she seems ecstatic nonetheless.

"Thank you. They're beautiful. I'll put them in water. Want a glass of the wine? It should go well with dinner." She walks to the kitchen and I follow behind, watching her ass sway gracefully just above the hem of her dress.

"Perfect." She thinks I meant the wine and dinner combination. I'll let her think that.

It's taking a lot of effort not to reach out to grab a handful of that gorgeous ass in front of me. Then she turns around, and I'm not sure if she caught me staring, so I quickly start on a new subject.

"So what's the plan tonight? You look so great; where are we going?"

"I was thinking we could watch a movie here. Is that okay?" I can't remember, though I don't think she's asked if any activity was okay before. Either she's let me plan or she's just told me what's going to happen. This is a sway of the tide, and I can't help but wonder if it's significant.

Or I could be reading *way* too much into every little detail. *It's probably that.*

"Sounds great." And it actually does. *Weird.*

"Well, I was thinking we could go to dinner and a movie. At a restaurant and the theater." She waves her free hand, the one not filling the vase she's grabbed, toward the kitchen windows. "But since you're popular enough to have a stalker, I thought it may be more fun to just stay in."

"I couldn't agree more. And I'm so sorry about her. I'd have understood if you'd wanted to cancel. She's fucking crazy."

I tell her about how Eva left work and how she melted down in front of everyone. Bee laughs in the right spots and gasps with excitement, making me feel like an incredible storyteller. She has a knack for listening. She's more attentive, observant too, than anyone else I know. During my descriptions of Eva, a glint reflects in her eyes. It looks like she'd like to beat her ass.

"I wouldn't let anyone get in the way of something I want." The fire I've seen in her before flares up, and then comes right back down. There is something deep down she hasn't shown me yet, and I still want to know more. She pauses, and I raise an eyebrow. She wants me. But after a thought she adds, "Our date, I mean."

Okay, she wants me and my company.

"Right."

I don't argue. I want her, too.

chapter Fifty-Two;

We make our way to the living room where we eat another amazing dinner. I can't believe she's losing weight if she can eat like this for every meal. I may gain a few pounds if she keeps feeding me.

Eventually we finish, I clean the plates, and Bee picks a movie.

"Mind if I turn off the lights? Movies are always better in the dark."

"A lot's better in the dark." She pauses and speeds up as if to correct herself. "But don't get any ideas, Shep." The nickname rolls around my ears as if it's been covered in honey, and I want to hear her say my name, any form of my name, a lot more.

"Scout's honor." Only the gesture I make with my hand is nothing any Scout would've made.

Bee throws a pillow at me in response as the movie starts. I plop next to her, and put my arm around her shoulders as the opening credits roll, though I resist every urge to do anything more. I have no idea why, but I want to do this right with her.

For some reason, this one matters.

Bee curls her feet up under herself and fidgets under a throw blanket. I can tell she's itching for something, but I'm not sure what. I know she'll get it out eventually, whatever it is, so I just let her work it out without prodding.

The movie is boring, and I'm not sure what's happened by the time it ends. The camera moves out as the music swells, and a couple kisses. Typical chick movie. Hopefully she liked it, at least. But when I look to Bee, she isn't watching the screen. She's looking down at her hands in her lap, and I can see the wheels turning in her head.

I reach for her chin and pull it toward me until she looks into my eyes. "Whatcha thinking about?"

"I know it's only our third date, second if you don't count the first...."

I interrupt her only once; after this, I plan to let her speak. "I do count it."

"Okay, so I know it's our third date, which is early, but I feel something I haven't before with anyone else. There's something pulling us together. I don't know if you feel it too, or if you'll just think I'm crazy after this. I think we could have something pretty great if we give it a shot. I know you're a lifelong bachelor, and I'm a little quirky." She laughs for a second before continuing. "Okay, I'm a lot quirky. And I'm not the prettiest belle of the ball, though I know I'm a pretty good catch. And so are you. So...god, I'm rambling...I was just thinking, and I want you to be honest, so say no if you don't feel the same. I was just thinking I'd like to be exclusive if we continue dating. I'd like to give this a real chance and be in a real grown-up relationship. Though, that's new to me too. Anyway. What do you think?" I blink once. Then twice. I'm blown away, except not for the reasons I should be.

I'm shocked, because until she blabbered all that out I had no idea I'd wanted similar; then as she finished, I realized I'd like nothing more than what she just offered to me. I have no idea when something inside of me changed, but it did, and I want to be someone's boyfriend. Even thinking the word, it's the first time I haven't flinched away from it. I may not want the house with a picket fence or noisy little brats running around, but I do want this woman to be mine.

Holy fuck.

And she's right. There is something pulling us together. Some invisible, red cord connects us, and I'm not sure why yet, but I'll figure it out. I don't feel bad for what I do in my spare time when I'm with her. It's a secret, yet she makes me feel like the two parts of me can both survive without annihilating each other. She makes it feel possible, that both parts are necessary. She makes me happy just to be me.

Holy fucking fuck.

"Okay, forget I said all that. Never mind." She takes my silence as hesitation, and moves away infinitesimally, signaling her hurt feelings.

I blurt out the first corny thing that comes to mind. "Bee, will you go steady with me?" And though it sounds ludicrous coming from me, I'm dead serious. "Will you be my girlfriend?"

"Are you making fun of me? She squints her eyes, pursing her lips in her most dubious look.

"Not in the slightest. I completely agree with everything you said. I just didn't know I wanted it until I heard you say it. But I'm serious. If you still want everything you just said, so do I."

She squeals in response, flinging her arms around my neck. As she pulls back, I know she's going to kiss me, and once she starts I won't be able to stop, but there's something nagging at my conscience I have to come clean about first.

"Wait."

Her face falls. "Shit. What? Changed your mind already? That was fast." She tugs at her dress uncomfortably, trying to hide it with her joke.

"Absolutely not. I just want to start out our relationship with full honesty."

Well as full as I can get, at least. Excluding admittance of committed crimes.

Now she switches from looking uncomfortable to looking scared, or maybe fearfully annoyed.

"What is it?"

"If you change your mind, I'll understand and walk away respectfully. I just ask you keep this between us." Her nervousness, already apparent across her face, kicks up a notch.

She doesn't answer aloud. She just nods for me to continue.

It's incredibly hard, but I confess my affair with Amelia to Bee. She looks a little sad, though she never once looks like she's going to turn tail and run. She even holds my hand the entire time. After I finish, it's her turn to think before speaking.

"I understand if you don't want to see me anymore."

When she still doesn't answer, my face falls despite my efforts. I'm overrun with disappointment, new to me, and I start to get up to leave. I should've seen this one coming. I knew this was all too good to be true. I was never meant to be with anyone except those about to donate to me.

"You two are done?"

I turn around to answer.

"Yeah." She may not know it yet, but yes, I'll break it off with Mel.

"Then I'm still in."

"Really?" I try to hold back the enthusiasm in my voice. I've officially become a teenage girl. I take back all the pessimism from a second ago.

"Yes, stupid. I'll be your girlfriend."

Bee smiles the most radiant smile I've ever seen. I could swear she's glowing.

I lunge at her and tangle my fingers into her long hair. She may not be up for a kinky threesome, and she may never know my dirtiest secrets, but something about this girl has me on a hook.

Before I know it, she's on top of me and we've fallen to the floor.

"We don't need to. I can wait." What the fuck am I saying? My dick is begging to know her better, deeper. I don't fucking *want* to wait.

But my brain has taken over, despite my dick's protests, and the words just fall out.

"Fuck waiting."

Her response is priceless, and our clothes come off. She's definitely the girl for me.

chapter Fifty-Three;

It's nearly the weekend again, and once more I'm surprised by how much I look forward to them. Even with a free day in the middle this week, Friday looks so good from where I stand. Yet something is nagging at me despite my happy anticipation. I want to pair the high I'm feeling from my budding and legitimate relationship with Bee to the adrenaline rush of a new kill, but Eva is making it impossible.

I've had the best idea ever. I want to collect a donation, give it to Bee, and swim in excitement every time she wears it. It would mesh my two worlds, my two personalities, together so vividly. I'd never have to come down. It's the most intoxicating thought I've ever had. And I can't do shit about it. Eva's still following me, and it's starting to get under my skin. I mean, I know I've hated her for a while, but this is just pushing me further over the edge.

I know I have other things to deal with today anyway, so I set the idea of another playmate to the side until after I deal with the other matter. I need to break it off with Amelia. We've only been together twice, but I'm serious about giving this thing with Bee a shot, so I need to be clear with Mel that our torrid, short-lived affair ends now. It was fun, but we both knew it wouldn't last forever.

I know I need to do it, I want to do it, I just have no idea how.

I can't send her an email or a text. I have such little desire to do it in person, but I know I should. Everything else is just so impersonal. And what we did was personal enough to warrant a face-to-face conversation.

That doesn't have to make me excited about it, though.

I pull up my email and compose a quick note first.

From: Aidan Sheppard
To: Bee Iverson
Subject: Honesty

Since all of the cards are out on the table, and for some reason you still want to be with me, I have one last thing I need to do to set everything straight. I need to see Amelia to end it in person. I don't want to, but I think it's the only respectful way. As your boyfriend (do you like the term yet?) I wanted to let you know the plan, and offer you to be there too if you want. Just let me know.

Also, do you want to come over tonight? I'll cook you dinner this time, you just have to pretend it's good.

Yours,
Shep

Since I've planned to be as honest with Bee as I can, about everything except my extracurricular activities, she needed to be forewarned. Then it's not as if I was trying to see Mel on the sly one last time, and if she does decide to come, she can see for herself nothing happens.

In less than five minutes, Bee's reply dings in my inbox.

I have a little rush of nervousness before I open it. What if she thinks this is unacceptable? What if she's pissed I want to see Amelia to end it and wants to end it with me?

Calm the fuck down.

I remind myself to be a fucking grown up, and open the damn

email.

From: Bee Iverson
To: Aidan Sheppard
Subject: Girlfriend.

:) First, I love the term already.

And again you surprise me, in a good way. I do want to be there, but not for the reason I'm sure you think I do. I trust you, and I don't need to be there out of suspicion that anything would happen. I'd like to be there for your moral support. I know it's not going to be a fun conversation, and I'd like to stand next to you through it since I'm your girlfriend (the question is: do you like the term yet?) now.

And yes. When should I be over? I hope you're as good in the kitchen as you are on the floor.

See you tonight,
B

Again I feel like a teenager, giddy from a simple conversation with a girl, and again I ask myself *what the hell is happening to me*?

I respond to Bee, telling her to come over after work around five. Next I pull out my phone and text Amelia, asking her to come over around six. I don't want her to feel ambushed, though I'm even happier Bee will be there now she's agreed. I'm already feeling uncomfortable with the thought of what I'll need to say, and I'm glad Bee will be there to help ease my discomfort.

I may be a selfish prick, but at least I'm a selfish prick with the support I want.

***

I make a quick stop to the grocery store on my way home, hunting for ingredients to the unknown perfect dinner for Bee. She's proved such a good cook on our two dates at her place, so nothing feels good enough. The prefect meal eludes me.

I finally decide on steak, since I can make it pretty well on the grill. This grocery stop isn't as quick as I'd intended with all of the meandering around, but on top of that I pick up the components for my mom's double-fudge brownies. Bee hasn't baked yet, and maybe I can beat her on it.

After purchasing everything and heading outside, I can't stop myself from waving to the continuingly annoying Eva. *Still there.* She makes no indication she's seen me. She just continues to glare from behind the safety of her windshield.

I don't know if she can hear me from behind the glass, but regardless I can't stop myself from saying something. I knock on the glass first.

"You know, if you keep the same look on your face like that, it'll freeze."

She isn't looking at me, she didn't turn, she's looking forward as if she can't be bothered with my presence, despite the fact she's following me, but I see the irritation ripple across her features after I speak.

Score one for me.

I hop into my car after the satisfying exchange, knowing it'll likely come back to bite me in the ass. But it felt good for now.

As I start to make my way home, I notice Eva doesn't immediately follow. Maybe my talking to her made the realization of what she's been doing register. Or maybe she's gone off somewhere, shopping on her own for something to bother me with even more. Maybe she'll show up with a foghorn in the middle of the night.

Or maybe she just decided it's time for a shower.

Either way, I'm happy for the break, no matter how short, from her ever-dampening, ominous presence. Though, I'm torn when I remember what I was grocery shopping for. Yes, I'll be making dinner for Bee, which will be great, but it won't be great until after I have an honest and emotional conversation with Amelia.

Ugh.

chapter Fifty-Four,

After I made it home, and Bee came over, we sat and planned out our evening. It was a nice change to have someone else who isn't passive or shy helping me make decisions. With Jason, he always looks to me to make a call, but with Bee she's as confident and as opinionated as me. And she's willing to take both seats when either is appropriate; she can sit back and listen or speak up and make a choice.

At one point I was watching her pouty lips move as she spoke, and when my gaze moved to her eyes the thought that she's part of what I've been missing crossed my mind. Though taken aback, because I'm still not sure I ever want a lot of those things couples want, I still find myself wanting a lot more of Bee around. I found myself wondering if she'd be okay with a life together without kids and just each other. I thought about the future.

She and my playmates are the two things lately I've noticed I feel better after discovering. But how different those two things are.

"And then I slit his throat, and he died right there."

Wait, what? My stomach lurches. What the fuck did I miss?

"I knew you weren't listening," she says.

I almost pass out as relief flushes through me.

"You're hilarious."

"She's going to be here any minute. Are you nervous?"

She's worried about my feelings. That's sweet.

"No, not nervous exactly. I'm just ready for it to be over and for her to be gone." Bee nods her head in understanding, reaching over to squeeze my hand. I think she's more anxious than I am. I want to ease her worry since she didn't have to be here. She could've come over after the dust settled. "You know, I've never been with anyone as amazing as you are." She neglects to answer, just smiling. "I'm serious. I've never had an actual girlfriend before. You're the only one to get me to sit still." Though it wasn't the best explanation (feelings are too convoluted, weird, and squishy to talk about for long or in exact terms), I think she knew what I meant.

She's pretty much it.

"You're pretty awesome too, you know." And she leans in to kiss the corner of my mouth. Her hand slides up the back of my shirt, and it nearly burns where fingers touch bare skin. My nerves tingle where she's been.

And then the fucking doorknob jiggles, and we break apart as if our parents have caught us in the act.

"Fuck." I breathe out the word on a wave of frustration and uneasy anticipation.

"It'll be quick and painless." She has hope pouring off her tongue, but I have a feeling it will be unrealized hope. Maybe I'm wrong.

I wish I could push all of the responsibility on Bee, but I got myself into this. I gave into the temptation, and it was definitely fun while it lasted. I'm just not one to anticipate the unease of ending something.

Reluctantly I stand and walk, a little slower than I should, toward the door. She expected it to be open. Hopefully when it wasn't, it gave her a clue as to what's coming. Maybe she'll prepare herself accordingly. Plus Bee's car is parked in the driveway, which should have indicated something different.

But then again maybe not, with how our last encounter

developed.

As I open the door, I steel myself for whatever will come. I embrace a formal tone, hoping to clue her in. "Hello, Amelia. Thank you for coming."

She's wrapped tightly in a trench coat, and as she moves in toward me, maybe for a kiss, I quickly sidestep it backwards into the house. She follows me and makes no attempt to sweep the room with her gaze. Instead she drops the trench without saying anything and before I can stop her.

Underneath she's wearing nothing but a cheerleader skirt; she's topless...*and this situation just got real awkward.*

"Mel, don't," is all I get out before Bee clears her throat. I turn my focus on her to see a smirk on her face, and the knot that was forming in my stomach unclenches. She's amused. This may go worse for Amelia than I anticipated, but better for Bee and me.

And in the end, that's what I care more about.

"Shit." Amelia scrambles to pick up her coat, wrapping it around herself once more, while a shade of red I've yet to see on anyone before spreads across her cheeks. Maybe her embarrassment will contain her reaction.

"What the fuck's going on?" She shouts.

Or maybe not.

"I wanted to have this conversation in person, and Bee is here because she's a part of my life now." I hear a little cough of triumph from behind me on the couch but keep moving forward with my speech so it's over as quickly as possible. "I'm sorry I didn't give you more notice about what was happening tonight." I have to concede that, at least.

"So what did you want to tell me? You've found a happily ever after and you're done with me?" She has a bitchy little sneer on the edge of her lips I'd like to smack off.

"Yes. I wanted to tell you I won't be seeing you anymore, because Bee and I have begun an exclusive relationship." I hear Bee stand from her seat on the couch and walk over to me. She doesn't say anything because this is my mistake to fix, but her close proximity relaxes me a little more. She stands behind me with her hands on my back. The touch is all I need to get this over with.

"Are you fucking kidding me? Her? Over me? Seriously?" Uncalled for nastiness erupts from Amelia in the form of surprise and disbelief. She's obviously hurt, but it's not something I plan to allow.

"I'm not kidding. And, yes, Bee. You've chosen your path in life Amelia, but just because you're hurt or disappointed doesn't mean you should diminish mine." I take a steadying breath before continuing, and all amusement leaves Mel's face. She can see I'm dead serious. "And you need to hold your tongue on any further disparaging remarks about my girlfriend, or I won't remain so civil." Bee reaches around my waist with this, stepping forward a bit to stand at my side instead of behind me. It's a uniting stance, and it's intimidating to Amelia as she takes a hesitant step back toward the door.

After a moment to let everything sink, in Amelia lowers her voice and sounds menacing as she spouts off once more. "This is fucking ridiculous. I'm don't need to listen to this shit." And with that she whips around, storming out of my house, leaving the front door wide open.

I wasn't wrong about how it would go.

"At least it's over. I'm glad you were here," I say.

Bee walks around to face me and there's contentment evident in her eyes. She looks happier than I've seen her yet, and for some reason it sets a sea of serenity bobbing inside of me as well.

"I am, too." She reaches up, pulling my head to hers a bit more forcefully than her sweet touches were just before Mel arrived. My dick twitches in reaction as our tongues intertwine.

I'd gladly skip dinner.

As if she heard my thoughts, she pulls away to state, "Time for eats, kid. I want to see what skills you brought to the table." She looks playful as she hurries to the kitchen. She grabs a knife, pointing it at me. "And if you don't stack up..." But she ruins her threat with laughing.

"I have better skills in a different room." Feeling playful too, I wink at her, before turning her to press into her from behind.

"First we eat. Then we play." She turns and smiles sweetly. I can't resist her charms and walk outside to start the grill.

But I can't help myself as I throw over my shoulder to her, "Did I mention I like you a lot?"

chapter fifty-five:

After taking the evening to regroup, Amelia texted both me and Bee, apologizing for her rude behavior, for her nasty words. She explained her hormones had led to her outburst, and she was sincerely sorry. Adding she hopes we're happy and assuring us everything would be kept from Jason.

Good.

She ended the note with an invitation for both of us to have dinner with her and Jason sometime in the near future. *That would be so awkward.*

It'll never happen, especially since she told me the last time we slept together she plans to leave him soon. I guess it was her way of being polite, of making amends, but time needs to pass, and the dust needs to settle.

I watch Bee, snuggled on my couch in my sweatpants, watching TV, and can't look away. She looks happy, beautiful, watching a horribly gory scary movie and loving it. I jump over the back of the couch, landing right next to her.

"What should we do today? We have all day to do whatever you want." I wrap my arms around her neck and squeeze her playfully. She struggles to fend me off, but unfortunately for her I'm not ticklish. And the wonderful sound of her laughing proves she isn't worried I'll strangle her. The thought briefly floats from one side of my brain to the other that I have the strength to do it, though, if I wanted.

Strangle...What a great idea.

That'll be my plan for number four.

I move on from the thought so as not to stew in the possible excitement, since I have no idea when I'll be able to shake Eva long enough to have a number four, and I stand up to start whatever plans our day will hold.

***

After a lot of activity out and about today, I'm finally back home. Bee chose to head to her house instead of staying over again. Though I wouldn't have minded her here, I know she's more independent than most girls I've known, and she wanted some quiet time in her own space. That's a quality to respect, so I didn't say a word in debate.

With Bee gone, and my solidarity for the evening intact, I have some time to ponder a few things. The first question that comes to mind is: when will I be able to have another playmate? I can feel my nerves alight with the idea. But I also notice an underlying anxiety I hadn't realized was there before. I guess I've been too busy with Bee, Eva, and Amelia to truly feel how much I *want* another kill. Even right now I can feel the burning desire start to worm its way into my system. My mouth waters, and there's true discomfort deep inside me somewhere, between my groin and my gut.

These playdates are exhilarating. I feel a rush of emotion, sensation overload, and pure euphoria. Though up until now, it has been more of a want I've been fulfilling, not necessarily a need.

But it's shifted, and I *need* it now.

And I need it again *soon*.

It's an idea to begin looking for a hitchhiker tonight. I don't know how good or bad of an idea, but it is a possible idea. If I don't find one, then that's fine, but I think the search needs to start. *Soon*. I'll come up with some plan to evade Eva, the festering thorn in my side, if and when I find the lucky candidate to play with. Looking out the window, I see that sure enough her car is still parked across the street. Stupid bitch.

I walk back to the couch and flip on the TV for some mindless white noise company. My plan is to eat dinner and then head out for a searching expedition in the comfort of my car.

Thinking about the exciting prospect of finding someone as I slap a sandwich together, my heart stops as I hear breaking news cut into the fluff piece which was spouting nonsense only seconds ago. I run to the remote to crank up the volume. Then I rub my eyes to assure myself I'm actually seeing what I hope I'm not.

"Kate Masten's body has been found after spending weeks in the ice-cold water."

My breath hitches and I see spots in front of my eyes. My peripheral vision is starting to go black, and I grab onto the back of the couch for support then sink to the floor. I can't see the screen anymore, but I can still hear the horrifying words from the anchor's ruby red mouth.

"Authorities are divulging very little information right now, though it seems clear her death was not accidental or natural. The case is being treated as a homicide."

I unconsciously start to bang my head against the solid frame of the couch behind me as I face the kitchen from the cold floor. At the same time, I stamp my feet on the hardwood. I need to feel here, present, connected to something solid, or I may float away on a cloud of paralyzing fear and stabbing uncertainty.

I was careful.

I can't get caught.

Fucking fucker. Fuck, fuck, fuckity, fuck.

Every version of the word drops from my brain in a continuous string as the news report I can't turn off continues behind my back.

I try to control my breathing as I remember I anticipated her body would eventually be found. I didn't weight her down. I knew this day could come. *I just wasn't ready yet.* I try to remind myself no matter how much I freak out there's no true connection to us besides DNA, and I destroyed all of that evidence.

I think I need to melt down right now. Yes, that sounds like an acceptable reaction.

I shoot upright to my feet as my hands twist into my hair, and I have to resist the urge to pull it out in fistfuls. This isn't how I wanted to end such a pleasant day. I had plans for an amazing night.

My feet take control, pacing from the living room to the kitchen, back again, and continuing over and over without any intention of stopping. I'd be wearing a pattern if there were carpet under me. With all of the frustrations that've been building up in my life lately, this just seems to be the pinnacle, tipping the scales from rational into batshit fucking crazy irrational.

I stop my pacing midstride, whipping around to my front door. I don't put on shoes. I don't add a jacket. I move at lightning speed without stopping to think. My muscles take over, leaving my brain back in the living room to sulk. As the soles of my feet slap against the ice-cold pavement, I idly note I don't yet feel the sting of cold. I will later.

I'm to Eva's car in a matter of seconds, before she has a chance to register what I'm doing, and before I've even decided what I plan to do when I get there. Standing next to her driver's side, I start banging my fists on her window. I know it won't break from the force of my hands, so no real damage will be made, but it will get my point across.

Eva's face morphs from confident to terrified. Finally she seems to realize what she's been doing. I'm larger, wider, stronger, and much fucking crazier than she'll ever be. She never should have started this idiotic revenge shit.

As each thump continues to land against her glass, my mouth moves of its own accord. I'm not thinking about what I'm screaming before it comes out, but that doesn't make it any less satisfying.

"You fucking psycho bitch. I'm done with your crazy fucking shit." Each satisfying utterance of fuck is accompanied by a connection of skin to glass. And each loud crack forces Eva to shrink further into herself and away from the window she seems sure will break into her face. "You need to stop fucking stalking me or you're going to fucking regret it when the fucking police drag you away. You've already lost your fucking job, which you weren't even qualified for in the first fucking place, so why do you feel the need to also lose every small fucking piece of dignity you had left? You're fucking pathetic, following me around like you're going to fucking intimidate me." I'm almost out of breath as well as steam, though I push on for one last insult. "Get a fucking life, you useless piece of shit."

Instead of waiting to listen to a rebuttal, I turn and tromp right back through my still-open front door into the warmth of my house. Once inside, my toes start to sting, but I relish it. At least there's adrenaline pumping through my veins now, and I've lost the frozen paralysis. I have a feeling other than fear crushing me.

After locking my door, I put on socks, grab a blanket, and camp out on the couch in front of the television. I need to know all of what's known about The-One-Who-Doesn't-Count's murder.

chapter Fifty-six:

I watch horrified, yet glued to every second of the horror. My eyes are dry, and they sting from bulging without blinking for so long. My thoughts move slowly, and I don't feel anything but numb.

I know where my missing watch went now. The police found it for me. It went down with The-One-Who-Doesn't-Count. It went into the water with her body. It went there and now it's been brought back. With her. The two are connected. Forever.

I can never take back the costly mistake.

There weren't pictures of it on the news, thankfully. Still, I know it's mine. There's no one else it could belong to. The reports said among the debris the police located a men's watch, and they're sure it didn't belong to The-One-Who-Doesn't-Count.

They're sure.

And they're testing for DNA.

I don't know if there will be any left after so long in the corrosive ocean water, but they're looking. And they hope to find some, so they'll look extensively. There isn't a silver lining for me tonight either, because even if they come up empty on a bright red DNA arrow pointing to me, they'll start trying to locate the owner in other ways. I have no idea if my watch had a serial number or if it's traceable, but I fucking hope not.

I watch.

And I watch.

And I watch, wishing I had been more careful.

***

Ten hours after learning of her waterlogged body's find, I feel just as awful as when the news first broke. I've reminded myself over and over I took extensive efforts to destroy almost every link to myself. All but the damn watch. I try to hold desperately onto the knowledge it should be impossible to find me, to blame me, to connect me to The-One-Who-Doesn't-Count.

I should be okay.

I should still be safe.

But I don't feel that way yet. Not at all.

The thought that works to calm me down enough to sleep is: if they're going to tie her to me, there's nothing I can do about it now. I don't need to look suspicious. In fact, I need to live my life *normally*.

Choosing the path I have will always keep me at some level of risk. I can't get rid of it all no matter how smart I think I am. I could be caught at any time for any of my playmates. So I need to live every moment to the fullest and remember to make myself happy at every turn.

I can't live in fear, and I resolve I won't.

***

"Leave me alone. I can't take it anymore." My voice is hoarse, scratching my throat.

"Why on earth would I do that? I'm just getting to the fun part."

Looking up, I see someone familiar straddling me. A knife at my throat. In the back of my mind I tell myself I should know who she is. Yet that small voice is overpowered by the louder, angrier one screaming in my face determined to hurt me.

She stabs me over and over. I should be dead. There's blood everywhere. How can there be any left in me? I keep trying to fight, but nothing's working. My arms are heavy and my legs are bound together.

It's much more fun being the enforcer of pain than the one feeling it.

"You can't take what you dish out?"

"I'm not meant to." I scream in her face.

This isn't how it's supposed to be.

"I'm making you better. This will make you stronger. You'll be better because of me. You're *better* with me."

And it comes to me. I know who she is. And I know what she wants.

I try to say her name, only I can't because she's severed my vocal cords.

***

So I was able to sleep. It was fitful, and not without nightmares or thrashing, but I slept nonetheless. I stayed in bed until the sun started to go down once again. It's now Sunday evening, and I've wasted the entire day.

But I'm finally starting to feel safer. Safe enough to be me again. So the day had purpose.

I may have decided to live fully, but that'll start tomorrow. I won't be looking for my next playdate tonight. I don't think my heart would be in it.

I get up, dragging myself to the living room. There's no need to get dressed. I'll be alone until work tomorrow. Since Bee is working today, I have no one to impress. I look out the window, and a smile breaks the plane of my face for the first time since Bee went home yesterday. Eva's still gone.

Thank fucking god.

She peeled away after my violent outburst last night and hasn't come back since. I don't want to hold my breath, but I seriously hope she's come to her senses and is gone for good. Maybe I scared her straight, or I could've just scared her shitless. Either way, if it prevents her from following me anymore I'm fine with it.

Back on the couch, I decide not to watch the news tonight. Any update on the autopsy or investigation of The-One-Who-Doesn't-Count can wait. I need to regain more of my previous and natural resolve before watching any more that will send my stomach to the floor.

I don't regret what I've done, and if I could take it back I wouldn't, so I need to stop worrying. I just need the time to calm down and return to normal.

chapter Fifty-seven:

After three or four beers, and well into my second action movie, I'm feeling a lot closer to the normal I wanted to return to. I'm starting to wonder if there's a healing quality to Sundays. Something about them just makes life easier.

My movie ends, and I switch from the DVD to live TV while I make myself something to eat. The alcohol is going a little too quickly to my head without food in my stomach, and I have to work tomorrow. Banter between fictional characters fills the room as I dig for leftovers in the fridge.

Maybe I should just order something. My fridge looks like a bachelor lives here.

As the sitcom moves into a commercial, I regret ever switching from the menu of my movie.

Are you fucking serious?

"News tonight at ten. Another woman missing shortly after the retrieval of the last. Should women be fearful? Learn more at ten."

I can't take it again so soon.

I saw Kristi's face and my suspicion was confirmed, with taunting from the same beautiful anchor who's been mocking me lately. Her concern is like spit in my face. I can't escape. It's just one blow after another, and I'm struggling not to run from the force weighing down on me. The urge to hide in a deep hole is getting stronger as complications arise.

But I know running, and hiding, will only bring suspicion. I can't give in.

I flick the TV off, forgetting my thoughts of food. Instead I head to the shower. I can't help but cling to the idea a hot shower can wash my worries away. A hot shower can drown out the outside world.

Under the water, I turn my face to its heat. I imagine every negative emotion pent up inside me washing away, down the drain, after being expelled with each loud exhale. As my breathing becomes deeper and more rhythmic, I notice something better and more confident returning.

But of course those happy thoughts aren't long-lasting. What the fuck else did I expect this weekend?

The window in the bathroom fills with red and blue flashing lights. They seem to beat against me harder than any fist could. I'm stuck, rooted to the spot, by confusion and terror. I can't hear the sirens over the pounding water around me, but I know they're going off outside.

Is this it?

Am I finished?

Have they connected me to my playmates? Is my world about to end?

I turn off the shower once movement seems to connect with my brain again and rush, naked, to the bathroom window. I was right; I can hear the sirens now since the water isn't running to cover it up. And they're loud.

The cars are right outside.

Everything seems to dull in my peripherals. Colors all fade to gray, and the sounds of the police cars wane. I watch in amazement as the room tips sideways, the ceiling getting farther away.

Then there's nothing.

Chapter Fifty-Eight

I fainted. I fucking fainted.

When I realize this, my head is pounding. I check in the mirror and there are no cuts, though there may be a bruise later. I have no time to examine any longer, because hard thumping knocks sound at my front door.

They're ready to take me away.

But I won't run. It would only look worse.

Even if they drag me away right now, even if they charge me, who's to say it would stick? Their case isn't airtight. A watch isn't enough to lock me away. No jury would be convinced with the little evidence they have.

I quickly wrap a towel around my waist, trying to breathe normally as I walk to the door. As I turn the knob, I wonder if they'd let me put clothes on before shoving me into the backseat. It's freezing, so I'd hope so.

"Police." A deep voice booms from the other side, just before the door opens.

"Can I help you, officers?"

Breathe.

"Mr. Jacobson?" The older of the two men speaks. The other stands silently, taking in my lack of clothing and confident posture.

I glance at their nametags, stalling for time. Officer Brown and Officer Lawrence look ready to strike.

Keep breathing.

My time is up.

"Mr. Jacobson, when was the last time you were at Delta's?" The other officer cuts in.

No.

"It's not a good idea to lie to us. Just answer the question. We know you were there, and we know what you did while you were there." The older cop takes over once again. They are almost tripping over each other.

I feel faint again.

Kristi is the only thing I can think about. Her face is the only thing I see. Her haggard, wrinkly skin replaces first one officer, then the next, leaving two uniformed dead women interrogating me. I *was* at Delta's, they're right. And I did do something really bad to the waitress who used to work there.

"Are you listening to me, Jacobson?" The younger one reaches out and shakes my shoulder. His contact is the jolt I needed.

Wait...did he say Jacobson?

"That's not my name. I'm Aidan Sheppard."

Could it be?

Lawrence looks to Brown for reassurance before continuing. "Is this 3057?"

Holy fuck, it could.

I point to the mailbox on the street and its brass numbers. "I'm 3061. Fifty-seven is next door." Again I point them in the right direction.

I don't need to remind myself to breathe anymore.

"Thanks. Sorry to bother you, sir. Have a nice evening."

And then they leave. They walk down my steps, down my driveway. Neither turns around. Neither stops and comes back to arrest me. As I strain, I can hear yelling from the house next to mine as well. They weren't looking for me. My heart soars, and I slam my door closed.

The police weren't here for me.

They weren't here to arrest me for murder.

Holy fucking shit.

I jump up twice with my hands in the air and a smile on my face that could crack concrete. But my luck runs out as my feet meet hardwood for the second time.

I slip and fall hard on my ass.

Fuck.

Nothing more than a groan comes out as the pain twinges, radiating from where I touch floor. There was too much water dripping from my skin to the now-slippery surface beneath me.

It hurts, and I'm annoyed at my own behavior, but I'll take a bruised ass over life in prison.

As I slowly get up, I realize how close my nerves came to breaking. It was all too much. The sheer panic, the rush of relief, it's all been overwhelming. I've come so fucking close to losing everything this weekend.

More than once.

As the emotions ebb, exhaustion sets in. I can barely stand any longer, and I take the cue to limp to bed. I can't take one more thing today. I wiggle beneath the sheets, still wet and naked, and I couldn't care less.

As I drift off, the sirens stop, yet the lights keep flashing in my room. With the fear gone, they create more of a hazy quality to the room. And I can still hear the shouts left over from some domestic dispute feet away from my bedroom.

But the yelling isn't what rips me from the precipice of sleep.

Two sharp staccato raps at my front door jar me awake.

You've got to be fucking kidding me.

Instead of dressing, or even looking for my discarded towel, I drag my sheets with me and hold them in front of my dick. Anyone stupid enough to be bothering me right now deserves any shock they get from my state of dress.

"What?" I try hard not to yell, though I still say the word too loud. There may be some accusation laced in the syllable as well. I just want to sleep.

No one answers. There isn't anyone standing on the other side of my door. There isn't even anyone running away. It's just empty, and it's cold. Maybe I imagined the sounds. But then the frigid wind whistles by, whipping something into view.

A note's taped to the outside of my door.

Someone was here. But they're gone now.

I grab it, letting the door swing closed. Something stirs in the pit of my stomach, knowing I don't want to read this. So I lock the deadbolt and limp back to bed before looking. But I can't wait forever; it can't be ignored.

It's typed. I won't be doing any amateur writing analyses then.

I hold my breath and begin to read.

Aidan,

I know whose watch they found in the water. I know what you've done. I know what you are. I've been watching you.

I read it twice, then crumple it up, turning off my bedside light. But seconds later I sit up, switch it back on, and reread it three more times. I don't learn anything new. The words never change.

Someone's been watching.

Someone other than Eva has been watching me, and for longer. It can't be her, because I haven't had a playdate or collected a donation since she became my shadow. Someone else out there knows. Someone knows my darkest secret, knows who I am inside, only they didn't threaten me. They didn't ask for anything.

They just told me they know.

I burn the note, flushing the ashes down the toilet. Though after I finish, there isn't much else I can do besides sleep. If they're watching, and they know, then all I can do is wait.

They'll have to have a playdate eventually, but first we'll have to be introduced.

I can wait. I can be patient if they aren't going to the police yet.

I'll deal with it, but only when the time's right.

With that resolution, sleep finally catches me and wraps me up in oblivion.

Chapter Fifty-Nine:

Monday morning's light breaks too soon after my eyes closed. They feel as raw as my ass, but despite the ache my nerves are surprisingly calm. Nothing a little aspirin and coffee can't fix, which is exactly what I grab on my way out of the house to work.

I still believe my anonymous admirer is going to keep quiet. There probably isn't any DNA on the watch. And Eva is again missing from the neighborhood's landscape. I've received no calls, no knocks on my door for questioning, and I'm beginning to think there never will be. No suspicion has been thrown my way despite the ample amount of time there's been for it. No repercussions seem to be blowing toward me, and because of this my steps into work are much lighter than they would've been had I been walking in this weekend.

Life isn't so bad.

As I walk up to our adjoining offices, I notice Jason is already inside and settled. He must have gotten in early. Show-off. So much for work as usual. I knew he'd cave. I lean into his office to say hello, still in an upbeat mood.

"How was your weekend?"

Right now I have no qualms about stupid chitchat with Jason. He can talk up and down about Kama Sutra positions with Amelia, and

I won't blink an eye.

"Boring. Didn't do shit. What about you?"

Taking a second to look at Jason instead of past him or into my own thoughts, I notice how weathered he looks. His normal exuberance is missing. It's been replaced by fatigue and annoyance. He's hunched as if a lot is sitting on his shoulders. I debate asking Jason what's wrong, but think better before I do. He usually shares with me when he's ready. And if he hasn't yet, then he isn't ready.

"Well, Bee and I are officially a couple now. I have a girlfriend. How weird is that?"

Jason's jaw drops as his eyes widen. He sits still, staring at me shocked without answering, and I struggle against laughter but end up losing the fight.

Probably in response to my amusement, Jason snaps his mouth closed, jumping up to come toward me. "Wow, that's great. When did this happen? His heavy hands slap me on the back, and then he envelops me in a hug. As he pulls back he adds, "When can you guys come over for dinner to celebrate?" His last question echoes the sentiment in Amelia's apology message after the blowup. I guess when you've been together long enough you start to think alike.

I'd love to answer *never*, but I bite it back.

An odd question floats through my mind before I come up with a better answer, and I wonder if Bee will start to think like me if we stay together long enough.

"Thanks. We'll have to get together soon, for sure." Quickly Jason looks distracted again, and this time I have to point it out. "Something on your mind?"

"Yeah…Sorry." I wave off his apology and wait for him to continue. "Dan sent out an email already this morning. They're announcing who will fill Eva's spot later today."

"Wow. That's exciting, right? Who do you think it'll be?"

I doubt it's me; I wasn't on my game like I was months ago, and I don't want it like I did then either. I seriously don't know who they'll choose this time. It feels much closer than before. I wonder if it'll be Sarah.

"I'm guessing you or Sarah. Who do you think?"

Maybe it will be her.

"Definitely not me. I didn't care enough like I did last time. I'm happy where I am, actually. Sarah would make a good boss, though." Jason's face falls a fraction of an inch, and anyone else watching wouldn't notice, but I've known him too long not to.

"Yeah, she will." I start to turn, then hear Jason open his mouth to add something. "Hey, it seems you're not the only one who's lost his watch lately."

I stop breathing. Stop thinking. At least my mouth still works.

"What?"

"Yeah, didn't you see on the news? They found that missing girl, and the sicko who killed her left his watch with her body. I bet it's some freaky calling card and we're about to be bombarded with reports of other missing people and a warning to beware."

"That's insane."

"I know. I bet they'll come up with some weird name for him, too. Maybe something like: The Watch-er."

"Shit."

"Exactly."

I have no idea what else to say. Jason continues babbling, and I watch his every move. Listen intently to his every word. Does he know? Is he the one who left the note? I swallow down bile every few seconds as it threatens to explode from me. But he never looks suspicious. He never again brings up I've also lost my watch. He just gossips about the news with his friend.

He doesn't know. It wasn't him.

He's as clueless as ever, and I let the wave of emotions subside.

After a few more moments of Monday morning catch-up, to cover up my wave of idiotic fear, we head to our respective desks to begin the workday.

chapter sixty;

Just after lunch, our department is called into the conference room for the big announcement. I have zero anxiety, because I know it won't be me, but I'm full of curiosity about who has been chosen to fill Eva's shoes. Whoever steps up will look amazing compared to her.

After everyone sits down, Dan clears his throat, signaling he's about to begin. "I know we've had a rough road behind us guys, but I have an immense amount of confidence backing my decision for who will lead us down a new road to the future. Everyone who interviewed would make a great leader, and my decision was incredibly hard. It wasn't hard because I had a lack of talent to choose from, but instead I had so much I couldn't include it all in one choice." He's building this up. If whoever he chooses fucks up he's going to look like a huge idiot. Again. "So without further ado, I'd like everyone to congratulate Jason Moore on his new promotion."

Holy shit.

Everyone starts clapping, and it's obvious a good decision was made. Jason will do well, and he'll be respected. I stand before anyone else, while it still seems to be sinking in for him, to clap Jason on the shoulders. "Congratulations. The best man won." I smile proudly for my friend.

As everyone titters with excitement, taking their turns to say how excited they are for Jason, I make my way to Dan. I extend my hand in a request to shake his, and without hesitation he returns the favor.

"It was close." Dan's volume is low enough so I'm the only one to hear. "You were our next choice, Aidan. Jason just seemed to want it more."

"I couldn't agree more. He deserves it. He's the best man for the job." And I mean it.

Dan sobers. "Have things been any better for you? I can't believe after harassing you at work Eva's turned to stalking you."

"It's awful. She's crazy. But hopefully it'll stop soon." A little sympathy never hurt anything.

"Hopefully."

After nodding, Dan moves to speak with Jason.

***

After a great day, I couldn't be happier sitting on Bee's couch with her legs across my lap. I even let her pick some stupid show about cooking without making her beg. I felt generous, because as I left work Eva was still missing, as well as a police presence.

"Are you bummed Jason got it over you?" Bee's already asked something along these lines twice, and both times I've said no. She seems to think I'm hiding hurt feelings. But actually, I'm content.

"I'm not. Seriously," I add when her eyes narrow. "More money would've been nice, but without the extra responsibility I get to spend more time with my distrusting girlfriend." I sneak my fingers up the side of her shirt to tickle her soft skin.

After she's gasping for breath, I finally relent.

"Okay, okay. I believe you." She hiccups from all the air she's gulped before continuing. "Good answer, by the way."

"Haven't you learned yet? I always know what to say." She laughs and hiccups at the same time, but I don't get to enjoy the sound as my cell phone starts ringing.

After looking at it, I report, "It's Jason. Should I answer?"

Bee nods. "Yeah, I bet he's calling to tell us where to meet him and Mel for a celebratory drink. Not that that won't be awkward. We can fake it, though." Her smile is a little sinister. She's cooking something up.

I answer expecting the same as Bee, but we're both way off. Before I can even say hello, I'm greeted by choked sobs. "What's going on? Who's hurt?" The concern in my voice is evident, and Bee's features quickly match mine. We both sit up straighter, waiting for his response.

"Amelia's gone." He doesn't say anything else. I know Bee heard too. She's already up and moving toward the front door.

"We're coming over." I hang up the phone and join Bee. Since we're only a few houses down we walk the short distance, jogging really, and go into the Moore house without knocking.

It's empty, eerily quiet. Mel must have taken the girls with her. We walk in past the entryway and see Jason sitting on the stairs to the second floor facing us. He's pulled himself together a little bit since we hung up moments ago.

"I didn't even get a chance to tell her about my promotion. She just said it's over. I know we've been fighting lately. I just never thought she'd leave. I couldn't convince her otherwise. Aidan...I...she's gone." He refrains from crying audibly, but a few tears leak from his lids and spill down his fat cheeks.

"I'm so sorry."

I walk over, sitting next to him on the stairs. I sling my arm around his shoulders and just sit there with him. I don't say much more. I look to Bee, and I can tell she feels the same. We want to be here for him, but we keep quiet more than we would for someone else, because we know too much.

Bee interjects an amazing idea. "Let's go get drunk at Z."

Jason lets out a halfhearted bark of laughter.

"That's the best idea I've ever heard, Bee. You're pretty great."

He stands slowly, and we all move outside.

"I'll drive." Bee starts to protest, but I shake my head. I lean in toward her and whisper, "I'll drive so you can drink with Jason, and I'll take advantage of you later." I wink at her as her smile spreads wide. I add one last thing before we all get into my car. "He's right, you know. You're pretty fucking great."

chapter sixty-one:

We all got through the night. Bee and I both stayed with Jason after getting him home from Z. The empty house upset him too much, and we felt too bad to leave him alone. I didn't get to take advantage of Bee like I'd hoped. But we made it through to the next morning. Everyone alive and breathing.

And since the news, Jason's been stellar at work. He *did* deserve the new position. Though, after work for the past two nights he's attached himself to me and Bee like his life depends on it, like glue. He's been clingy, but he's agreed he won't be intruding again tonight. And I can't really blame him. After ridding myself of Eva I don't want to add a new tail, so I asked for one night off. He seems to be doing much better.

I don't think he'd ever admit it, but maybe he'll be better off.

***

Just before leaving work, I check my email.

But I wish I hadn't.

From: Anonymous
To: Aidan Sheppard
Subject: Don't forget I know

Aidan,

I thought you would appreciate this video. When I stumbled across it, it reminded me of you.

Enjoy,
Your friend

I click the link embedded and watch as a video pulls up.
What the fuck am I in for?
I know I shouldn't, but I hold my breath as the seconds tick by while it buffers. There's no way this can be good for me. Then finally it's ready, and I start breathing again but too quickly this time. As it starts with a black screen, a raspy voice croons things about abusing and being abused.
Well isn't that just a peachy little bit of music.
Fuck.
The screen comes to life with color, and I have to slap my hand over my mouth to prevent drawing any attention to my office. I bite my lip, hard, to keep silent as blood flows across my computer's monitor, and it tastes like iron in my mouth. The video is a compilation of death scenes in scary movies. Every clip is gory. Every death stabs me deeper. There are so many I lose count. Some have drawn-out monologues, but others are quick with no preamble. It's a movie of my life, what it is and what it can be, acted out by others.
I feel like I might faint again.
Or throw up.
Or have a heart attack.
This is terrifying.
It's thrilling.
The video is over ten minutes long. I watch it in its entirety. And

then I watch it again, silent the second time.

I don't stand up to leave the office until half an hour after I normally do, and I'm sure I look like a zombie the whole way out.

***

The video, that disturbing video, didn't deter me. Maybe it should have, maybe I've lost my damn mind, but my plans for tonight remain the same. I need an outlet. I need to get back to what I'm good at. In other circumstances, I would have drawn inspiration from the scenes in the video. It could have been something helpful, something special. But instead it was a reminder someone is on to me.

I tried to respond, but immediately after sending the link my *friend* disabled the email account. I couldn't have someone else trace the address without raising a lot of questions, either. Next, I tried to attack through the video after email failed. There were no comments posted below since it was only uploaded today. And the account that created it is both blocked and anonymous. That's where I hit a second dead end.

And then I quit, with nothing else I knew how to do.

It evoked a sense of helplessness and rage throughout me. It made me want to scream. It made me want to cry out for help. It made me want to turn tail, running to an uninhabited part of the world where no one has ever heard of Aidan Sheppard.

And it made me want to kill.

Which is why, after calming the fuck down, my plans for tonight stayed unchanged.

Bee has to work on another writing deadline, so I have the evening to myself, and since Eva's still gone, I'm using it to take a drive. Regardless of finding a hitchhiker or not, *I will* have fun tonight. I'll find some nobody and take her to the woods.

This isn't an *if*. It's a definite.

Then she won't be a nobody anymore. She'll be a somebody, a

somebody to me. She'll be a playmate.

I've been waiting long enough and my need, my hunger, is pulsing stronger than it ever has before. I can feel it all the way down to my toes. Tonight I'll satisfy my inner darkness with warm, slick blood. I'll wash my hands in it as it seeps out.

This is the thought I cling to as I pat my kit next to me on the passenger seat.

chapter sixty-two;

After two hours of driving along the highway, my excitement and adrenalin have subsided, leaving a void in their wake. I feel emptier and hungrier than I did before embarking on this search.

I'm disappointed.

And I still feel the *need* for a donation.

Maybe I should've looked for someone else. I could've looked for another prostitute, or another homeless woman living in a cardboard box. Either one would've been a surer bet. But I didn't go that route.

I didn't, because I've already walked down those paths. I don't mind if I stumble upon a happy coincidence and find a female who happens to fit into one of those two categories. But I don't want to go looking for the exact same occurrence I had before. I want each experience to be as different as I can make them. That's what my adrenaline thrives on.

I'd prefer to find a hitchhiker, or someone in a parking lot, or walking down the street, anyone new, anyone different, anyone exciting.

Once I hit the three-hour mark, I decide it's time to turn around. It's time to give up. It just isn't meant to be tonight, and I can't afford to push it. Not with so many variables flying around lately. With Eva, my new anonymous friend, and the news reports, I can't take another possible problem. Up until this point I used to have a lot of luck on my side, and I don't want to push it away. No, I want as much luck as I can get, so if it isn't supposed to happen tonight then I shouldn't force it.

Three hours away. *Fuck.* I shouldn't have driven in a straight line away from home. Now I have three hours to drive back with nothing to show for it and nothing to keep me happy.

I flip my turn signal and U-turn in the middle of the highway, prepared for the long drive home. At least I'll have plenty of time to think of future plans, weapons, and execution styles. It won't be a completely wasted chunk of hours.

No more than one minute down the other side of the highway, I almost shit my pants. There's a hitchhiker. A petite, young, female hitchhiker, with long hair whipping in the cold, is walking the opposite way from which I was just driving. If I hadn't driven this far before turning around then I'd never have spotted her. I have no idea how I missed her before, even though she was on the other side.

Fate gives me a kiss yet again. A wet sloppy kiss which leads me to number four. Perfect little number four.

I slow down next to the hitchhiker and let my passenger window roll down slowly. "Where ya headed?" I keep my tone light, hoping a single man won't be too intimidating to accept a ride from. I'd rather not have to get out and chase her, chancing a car spotting me.

"As far as you can take me in that direction." She points the way she was walking, the direction toward home.

I click the unlock button, and she immediately reaches for the door. I can see the confidence rolling off her as she does. Independent and smarter than everyone else. She thinks she can handle it all, and she isn't worried about me.

What stupid assumptions.

"It's freezing out there. How long have you been waiting for someone to help you out? Hopefully not too long." As we pull back on the highway, my car automatically locks itself. Such a convenient technological feature.

"I've been walking for about an hour, and it *is* fucking cold. Thanks for picking me up. I think if I had to walk much longer some of my toes would've fallen off. I'm not exactly dressed for this." She gestures down her bare legs.

"No, you're not." I keep my eyes forward, but my hands are itching to wrap themselves around her legs, her throat, her heart.

"Thanks a lot...what's your name?"

You don't need to know, bitch.

Instead of answering, I brace myself and then slam hard on the breaks.

Hitchhiker's head slams forward, hitting with a crunch into the dash. I'll have to clean that up later. Should've stolen Jason's car again. Oh well, blood can be cleaned.

And the beautiful blood I've needed starts to ooze from a fresh cut on her forehead. Her eyes roll back, and she loses consciousness, but I know it won't last long. In a moment of weakness, I take precious time to slap her face hard once. She doesn't stir, and the handprint forming is satisfying. It's almost as satisfying as when I rip her shirt open, exposing her milky white skin.

Shit. I need to get off the main road.

I drive a few blocks and find a patch of thick trees to conceal the dirty deeds I'm about to indulge in.

Hitchhiker starts to stir as I pull her from her feet out of the car after parking it. I don't take the time to savor; I'm starving for this, and it's going to be quick. Her head hits the ground with a loud crack against the gravel. The disturbance is enough to bring her back to consciousness.

She starts to thrash around, though no amount of kicking will free her ankles from my gloved hands. For some reason, she hasn't started screaming, which is helpful this time. Typically I'd like to savor in her torment, but at the moment I don't know how close or far away a house with inhabitants is, so quieter is better tonight.

Before she has a chance to change her mind, I rip off a long strip of duct tape and slap it across her face, dropping her ankles for her wrists instead. That way she can't tear the tape off.

And I continue to drag her across the harsh landscape. I laugh as rough bark, rocks, and whatever else pull and rip at her skin as her own weight works against her. I watch as tears stream down her face. She should have known better than to hitchhike. It isn't safe. And with me she never had a chance. The minute she walked up to my car, her hope flew away with the cold wind.

"Normally, I'd banter back and forth with you, give you a speech about how much fun I'm about to have, delight in your last efforts to fight, but not tonight. My delay of gratification skills seems to be diminishing the longer I go between playdates with pretty little things like you. So tonight, fuck the side dishes, we're going straight to the entrée."

Her eyes go dim as I finish. Their spark faded, yet I still need the blood.

I kneel down, wrapping my fingers around her throat. My gloves are cold against her skin, and her fight fails quickly. She kicks and claws at my back for a few moments, but as her brain struggles without oxygen she goes limp. All that's left with movement are her eyes. I watch her eyes closely, my adrenaline surging. It spikes in an addicting pattern as I watch her face turn red. Her pupils dilate, and her gaze goes unfocused.

Finally she welcomes the death I'm about to bestow upon her, and again my body feels alight with electricity. I'm amazed how I've been lucky enough to have another different experience. This will *never* get old.

Soon she's dead, yet I continue holding her throat. I never want to come down from my high. But a new feeling creeps into me. Again I've had an exhilarating experience of taking a life, and again I want to pair it with a sexual one. But I don't want to chance any more evidence than necessary, so I refrain.

I'll just have to see Bee when I get home tonight, no matter the hour.

The thought kicks me into a hurried cleanup mode, and I get to work.

As I start to dig the hole to bury her in, I hear the snap of a twig and my heart stops. But before I can turn around, a horribly familiar voice scrapes at my eardrums.

"Holy fucking shit. And you said I was crazy."

"Hello, Eva," I answer.

Chapter Sixty-Three:

I turn around slowly to a gun pointed at my chest.

How the fuck am I going to get out of this one?

"Now they'll have to give me my job back, or at least give me your job, when I tell the police *and* Dan what you've been doing when you're not at work."

My god, she seriously is a crazy fucking bitch.

I thought she'd stopped following me. I thought my luck had turned around.

I guess I thought wrong.

"I think we can come to an agreement here, Eva. I know your survival instincts are as strong as my need for self-preservation." I need to come up with some plan. How can I take her down while she holds a gun...without getting shot in the process? My mind is racing, but nothing of substance comes to the surface.

"No, what's going to happen is you following me to my car, then I'll handcuff you inside and take you to jail where you'll confess everything." Her voice is more menacing with each syllable, and her features get wider. Her face muscles twitch, and she glances around a few times. Is she hearing things? With shifty eyes, shaking arms, and bared teeth like a dog, I can tell she's about to lose it, and I don't want to be standing in line with the gun when she does.

"I don't think so."

I strive to sound calm while every muscle is strained to the breaking point.

And then to my left I hear another rustle that shouldn't be there. Someone else is here. *Who the fuck else could it be?* Have the police followed Eva and come to take me away? But I recognize the pattern of the steps, and it's much worse than the police being here.

Before I can take another breath, Bee launches herself at Eva, knocking her over in one swift move. When they both tumble to the ground I reach for the discarded gun, ready to shoot Eva, except I don't have a shot. I won't hit Bee, and the two aren't separated enough as they wrestle in the dirt.

First Bee is on top, and then somehow she's underneath Eva again. Dirt is flying, and I do nothing but hold my breath. Hair gets pulled. There's the dull thump of fist finding thinly covered bone.

But then Bee gets the upper hand, straddling Eva.

"You picked the wrong girl's boyfriend to mess with."

Bee's voice is as calm as mine was when trying to reason with Eva, but I have the suspicion she isn't faking hers. She's the one in control.

"Who the fuck are you?" Eva's question comes out in a shriek.

"The last person you're ever going to see." Bee pulls out a plastic bag from her pocket and presses it against Eva's face, blocking every hole for oxygen. I continue to stand there without saying a word.

I'm dumfounded.

I'm confused.

I'm horny.

I'm in fucking shock.

Bee watches as Eva takes her last strangled breath, and then Eva's life is gone as quickly as the hitchhiker's was. Bee then stands slowly, cleaning herself off before turning around to face me. When she does there's questioning on her face.

It all happened so fast I feel like we've been on fast-forward, and I'm just trying to catch up.

She looks to the ground, shielded by her lashes, and she can't stop wringing her hands. She wasn't scared when attacking Eva. She wasn't anxious killing her. But now she's nervous to face my reaction.

She takes a deep breath, starting to speak while looking at the ground.

"I've watched you before tonight. I've been keeping tabs on you since we were introduced. I felt something kindred right away. I believed you were like me. Then, when I found out I was right, when I saw what you did under the protective darkness of night, I was ecstatic. I'd confirmed we like the same things. I knew who you were, and I still wanted to be with you, because we're the same. I'm the 'anonymous friend.'" She uses her fingers like quotation marks, pausing before going on. "I wanted to prepare you for when I'd tell you everything. I *am* just like you."

She pauses again, finally looking into my eyes.

But the pause is briefer this time. "I know when you look inside yourself you see nothing but darkness." I take a step toward her, discarding Eva's gun at my feet. "Only that's not what I see as I look inside you. I see perfection. I see a beautiful darkness that matches my own. I want to be with you in all areas. I want to do this together, instead of both of us on our own." She looks down at her hands again as she wrings them, waiting for a reply.

She's so nervous it's affecting me.

She's like me. She kills people. In fact, she just watched me murder someone, then did the same, and now she's nervous about what I'm going to think.

"I love you," she utters.

My brain is somewhere back in the hole I was digging for the hitchhiker, but I don't give a fuck. My gut has done me well at every turn, and I've never felt stronger about anything else in my entire life. I know what I want, and I'll never let it slip away.

"Bee, will you marry me so we can live a life together with date nights like this all the time?"

She flings herself into my arms, laughing, and we fall to the ground. My pants are down around my ankles faster than I knew they could fall, and her skirt is up around her waist.

I reach behind her head, burying my hand in her hair while I push myself inside of her.

"Yes."

She answers my question over and over as we make love in the cold air, on a winter night, not far from Eva's lifeless body.

Acknowledgements

First of all, I'd like to thank all of my amazing critique partners for every bit of help, every insightful comment and criticism they've given me over the years, and will hopefully continue to give. I couldn't continue writing without such phenomenal friends. The list isn't exhaustive, but these wonderful people include Kathryn Trattner, Carly Green, Kristin D. Van Risseghem, Heather DiAngelis, Irina Hall, Kim Graff, and Christina Robins. Thank you for liking my characters as much as me, and for always pushing me forward. I also want to thank Heather again, who doubles as my editor. Thank you for your attention to detail and your ability to help make this book strong enough to face the world.

Thank you to all of my supporters and friends that give me everything I need to paint with my words. Thank you especially to Scarlett for dragging me to events that help me cultivate my creative side. And to my family, who pushes me to be a better person and support me even when I'm not always the best I can be.

Also, a special thank you to Tory for pushing me, inspiring me, and telling me I could and should do this. I'm so ecstatic to have a friend reminding me to do things for myself, things that make me happy. You rock, and I'm lucky to have you in my life.

I swear I'm almost done, but I can't leave out the strongest women I know—my gang of embroiderists. Thank you for being amazing examples of the *best* kind of women, women I am lucky to know, and women I strive to be more like. You help me grow and improve all the time.

Most importantly, thank you to my amazing husband (and our

monster) who supports me without fail through every adventure and endeavor. Without you and your never-ending love, my creativity could never have the space to flourish, and projects like this book would never be finished. Thank you for loving this book even more than I did. For everything, thank you, and I love you.

And, finally, thank you to my readers. Thank you to every single person reading this book, giving your time to me and my words. Thank you from the bottom of my heart. Never stop reading.

About the Author

Maria Green lives in Minnesota with her husband and little family—including three cats who always want to sit on her computer while she writes. She's always loved to read and write, as far back as she can remember. She loves how writing makes her feel and how creative it lets her be. Nothing is as exciting as creating a whole world and entire people in the midst of a twisting plot.

There's never a time you won't find a paperback thriller in her purse. And if you look for her, and she's not writing, you'll probably find her curled up with one of those books and a cup of hot coffee or a glass of sweet white wine.

She aims to paint with her words, so her readers can feel connected to her passion for writing. Maria continues to believe that though not every story is for her, and her stories aren't for everyone, every story has a reader. And she hopes you find your story.

Dear Reader,

I hope you enjoyed reading Nothing but Darkness!

I'd love to hear from you, or connect with you on my social media pages. You can write to me at

maria.ann.green.author@gmail.com

Find me on –

Amazon - https://amzn.to/2HVVXCS,

Facebook - www.facebook.com/MariaAnnGreenAuthor

Twitter @missmariaann,

Instagram @mariainmadness.

If you have enjoyed this book, look for the next in the series, Deeper into Darkness, coming soon. And if you're so inclined, please feel free to leave a review as well.

Thank you so much for reading and spending your time in this little world I've put together.

Sincerely,

Maria Ann Green, Author

Made in the USA
Columbia, SC
13 October 2020